'Beams's first novel is a meticulously crafted
suspense tale seething with feminist fury.'
O, The Oprah Magazine

'Stunningly good – a brainy page-turner that's gorgeous and
frightening in equal measure. *The Illness Lesson* dazzled me.'
Leni Zumas

'Reading *The Illness Lesson* I experienced the exquisite sense of
vertigo that is only ever sparked by a writer who's so in control
of her story . . . That bond of trust did not disappoint: *The Illness
Lesson* shines with generosity and rage, and I was both chilled
to the bone by it, and felt comforted and held.'
Livia Franchini

'Beams excels in her depiction of Caroline, an intriguingly
complex character, and in her depiction of the school, which
allows the reader a clear view of changing gender roles in the
period, with parallels to today's sexual abuse scandals. This
powerful and resonant feminist story will move readers.'
Publishers Weekly

'This suspenseful and vividly evocative tale expertly explores
women's oppression as well as their sexuality through the
eyes of a heroine who is sometimes maddening, at
other times sympathetic, and always wholly
compelling and beautifully rendered.'
Booklist

'Clare Beams' writing is a revelation . . . *The Illness Lesson* is a
strange novel, although its strangeness is a crucial part
of its appeal. A fascinating mix of genres (the school story,
body horror, paean to feminist anger), it manages to achieve
all the things that the best historical fiction should.'
Irish Independent

Praise for *The Illness Lesson*

'Astoundingly original, this impressive debut belongs
on the shelf with your Margaret Atwood and
Octavia Butler collections.'
New York Times

'A brilliant, suspenseful, beautifully executed psychological thriller.
With power, subtlety, and keen intelligence, Clare Beams has
somehow crafted a tale that feels like both classical ghost story
and like a modern (and very timely) scream of female outrage.
I stayed up all night to finish reading it, and I can still feel its
impact thrumming through my mind and body. A masterpiece.'
Elizabeth Gilbert

'Subtle, clever, suspenseful . . . builds to a shocking climax.'
Diane Setterfield

'Narrated from a painfully intimate perspective, *The Illness
Lesson* explores the consequences of an outrageous medical
treatment inflicted upon adolescent girls in 1870's New
England to cure "hysteria". In Clare Beams' luminous and
suspenseful prose, the unspeakable is spoken, falteringly at first,
then with triumphant strength. Its timeliness will be evident
to readers for whom the suppression of female sexuality/
identity is an ongoing and urgent issue.'
Joyce Carol Oates

ALSO BY CLARE BEAMS

We Show What We Have Learned & Other Stories

THE ILLNESS LESSON

Clare Beams

doubleday

TRANSWORLD PUBLISHERS
Penguin Random House, One Embassy Gardens,
8 Viaduct Gardens, London SW11 7BW
www.penguin.co.uk

Transworld is part of the Penguin Random House group of companies
whose addresses can be found at global.penguinrandomhouse.com

Penguin
Random House
UK

First published in Great Britain in 2020 by Doubleday
an imprint of Transworld Publishers
Paperback edition published 2021

A CIP catalogue record for this book
is available from the British Library.

ISBN
9781784164386

Printed and bound in Great Britain by Clays Ltd, Elcograf S.p.A.

The authorized representative in the EEA is Penguin Random House Ireland,
Morrison Chambers, 32 Nassau Street, Dublin D02 YH68

Penguin Random House is committed to a sustainable
future for our business, our readers and our planet. This book
is made from Forest Stewardship Council® certified paper.

MIX
Paper from
responsible sources
FSC
www.fsc.org   FSC® C018179

For my daughters,

Tess and Joanna

Divination seems heightened and raised to its highest power in woman.

—AMOS BRONSON ALCOTT, *CONCORD DAYS*

"Birds in their little nests agree," sang Beth . . .

—LOUISA MAY ALCOTT, *LITTLE WOMEN*

BIRDS, AGAIN

ASHWELL, MASSACHUSETTS, 1871

≈≈≈

Wonders, wonders!

—MILES PEARSON, *THE DARKENING GLASS* (P. 4)

The first of the birds Caroline mistook for her own mind's work. When the streak of red crossed the kitchen window-pane, fast, disastrous-bright, she thought it was some bloody piece come loose inside herself.

Then her father appeared from the study and held the door-frame, leaning in. "Caroline! Did you see?"

They found it in the yard, real after all: high in their birch tree, pecking judiciously at the bark. The size of a dove, the shape of a crow, and a brazen crimson tip to tail feathers, the shade a cardinal might bloom to if dipped in wine. It had a crestless head, all sharp planes. As the Hoods watched, it took a choosy bird-step forward, then craned neck over back to root around in its wing.

"No question at all," Samuel Hood said. His hand on Caroline's arm felt slight. This shock had dislodged his usual serenity, and in his face she saw old age, the way his features would fold in on themselves. To brace them both she gripped his fingers. "Trilling hearts. Who'd have believed?"

"*A* trilling heart," Caroline said.

She had just one hazy red-tinged memory of the trilling hearts' only prior appearance in Ashwell, twenty-five years earlier. Standing barefoot in the grass of the front garden, four years old and afraid to go down the path because of the bird that stood guard there, chopping up a worm with its brutal beak. *Snip, snip, snip*, worm bits on the gravel. On the steps behind her, sewing in the sun, her mother.

"What can this mean?" her father asked.

"That there's a red bird in our tree."

Samuel put a hand to his shirtfront. When he was a boy, his appendix had almost burst before the surgeon managed to remove it, and in moments of great excitement a heat-and-pain phantom seemed to revisit him. Sometimes Caroline found him with his fingers pressed there while he wrote and knew he was imagining readers, roomfuls of them, schools of hands turning reams of his pages.

"There is some significance," he said.

The immensities of God's creation often whittled themselves down to make a message for her father. But this—in this wouldn't anyone read meaning? The red flash, the answering thrum.

"You know it was your mother who named them," Samuel said, as if speaking about a person who'd stepped into another room.

Caroline tried again to turn her four-year-old head, to leave off staring at the bird and catch sight of her mother's face.

"You never told me," she said.

"I must have. Well. When we first saw them—a group of us out walking in the afternoon, just happening upon them in the fields, you can't imagine—she said they put her in mind of hearts, scooped right out of chests. Disembodied, trilling hearts, she said."

The bird's shape was wrong for this description, but its feel was right. The trilling heart looked like something safer left hidden.

"Do you think David will be here in time to see?" Samuel said. As always, David's name sounded louder than the rest of the words. "And I must tell Hawkins. I'll write him today. Hawkins will know if there've been others spotted. He's told me nothing grows or flies or runs in Massachusetts without his permission."

Caroline hadn't seen George Hawkins, or any of the Birch Hill men, in years, but she could picture the set of his mouth in delivering this not quite jest. He was a physician, only an amateur naturalist, but the sort of man who never considered himself an amateur at anything. They all were.

The bird raised its head again. Its black eye had the sightless sheen of a drop of oil. It tossed some bit of bark or insect back and swallowed it down, muscular throat squeezing.

"I ought to send a drawing with the letter. Caroline, would you? You have a fine hand."

She breathed in on the swell of pride that came when her father praised her and stared at the bird, to memorize it, so that in the drawing itself she might earn that praise again. She noted the shape of the head; the shining, sharp-looking lines of the wings; the beak like a long, cruel tooth; the sweep of the tail feathers; that red, improbable shade.

*

The bird flew away before David arrived, so they went back inside to wait. Samuel wrote, and Caroline drew. "I wonder what's keeping him," Samuel said, but this was David he was talking about, his last disciple and unexpected hope; he didn't say more.

In the confluence of Caroline's two projects, the drawing and the waiting, a strange suggestion was taking hold. Only one bird, she reminded herself. Still, she tried to capture the line of the bird's beak and thought, *Perhaps*; she shaded its eye and thought, *Perhaps*.

Considering slowed her hand. Her trilling heart had only the basic outline of a back and head by the time her father hurried to meet David at the front door. From two rooms away, Caroline heard them clearly—the founders of the Birch Hill Consociation had tried to plug the drafts of this hundred-year-old farmhouse when they'd bought it, but they were men with a greater affinity for ideas than for planks. "Astonishing," her father was saying. "I never thought I'd see them again, not on this earth. I'd forgotten their look. Such a red."

"I wish I'd seen," David said, and Caroline wished for a basketful of trilling hearts that she might carry to him, pinned against the shelf of her hip bone.

"Caroline must have nearly finished sketching by now."

Before the door opened and they were upon her, she just had time to cover the page.

"Caroline—" her father said, flushed and smiling.

"Not yet."

David inclined his head, but her father went on. "Surely you've caught at least some part of the essence. Enough to give David an idea."

No two men in all the world to whom she would have been less willing to show a half-formed thing. "Just another half hour. I'll bring it to you in the study."

Her father darted with a boy's nimbleness and caught the drawing out from where she'd hidden it. He held it in the air and squinted. "Ah, well, not done. This is the basic shape, though, David. Nearly."

Caroline's father had written a great and famous essay against cruelty, which scores of New England schoolchildren could quote from memory. She had seen him stop a man in the street who was striking his horse.

"Oh yes," David said.

Samuel set the sketch gently back down on the tabletop. He led David to the study and closed the door.

Caroline left the house. She strode off across the grass. She drove her legs forward as punishment—her own fault, always mostly her own fault—and sweat prickled the back of her neck, beneath her heavy hair. *A deep, dark forest of hair*, her father used to say, when she was a child, and kiss the top of her head. She'd thought he meant she had magic, or magic would happen to her.

As she passed the line of trees that obscured the house from view, she didn't slow, not until she had climbed to the top of the main hill. Below, their fields were spread, rich enough for eating, as if someone had taken up a heaping knifeful of sweetness and stroked it across the ground to tempt the appetite. The whole of the Birch Hill experiment needed no more explanation than that the weather must have been fine on the day they first saw the land. The sloping green of the fields in the sun, stands of trees clustered here and there, each casting its shade like the dark wet spill of an overturned bowl; the hills that grew greener and larger, greener and larger, in the distance, until at last they became mountains, and blue; the air thick with its grass-and-heather, baked-dirt smell; the chorus of humming, chirping, buzzing things in the grass, a small riot like the voice of the soil itself. The land had the same overabundant beauty as Samuel Hood's essays, and so those men had all come here to found a bright-colored world on both. And when the trilling hearts had arrived, a month into their project, it had felt like God Himself was telling them, *Oh yes, just what I envisioned, here, my final touch, by all means proceed.*

Important, Caroline thought, to remember this time how that time had turned out.

She let herself run down the far side of the hill. The ground gave a little beneath her feet. The neighbor boy had come a few days earlier to help them with the July haying, and there was nowhere Caroline could go, not even her bedroom, without tasting cut grass.

Caroline crossed the little valley, climbed the farther hill. And there, in the apple orchard at the crest, she found two trilling hearts twitching amongst the leaves of the largest tree. The first the brilliant color of the bird from this morning, the other—it must have been a female—a tamer red brown. Not just one bird anymore, then. Whatever was happening here, it was doubling, doubling. The tree they occupied, at the orchard's center, was the only one the Birch Hill founders hadn't planted—the farmer who'd sold them the land had done that—and the only one that had ever thrived, bearing full ripe fruit in the fall. The birds knew better than to trust their weight to the others' spindly branches.

Caroline watched them move, in lines instead of curves, start-stop, pecking at the surface of the world. Those beaks she could almost feel, somewhere along her spine. She saw that she'd gotten the angle of their backs slightly wrong in her sketch.

David wanted to see them. He could see them now, if she brought him.

But back at the house, she found David and her father on the front lawn, watching more birds. Five trilling hearts hopped from branch to branch in the oak by the front door. All on their own, without her help, David's eyes followed, and childish disappointment made her throat ache.

"Look, Caroline!" her father shouted, though she'd stopped right beside him.

"More in the orchard too," she said.

Samuel turned to David. "Now, I think. What better time? They've almost made our announcement for us."

David nodded.

The certainty settled heavy in Caroline's chest: *My father has hatched some scheme, and David is leaving.*

Samuel whistled into the sky. The birds flapped a little at the sound, as if it were a greeting. "I feel twenty years younger."

Crisply, Caroline said, "What are you talking about, please?"

"We have news, Caroline. We've been making plans, David and I—to open a school. The first of its kind, for the training of intellects and souls, hearts and minds. A school, here, for girls."

"What girls?" Caroline said.

David laughed.

"Any of them! All of them," Samuel said. "Any who want what they couldn't find in any other girls' school. A true, transforming education, dearest. Like the one you've had." His fingertips grazed her arm.

The education that had grown a wilderness in her head, too large to fit into any available space she'd yet found, so that she'd always wondered what her father had planned for her exactly—if he'd planned anything, if he hadn't just taught her all of it because she was there and because he could.

"We'll be filling a hole in the educational landscape," Samuel was saying. "No one, no one, has done this before. Formed girls into women who can become their own best selves, who can be true partners to their husbands and true mothers to their children. Our school will be a pursuit of the divine in the human. We'll teach thinking, not sewing or physical graces, not shallow parlor-trick erudition. We'll teach them to read the text of the natural world."

Samuel Hood, essayist.

"It's unprecedented," he said.

But Caroline thought all this would have sounded familiar to the Birch Hill men, only the direction of its application had shifted.

"Of course there's the matter of what they're to do with all that after," she said. She did not look at David.

Then her father surprised her. He stepped forward and caught her hand. "I know," he said softly. "My dear, I do know. That's why this school is so important, as a first step. There's nothing to do with it? We'll make something to do, while we're making the doers."

Another small beginning, meant like Birch Hill to ripple. Shouldn't her father understand that the ripples did not always follow? Birch Hill hadn't lasted two years. And yet. A bird adjusted its wings, and Caroline thought she almost heard the slight friction of feather against feather. One impossible thing might follow another. Her father did mean what he was saying, she knew—he always did—and about girls, who else said and meant such things?

She hadn't realized her father understood what it felt like to her.

Samuel gripped her shoulder. "You'll teach with us, Caroline. You'll help us shape what we're doing."

Caroline had briefly tried being a teacher. She hadn't been sure what else to try, equipped with the education he'd given her, tied to this place, so three years earlier she'd gone to work at the Ashwell grammar school. A few of the children she'd adored, but when she raised her hand one afternoon to strike a boy who'd thrown gravel in another boy's face, she only just remembered to open her fist. She'd returned to Birch Hill and told her father that the world wasn't served by the troughs and peaks that teaching seemed to bring her to.

"Teaching didn't suit me, remember?" she said.

David answered. "No one has taught the way we'll teach here."

Fluttering on its branch, one of the birds gave its call. A single rapidly repeating note, almost mechanical in tone but lighter, higher: the sound of a quick tongue ticking on teeth.

"Sir, for the name?" David said. He bounced on his feet as if testing the ground. "The School of the Trilling Heart. What do you think? In honor of the circumstances."

Joy suffused Samuel's face.

There were words that might have plucked him down to earth again, but Caroline couldn't bear, in that moment, to say them.

2

LAYING OF PLANS

~~~

On this morning, though he did not yet know it,
his whole life was to begin anew.

—MILES PEARSON, *THE DARKENING GLASS* (P. 12)

Hawkins wrote that he wanted to come see the trilling hearts for himself. *Nature having arranged a thing so unmissable, I think I must oblige.* He was plainly more interested in the birds than in the school. "That's all right," Samuel said, folding the letter and laying it in a drawer. "He'll see once he's here."

"See what?" Caroline said. She wanted to underscore for herself too that there was nothing substantive here, so far.

Samuel raised his eyebrows, the way he had her whole life when she was being difficult. He had always maintained his right to be taken aback by her.

Though they would open in two months, the school at this point existed solely in the plans that spun through the air of any room Samuel and David simultaneously occupied. There was much to do, and more, maybe, to avoid doing. Samuel had taught as a young man, at a secondary school in Boston, and had come away with a host of aversions: to lectures, drills, the McGuffey Reader, and the striking of students. "Hours spent in dim rows, copying out dusty verses, smother the intellect in its womb," he told David, as they paced the carpet in his study.

David had not spent many such hours. His only formal instruction had taken place in a one-room schoolhouse on an Ohio farmer's back field; at the same age at which Samuel had gone to Harvard, David had gone to war. Still, he knew what he thought about the point Samuel was making, as about most things. "What does regurgitation have to do with the mind?" he said.

David's mind, Samuel had long ago proclaimed, was as fine as any he'd ever encountered. This was especially impressive given that David had been almost entirely self-taught. David told Caroline once that his Ohio schoolmaster, in between getting sums wrong on the blackboard, took away the books David used to secrete in his desk, so that his earliest impression of school was of a place where it was unsafe to be caught reading.

"Nothing at all. We'll free them from all of that," Samuel said, with the relish of talking to someone who agreed with him, David in particular.

David had been with them almost exactly a year, though it felt both longer and shorter. He'd arrived at haying time, come to the front door and knocked in his strange, somber clothes, black and clumsy-sewn. Caroline later realized he'd fashioned himself after the author plates in the Birch Hill men's books. At first she'd believed he was peddling something, and her "May I help you?" on opening the door was not too kind. Only when he'd given her his letter for her father—at work in his study, not to be disturbed—had she gathered that he was one of Samuel's would-be acolytes, whose arrival had tapered and tapered through her childhood. David hadn't known Samuel had a daughter. "Well, he doesn't write much about me," Caroline had said, smiling at the lock of David's brown hair that lifted in a pocket of wind like a rogue antenna.

Thinking the smile was for him, David returned it, carving lines in his face beside his bold, bony nose. "Tell him he should," he said. "Surely at least a paragraph somewhere." His eyes gleamed at her as if she were his own discovery. Then he'd held the letter out to her, the backs of his hands sunburned, and told her Samuel might send word to the Ashwell Inn if he chose.

Caroline, pressing the wax seal while she watched him go, had considered not giving the letter to her father, though she wasn't sure why—only that the paper had the feel, in her hands, of change. It might not have mattered. A man doesn't travel from Ohio to Massachusetts only to leave again without speaking to the one he's come to see. Yet she did think still that David, with his mix of arrogances and wounds, might not have returned— might have boarded a train homeward and cast himself back into the life he'd left, and she might never have seen him again.

When she'd handed the letter to her father that night, he'd groaned. "These poor boys. These poor, poor letters," he said, as if they still flooded in. He broke the seal and began to read.

"Oh," he said. With that sound, the change flew into the open. Caroline had been watching that change since, trying to understand what it might be carrying for her, trying to decide on the exact shade of its feathers.

She was coming to suspect that its shade too might be a red so bright and so unexpected, so unlike the colors of her life, that it held a violence.

"At what age will our instruction begin?" she asked her father and David now, for many of these practicalities remained vague. She was sitting by the window in her usual chair, out of their lines of sight. They turned toward her. She wondered if they'd remembered until then that she was there.

"Fourteen, I think," David said, and Samuel nodded. "It's such a critical age, fourteen, fifteen. The entry to adulthood. A time when proper steering can work to great effect."

Samuel tapped his mouth thoughtfully. "I like that. The entry, the steering. Let's put it just that way. We'll have a brief essay in *The Examiner* this month," he explained to Caroline, as she was readying her question, "to announce our aims."

She wondered if the idea for the essay had come to her father before or after the idea for the school. "Where would you like to steer these girls?" she asked, leaning a bit on the last word.

"Toward the best of what's in them already," he said. "That's what education should be, for boys and girls alike. A molding of what they already have."

"No difference, then." She wasn't sure if she was challenging him or if she only wanted him to explain it to her.

"The sole difference is that we'll have to show these girls there's no difference."

A few days later, as they walked to the barn to assess their future classroom—the only space large and open enough for what Samuel imagined—Caroline asked David, "Did you ever guess you were coming here to open a school for girls?"

"I could lie and say I did," David said, watching Samuel, who had walked ahead. "But truthfully, I can say that the best parts of my life have mostly been things I couldn't have imagined."

He'd never imagined her, she knew; she'd seen that on his face when she first opened the door to him. She half turned to him now to see if she could catch whether that was any part of what he'd meant—but they were in earshot of her father now.

"We'll have to replace that door," Samuel said, gesturing broadly. "You see how the wood's going. But most of it's fine. Come in, both of you. Picture how it will be."

*

Hawkins arrived. His skin had thickened and reddened with too much good eating since his last visit, five or six years earlier. He brought luggage. He remembered where things were in the house, and when he wanted something—a book, a footstool, a piece of the bread Caroline had made—he went and got it without saying a thing to anyone, as if this were still his home. Caroline wished he hadn't come. He looked at her too long, and her skin crawled with his eyes on it.

Together, Hawkins, David, and Samuel went out to kill one of the trilling hearts, so it could be sent to an acquaintance of Hawkins's at the Boston Society of Natural History. Twenty-five years ago, when the birds had first been seen, the society had no record of this species, but the men thought records might by now have improved. Hawkins was the one who shot the bird; he carried it back to the farmhouse by its feet, like something he intended to roast and consume, small though it was. "Now we'll get some answers, if there are any to be had," Hawkins said, standing over the bird while it sopped blood as red as its feathers onto the rags Caroline had laid out for it on the kitchen table. Caroline leaned in over the limp body. At this proximity it had a gamy smell, and two tiny mites swam across the glassine surface of its open eye. She felt relief at seeing it this way, its strange magic all fled. She straightened again.

The answer, which returned quickly from Boston, was the one Caroline knew they'd wanted: there was still no record of the trilling hearts, though it seemed they were close relatives of a bird common in South America. No one had a convincing theory about where these birds had come from or why they should descend on two or three towns in Massachusetts, vanish for decades, then reappear. But there it was.

The men were credited with having sent in the society's first official specimen (any sent during the birds' brief stay last time having been lost or misplaced). In the ledgers, the birds became *Aphelocoma rubinus;* in the wider parlance, they remained trilling hearts.

"Your mother named a species, Caroline," Samuel remarked wonderingly.

*

The essay about the school in *The Examiner* appeared and caused a modest stir. David read it aloud to all of them that evening by the fire.

We have been lately reborn as a nation . . .

The mothers of this nation, the daughters, deserve . . . will give in turn . . .

Souls . . . souls . . . souls . . .

They applauded. David flushed.

Instead of letting the applause stand, Hawkins grunted, shifted. "Isn't it something," he said, "the way these birds are making people fall in love with Pearson again."

If they'd ever fallen out of love with him, Caroline hadn't heard. Miles Pearson, the youngest of the Birch Hill men, had been in his early twenties during the grand experiment and had abandoned it first of all of them. In short order he'd written a titillating novel called *The Darkening Glass*, a tale of the supernatural, very famous—so famous that more people knew his name now than knew Samuel's. He'd married, then died young, winning himself still more celebrity.

The Darkening Glass was the only forbidden book in the Hood household. Samuel refused to speak about it. Birch Hill was already dead when *The Darkening Glass* was published, but he could not forgive the novel for making that death final, or for its other crimes. Its heroine, a perfect golden glittering paragon named Louisa Blake, had been based, it was said, on Caroline's mother, Anna. The villain, Abner Blake, was based on Samuel, but Pearson had made him Louisa's uncle instead of her husband. Abner keeps Louisa locked away through various dark machinations; a young man named Hammond arrives and ushers in a season of attempted liberation; trilling hearts flap madly through significant scenes; nothing ends well. When she'd read the book—at sixteen, a copy she'd at last purloined in town, too desperate for what it might contain to resist any longer—Caroline had found little of her father in the sinuous Abner except a tendency toward speeches. Louisa, childless, unmarried, and slippery with virtue, had slid right through her fingers, though she'd tried so hard to clutch and hold. And then at the end of the novel Louisa had died. That part at least had felt familiar, even if Louisa's manner of dying—undone by either ghosts or Abner's potions, the question of which left unresolved—was more dramatic and tormented than Anna's, in the midst of an epileptic fit.

Now Samuel asked Hawkins, "Are they?" as if it made no difference to him.

"The bookstore in Ashwell has two shelves of only Pearson." Hawkins coddled his paunch like a lapdog. "People are giving *Darkening Glass* tours."

Caroline had seen the new crowds thronging Ashwell when she walked to the post office to send and receive her father's letters. So that was what the strangers were doing, tromping through fields to find the birds, pulling copies of the novel from their pockets to read relevant passages aloud to each other in the sunshine.

"What can there possibly be for them to see?" Samuel said.

"It depends which eyes are doing the looking, Sam," Hawkins told him, tapping a finger, for some reason, to his temple.

"If people are talking, they may talk about the school too," David said. "That can't hurt."

Samuel lifted his newspaper and was silent for a moment. Then he lowered it again. "Those tours ought to come this way. They ought to see themselves right to the front door and meet us. Don't you think, Caroline? If they're lucky, I might bestow a hair from my head, a fingernail clipping or two, for burning in their midnight rituals."

Caroline felt as if she were watching a poor tortured bear try to jig. She smiled. "Why give them away? We should sell them. Profit from what's ours."

"Very clever," said Hawkins, and there were his eyes again.

*

Hawkins, some of the other Birch Hill men, and several of her father's newer correspondents had gathered at the farmhouse once, when Caroline was about ten—five years after Birch Hill had ended, almost five after her mother had died. She'd gone down in a new white dress like a nervous little bride to recite the opening of the *Aeneid*, which she'd been studying with her father, before supper. Caroline stood in the center of the circle of dark-suited men. "Caroline would like to demonstrate what we've been working on," her father said. She'd neatened the folds of her dress, pinned her arms tight to her sides, and stood up straight, because, she imagined (she cringed to remember it now), this was the way Dido or Viola or Penelope or her mother would have stood. *"Arma virumque cano, Troiae qui primus ab oris Italiam, fato profugus . . ."* The white dress and the words fit themselves to her skin. When she was done, she knew the men would applaud thunderously, and then they would come closer to touch her arms, her hair. *So like Anna*, they would say.

But when she stopped after thirty lines, their applause was merely polite. "Very nice," said one of them. The others made encouraging noises. Caroline had twisted her hair up, hours earlier, and tucked in a blossom from their dogwood tree. Had her fingers actually crept to remove it or had they only wanted to? She couldn't remember.

"All right, Caroline. You may go back upstairs," her father said, in a kind way but with something like embarrassment in his face. Why? She knew she'd done well.

From there, she could still hear. "What a little creation, Sam!" somebody said. It might have been Hawkins; she wasn't sure.

"Someday her husband can refresh his schoolboy Latin at the breakfast table."

"He won't need to refresh. She'll talk to him in nothing *but*

Latin. Their children will speak it when they emerge from the womb."

Her father laughed along with them. "Let's go in to supper, shall we?" he said. Nothing else. She remembered that.

*

Samuel and David and Hawkins, clustered around the desk in the study to talk and talk; Caroline on the sofa, sun slicing through the curtains to lie on the carpet in big wasteful stripes. Filling her with that restlessness she knew as well as she knew any person—that sense that a gift was being given, and the moment for its use was passing, had passed.

"Would anyone like a walk?" she said.

But Hawkins was declaiming. "Thoreson of course holds that in education it's discipline that matters most. I was reading an essay of his the other day." All these men had this ability to seize on every essay, never letting one slip by, vigilant as housewives guarding their flour and sugar from pests. "Educating, he says, really should *be* disciplining, in every sense of the word. Teaching order, order in the mind."

"I read that too," Samuel said. *Swat, swat,* essay read, stores safe.

Hawkins sat back and eyed Samuel. "You don't agree?"

"Oh, order matters, of course. But the notion that it can be externally established—stamped down on pupils, each of them receiving it in exactly the same way, as if they're all just the same shape . . ." Samuel hissed air between his teeth, wincing a little at poor Thoreson's error. "And the precedence it's given. He seems to feel the only measurement of successful education is how quiet and unobtrusive the whole enterprise can be made."

"To what would you give precedence?" Hawkins said.

"To the truest, deepest self."

Hawkins sneered. "The *deepest selves* of these girls."

"They do have them," Samuel said. "We must encourage them

to think and question and find God in themselves, where He lives, after all. In educating women, we can make a great leap forward, because the next generation will be handed to them, in large measure, to raise—to shape as they see fit."

This dreaming was a fever Caroline had decided not to catch, and yet to her fury, her forearms rippled now with goose bumps.

"Well, yes, I knew you thought all of that," Hawkins said. "But in light of these new advances—Thoreson's new school is getting quite good results, it seems—"

"Good results," David said, smiling. "As in farming. Carpentry."

Hawkins regarded David impassively. *You are an upstart and new to your place here, and some of us have been here a long time.* It was a look that Caroline had sometimes wanted to give David too, among other looks.

"All right, so what will it be like in practice, then? This finding of true selves?" Hawkins said, turning back to Samuel. "Will you talk to them about their souls all the time?"

"Their souls are the aim, not the material. The bulk of the instruction will consist of reading and conversation about what we have read, as it would if the students were boys. Literature, moral reasoning, and scientific inquiry."

"And mathematics," David said.

"Yes," said Samuel. He had a way of forgetting mathematics, which David would be teaching and which had never been Samuel's strongest suit: too many rules in what one did with numbers.

"Though they *aren't* boys," Caroline said. No matter how many times she said this she was never quite sure he'd heard.

"The soul does not have a sex," Samuel said. "That's what we're going to show the world."

While Caroline walked that evening, she thought about the sexless soul. The idea had its own chill, like the air tucked into the shade beneath the trees now, foretaste of fall. She had no way, really, of evaluating its general truth. She knew only that her life had a sex.

She'd always understood it would, of course. Her father might have instructed her as he would have a son, but she'd known she was not one. Only she had never quite felt like a daughter either. Mary Sutton, from a farm a bit down the road—with whom Caroline had played and mapped these hills when they were small, running through imagined fairy glens, bedecking themselves in moss, and plaiting their hair with grasses and flowers—had been a daughter, able to roam only until her mother called her to come and help prepare the food, hem the trouser leg, sweep the kitchen. In Caroline's house there was no mother, and Mrs. Wilmer, the housekeeper, did most of these things; she taught them to Caroline only if Caroline happened to be by. The girls her father sent her to visit in Ashwell, they too were daughters, with their crossed ankles and their tiny smiles.

Years passed and Caroline had watched while the Ashwell girls were claimed, one by one, by their brothers' friends, their fathers' younger business associates, sometimes distant cousins. And the spring they were fifteen, Caroline and Mary's games, which always paused for the winter since they never had much to say to each other indoors, somehow never resumed. When they were seventeen, Mary wed a farmer's son. Caroline called on her, that first year of her marriage. Mary had come to the door of the ancient farmhouse where she now lived with her husband and his family and led Caroline back into a cabbagey-smelling dark, a sitting room in which every wall sloped and curved, suggesting the inside of a loose fist. She adjusted her skirts to sit, and Caroline could see the rounding of her stomach.

"A very hot summer," said Mary.

Caroline made a noise of agreement. A boy of perhaps eight ran through the room, pounding his feet as if in rage—one of Mary's nephews? A small brother-in-law?

"At the end of working the men are drenched," Mary continued.

Caroline wanted to ask her what it felt like, that swelling, that growth out of herself, unnatural looking as something that could kill her. "And you, are you well?" she said.

"Well enough."

The baby, a girl, hadn't killed her. Caroline sometimes saw this girl out in the fields now with the other neighbor children. She was eleven or twelve, tall and towheaded, not much like Mary. There were three boys now too, and the youngest did have something of his mother in the set of his eyes.

Samuel had always said that the tending of the souls of children was the highest moral calling there was. Caroline had expected that someday a means would appear of joining all of his instruction to the things that usually came for women, and that this union, in its particular shape, would turn out to be what she wanted. She would read and think and roam and mother, all at once. The world would give her a way of rounding out and filling in and firmly rooting.

And she was firmly rooted now, she supposed. She just hadn't expected the rooting to happen where she'd always been. If her mother had been alive, maybe she would have helped Caroline to see what different thing she ought to have done, at what crucial point along the way.

Caroline stopped beneath the tree on the front lawn and leaned against the trunk. There was one place where it fit her back exactly. In the quiet, she found herself listening for the trilling hearts' call, the invader's flourish. Listening that way all the time was exhausting in a way that felt familiar—stilling, tensing, attending—because she'd always known that another possible future might come for her instead. Her mother's epilepsy had begun in adolescence. Caroline should have felt calmer on crossing the threshold of each new year after her own adolescence was done, but waiting for something that didn't come made true calm impossible. There was no clear end to the wait, no clear beginning of safety—no official word that here, this year, this month, this moment, just here, was the line that separated her from any chance that what had happened to her mother would happen to her next. No one knew enough about what had killed her mother to know that for certain. Sometimes she even felt that it would be better to be sick, because then at last she could stop asking if she would be.

No call now, but there, in the tree a little ways across the lawn, a grouping of birds, six of them, seven, their red flattened a little by the dusk light. One stabbed at the branch beside it, stabbed again, then tore most of a leaf from its stem and rose with it into the air. Caroline suppressed an urge to pursue, to leap and try to reclaim that leaf and reaffix it to the branch. These holes in the regular order—she wanted the birds to stop leaving such marks of themselves.

Through the lighted windows of the farmhouse she could see David and Hawkins and her father, seated at the table. They looked like a painting. *Wise Men in Conversation.* David tilted back a little in his chair and stretched out his feet, offering up the plane of his body.

Caroline wished that someone had taught her how to know if such an offering, after all this time, was for her.

*

To Caroline's relief, Hawkins left after a week. Samuel and David set about assembling the list of the girls who would come to the Trilling Heart School. The list was not long. This, Samuel explained, was the way they wanted it at first. "From seeds, bountiful gardens, with care in the selection and sowing," he said, though it seemed to Caroline that they had not selected from a very broad array. Samuel exchanged several letters with each girl's parents (mostly fathers, a few mothers) to assure himself of fruitfulness.

*

The girls were:

Miss Rebecca Johns, daughter of the Boston banker who
handled the income from Samuel's essays.
Miss Felicity Ridell, whose parents had read the essay in
The Examiner and felt that their daughter had *something
of a historical mind.*
Miss Tabitha Seward, daughter of a newspaperman in
Larchmont who believed in being part of the vanguard
where possible.
Miss Julia Altman, whose mother had long admired
Samuel's ideas and could wish no better for her daughter
than to learn to live according to them.
Miss Livia Bunting, possessed of too many energies, and
too varied, for her current school to handle.
Miss Abigail Smith, at the wedding of whose parents a
passage from Samuel's essay "On Love: Plenitude and
Patience" had been read aloud.
Miss Margaret Sawyer, whose father played cards with
Mr. Howard Phelps, former Birch Hill resident, and
who feared the school she attended now was making her
silly.

"Their parents would make marvelous students, anyway," Caroline said.

Still, there was something about seeing the names. She would
be teaching Shakespeare and Wordsworth to a Tabitha, an Abigail, a Rebecca, a Margaret—handing all of it to them as if it
were theirs. She ran her fingers over that list in her father's hand,
those letters that spelled out girls.

*

Not long after Hawkins's departure, David moved out of his rooms in Ashwell and into the farmhouse. No one had thought to mention this to Caroline until the day before. "He's going to live with us?" she asked her father. She took care to keep her voice steady.

"It won't make any sense for him to be traveling back and forth once the teaching begins," Samuel said.

On that first morning Caroline awoke with the feeling that the earth had shrugged its skin in the night. She'd never been free to seek out new places for herself; this seeming newness of her usual place gave her hopes of terrifying size. She herself didn't seem at all new—her face in the mirror was the same, the just-darkening patches beneath her eyes like the fingerprints of a person who had pressed too hard, though no one but Caroline had ever pressed there.

Across from David at the breakfast table, she stirred and stirred her tea. David, it turned out, didn't drink it in the mornings. She raised her eyes and caught him looking at her, or perhaps his gaze was only tracing an arc from tabletop to window and her face happened to be in its path.

That night, she had a dream in which she stood on the front stoop of the farmhouse wearing a dress made of red feathers. She stroked her fingers down her arms to feel the smoothness of the sleeves, feathers lying one over another as if still notched in place on the backs of birds. The cuffs at her wrists were scalloped because of the feathers' points, and more shades of red than there were words for. She'd never worn anything so fine.

But when she moved to touch the bodice to see if it was just as sleek, there was no bodice but her own warm skin. The dress was only sleeves.

There she was, standing on the porch, only her arms clothed, waiting for someone. *I don't know who*, she told herself. She slid her hands down the sleeves, down her warm stomach, down to where the hair lay smooth and silky. She stroked the way she'd stroked the feathers. *I don't know who*, staring out at the horizon. The lie was coated in sweet shame that spread and spread with the motions of her fingers. Her knees buckled.

Caroline opened her eyes in the gray light of her own bedroom—her hands still in the dream, still working—and closed them again. She could tell from the house's stillness that the others weren't awake yet. She dressed, wrapped herself in her cloak, and went outside. She would find some of the birds and watch them until she had inoculated herself, taken all the mystery out of them, remembered that in spite of dreams and swells they were only tendon, meat, feather, flimsy bone. That they meant nothing at all for her. The grass was drenched enough to wet the tops of her shoes. All around her birds, waking up for their day, were calling.

But she walked and walked and couldn't find any trilling hearts. She roamed for ten minutes, began to feel ridiculous, and snuck back to the house and up the stairs with her hem soaked through. She crawled back into her bed and curled herself over to warm her feet. Only when she heard her father and then David going down the stairs did she rise and straighten her dress. She went down to meet them, pretending she too was just starting a day in which she would be too busy to watch the sky.

3

MISS ELIZA PEARSON BELL

❧❧

How beauty can stir a man!

—MILES PEARSON, *THE DARKENING GLASS* (P. 43)

The week before the school would open, Caroline's father caught a summer cold. She found him stumbling through the kitchen with a blanket clutched around his shoulders like a shawl. She seemed to be seeing a new, fine crack at the base of an enormous structure, so slight, and yet the structure's own weight was already almost enough to topple it.

"Back to bed with you now," she told him.

When she carried his tea up, he took it from her fretfully and sipped. "David and I were going to walk to Jeffers's to sign for the desks for the students. The two of you will need to do it, I suppose."

"All right."

"You can discuss your first week's lessons. You're planning on a sonnet?"

Caroline, it had been decided, would be teaching only English literature. David would take natural history and mathematics, Samuel would take classical languages, and the men would divide moral philosophy and history between the two of them. Though Caroline was meant to be a walking embodiment of the school's aims, that didn't mean her feminine fingers belonged in its meatier pies.

"David may have some thoughts for you. And you might have to rein him in a bit, if you can do it gently. We must prevent his brilliance from being anything but an asset." Samuel gave a moist cough and settled into his pillows like any old man. "Despite this little setback, it's very good to feel that I'm beginning this most important work just now. That God has made it possible for me to serve Him in this way, at this late hour."

Caroline remembered one supper when she was about thirteen: snow coating the windows, Samuel reading aloud a review of his most recent book of essays and trying to laugh, trying to pretend the soup was too hot and that was why his eyes were tearing. Caroline had said, "It sounds as if the writer has misunderstood your argument," and thought, *I will never, ever be able to leave him.* He wrote just as eloquently in the years after Birch Hill's failure, but people began to read him differently. They wanted writers whose feet were more firmly planted and who had not been models for storybook villains. The shift broke his heart, she knew. Watching it broke hers.

Now this plan for the school was allowing her father his visions again. There were worse needs. His visions had goodness, shine.

Yet the noise of his tea sipping, which she would have known anywhere, made her shoulders want to creep up around her ears.

"We'll change these girls," he said, "and send them off to change others—turn them inward, then turn them outward again. It's the way the world changes." Delicious words in the mouth, *change the world.*

"We can't quite know what they'll see when they turn inward, though, can we?" she said.

"Grace, of course."

Caroline pulled the blanket up to tuck it more snugly around him. "I've been giving some thought to the name," she said. "Wouldn't it be simpler to call it the Birch Hill School?"

Samuel's eyes sharpened and focused on her face. She would

plunge ahead wholeheartedly with this school, she would never speak another word against it, if he would just make himself say it now: simpler, yes, of course, to make the school's status as Samuel Hood's repeated, doomed experiment clear to everyone.

He put on a smile. "I'm surprised at you, Caroline," he said. "I would think you'd want your mother to have the naming of it." His fingers worried at the blanket. "My dear, let's give her this."

*

When Caroline told David her father was ill, his face tensed. "He's all right? Should we send for the doctor?"

"It's only a cold. He'll be well in a few days, I'm sure."

Out in the lane, David tore a branch off a tree, stripped it of leaves, and swished it through the grass beside the road as they walked.

"What are you going to do with them, the first day?" she asked. She was remembering red sleeves, but she knew he would never have been able to tell from her face or her voice.

"I'll begin with a nature walk."

"Really."

"We'll visit the fields, with the students instructed to collect samples that are of interest to them. My scheme is for them to keep journals of observation for analyzing and responding to what they collect. I know your father also intends journal keeping, but the two projects will be separate, and different, I think, in character."

Samuel's kind of journal was a record of self-inspection as a means to moral improvement. He'd kept one for thirty years, its volumes spanning a prominent shelf in his study, which dipped a little with their weight; Caroline had kept her own as part of her education at his hands. For years he read it weekly and left guidance in the margins: *When you feel impatient in this way, try to recall the everlasting patience of your truest Friend, which lasted through death itself.* The words always gave her the sense that he'd written them for her but also with some theoretical broader audience in mind. At fourteen Caroline recorded a dream about running in a hot field with their neighbors' son, William, a year older than she was. Her dress had caught on a stick and torn, and William took it between his hands and tore it further. Her father called her into his study after that week's reading and told her, without meeting her eyes, that he'd decided she was now capable of monitoring her own thoughts and feelings on the page.

Later that summer, Caroline had kissed William but run away when he took her hand and tried to tug her into the woods between their houses. She wouldn't be kissed again until, at twenty-four, motivated mostly by curiosity, she let Emmet Baker, her father's middle-aged bookkeeper, press his lips to hers in the back garden while Samuel was out walking. Had she known the dearth that lay ahead on that summer day, William's mouth sweet against hers, she might not have run. William and Emmet were both married now: William to his second cousin from Lattemore; Emmet to a wealthy Ashwell widow.

Caroline did not keep journals anymore, because she didn't like to set words down on the page where she'd have to look at them.

"You surprise me," she told David.

"In what respect?"

Your voice, your face, your step surprises me; in every way, you are to me a continual surprise.

"A *nature* walk," she said.

"A study of the way God lives and clothes Himself." He swooped the stick through the air. "Of the life the grandest ideas find in the smallest things."

"You think these girls will grasp that?"

"I'll teach them to," David said. He'd stopped walking, so Caroline turned back to face him. "It can be taught. As your father taught me, long before I ever came here. I was fifteen, coming out of the shop in town, and a man in a suit tossed *The Inner Pen-*

dulum down right in the middle of the street before getting back on his horse. To travel lighter, maybe. My own literary angel."

A book-jettisoning angel who hadn't considered her father's words worth their weight. Caroline smiled.

"You wouldn't understand what it was like, coming across his thinking for the first time. I didn't sleep till I'd finished. It was a defense of so many things I'd always instinctively felt were true."

"What things?" Caroline asked. He was right—she didn't know what it would be like to meet her father this way.

"Well, that moral truth belongs to all of us, if we practice the right kind of seeing. That's how we find God, not in dancing and screaming before some man on a stage who's thundering about hellfire." Walking faster now, David tossed his stick to the ground.

Caroline pulled abreast. She said carefully, "My father hasn't written much about hellfire."

"My family went to the camp meetings, that's all. They lived for them. I'm sure they do still."

Caroline saw in her mind a foam of writhing people, David standing apart, the only one not moving. "I've never been to anything like that," she said.

"You'd hate it too."

Her face heated.

David bent, picked something from the grass beside the pavement, and straightened again with his hand extended toward her. "From a trilling heart female, I think."

She took it from him. Not much like the feathers in her dream—in the palm of her glove it made a bedraggled, loose light-brown *C*—but a haze of red did somehow cling to that brown. "How would you describe that color?" she asked David.

"Oh, reddish-brownish."

Well, yes. She brushed the feather away lest the haze somehow cling to her too, but he bent and lifted it again.

"You'll keep it?" she said.

"To show the students, I thought."

She couldn't think how to explain the small recoiling she felt at the idea of the feather inside his pocket, inside some drawer in their house.

They were crossing the heart of Ashwell now, with its rows of quiet, matronly houses. Two fashionable girls, younger than Caroline, strolled down the other side of the street. Caroline didn't want to watch David to see if he looked at them. She pointed to the grand white house a little ahead. "That's where my parents lived when they first married, did you know? It had been my mother's family home."

David ran his eyes up the pillars.

"There was some money, and my father met her before his writing had earned much, so their marrying caused a stir."

"What was she like, your mother?"

Caroline should have known better than to talk about her mother. Stiffly, she said, "She died when I was six. I only have a few memories." Her mother standing far away, raising her hands to her mouth in a growing wind (a storm must have been brewing) and shouting for Caroline to come in. Her mother in the kitchen, handing her father a plate.

"Your father speaks very beautifully about her."

"Yes, though of course my father could speak beautifully about a washtub."

The white house was a house for a perfect girl. When she was a child, Caroline decided that her mother must have been one, who had grown into a perfect woman. And then one day a handsome man came by on his horse. (The handsome man bore no real resemblance to Samuel in her mind.) The man had just moved to town, so he stopped and stared at Anna, because she was the most beautiful thing he had ever seen, and then asked her where he might find the library. Anna pointed in the right direction, but the man decided the library could wait.

"She must have been very young when she died," David said.

There was an old woman out on the porch of the house opposite, beginning to stare and straighten up in her rocking chair. Caroline started them walking again, then said, "Twenty-six. She'd had the fits for years—since she was just a girl—but no one thought them dangerous. It was a very great shock."

"I'm sure."

"I don't mean for me. I mean, it must have been, but I don't remember." Her one fragment of a memory from that day held no real feeling: sitting on her bed, Mrs. Wilmer's fingers stroking her hair, while downstairs her father made shrieking sounds. The loss itself had always been something seen through fogged glass. Into that absence had crept a vivid imagining, a presence of a different kind. She could not stop anticipating how her inheritance from this unknown mother might arrive. Perhaps with a jerk of the fingers, as if pulled by twine. Or in the chest, a new thump, a foreign heart. In the legs, a sudden refusal to bear the body's accustomed weight. In the head, a hot white limitlessness.

Caroline was almost surely too old now for such a beginning, as she was for other beginnings. Still, when she rehearsed the possibilities, she was unsure if she was picturing her mother's body or her own.

"Your mother," David said, "she was Pearson's Louisa Blake?" Caroline had the feeling he was forcing himself to ask as if he had the right to instead of whispering.

"People say so. I've never thought Louisa seems like a creature who could breathe anywhere outside of imagination. You've read *The Darkening Glass?*" Even naming the book set off a thrill of disobedience. "Don't tell my father."

David nodded. "As a boy, before I'd read your father's essays, and I read it again before coming here. It seemed wise to know everything I could, if I was to meet him, really meet him."

"Well, what did you think of it?" she asked.

"Apart from the absurdity of Abner Blake?"

"Yes, apart from that."

He seemed to consider. "It's curious. You always feel that you're straining to make out the characters' faces in the depths of dark rooms. But Louisa—I don't know. Pearson must have been in love with her, your mother, don't you think?" Looking ahead again and not at Caroline.

"My father says they all were, a little." As she said this, Caroline suddenly heard its deflection. She had of course wondered before about her mother and Pearson, but then there were so many things she had wondered about her mother. "I can't remember Pearson himself at all, so I can't tell you firsthand. But I'm not sure it's exactly a lover's eye that's trained on Louisa. She's barely there at all. Just a sort of shimmery vapor that sometimes coalesces long enough to say 'Oh sir' or 'Oh thank you so much,' and then disperses again."

"Ah, you know the book well!" David said.

He met her eyes again and smiled, and there it was: a secret they would keep from Samuel, for only themselves.

They'd reached Jeffers's door, where Mr. Jeffers himself waved them in. He was a potbellied man with a splendid, healthy mustache who had made Caroline's parents' marriage bed and seemed to feel this made them familiar. The desks and chairs were grouped at the front of the store for inspection before they would be loaded on the cart and brought to the house.

"You try it," David said to Caroline. "We need a lady's opinion. The students will be ladies, after all."

Caroline sat. David looked at the places where the lines of her body hit the lines of the chair.

"It's comfortable," she said, though really she couldn't tell, intent as she was on holding herself still under his gaze, which hit her like a focused point of light, traveling.

"Is the back at the right angle?" he said. He reached out to touch her between the slats.

The delivery, Jeffers said, would take place the next morning. He was certain they'd be able to get all seven onto the cart at once.

"Seven," Caroline said, while Jeffers was in the back. There was something about hearing the number separated from the names. "Not very many."

"There will be more later, as soon as people see what we're doing," David told her.

A wet gray tissue of cloud had descended by the time they left Jeffers's. Everyone in the streets now scurried. With satisfaction, Caroline imagined the state of the girls they'd seen on their way in: they'd look melted, ribbons, curls, and ruffles all pasted to their skin.

When they'd almost reached the end of the street, a voice called from behind. "Miss Hood! Miss Hood, a moment! Please!"

Caroline turned to find a group of three people coming toward them: a prosperous-looking middle-aged couple and a girl of fifteen or sixteen. The girl had been the one calling out her name. Caroline didn't recognize any of them.

"Hello," Caroline said, and put a question in the word.

"I'm sorry. The man at the store said it was you who'd just left, and I had to meet you. I hope you don't find me very forward." The girl had dark hair, a large mouth, and skin that was almost translucent. Her gray dress gave away its expensiveness in the way it gloved her.

"Eliza, please," the richly wrapped woman behind her said, grimacing at the sky and dragging a little on the arm of the man, who was thickset and luxuriant-bearded and crisp-edged in his top hat. Somehow none of the three of them seemed very wet.

"Excuse my mother. She doesn't like weather," the girl said. "I'm Eliza Pearson Bell."

She put weight on that name in the middle, and through her shock Caroline thought that someone should tell her not to be so obvious. But when she saw the way Eliza was watching, she realized that the middle name was not habitual, was just for Caroline, because Eliza wanted to see how it would land. Caroline tamped all reaction down beneath her own expression. She had never met Pearson's widow and daughter, who'd been only a baby when he'd died. She'd thought they lived in New York now. They were like figments made real and polished, this vivid girl and her decorative mother. She must have summoned them somehow by saying *The Darkening Glass* aloud.

"This is my mother, Adelaide Pearson Bell, and my stepfather, Matthew Bell."

The man tipped his hat; the woman pursed her mouth in their direction.

"A pleasure to meet you," Caroline said. "And this is Mr. David Moore."

From between buildings, a flurry of trilling hearts rose into the sky, and Caroline started at the sudden fragmenting and animation, like pieces of a still painting that had decided to move.

Eliza turned to watch them. "Aren't they beautiful!" she said.

Caroline smiled. *Beautiful.* Why did everyone seem to think that?

"Really, I can't get used to them. We were on a sort of New England expedition anyway, because Papa had some business, and once we heard about the trilling hearts, of course we had to come out here and see." Eliza's speech and gestures might have belonged to someone ten years older; she seemed a small, perfect, unnerving copy of an adult woman. "We took a tour."

"You practically gave the tour," her stepfather said. His voice turned out to be high and froggy.

"I shared a few things I happened to know." Eliza waved a hand. "I thought everyone might be interested."

"They were," said her stepfather.

Caroline imagined Eliza raising her arms and a cloud of birds swirling up, conducted.

"But of course now none of that will be the highlight of our trip. *You* will be. I just can't believe I'm meeting you in the flesh."

"Please, Eliza," her mother said again. It might have been the word *flesh* that set her off this time.

"Yes, sweetheart, we should be going," Bell added.

As if they hadn't spoken, Eliza continued. "Miss Hood, may I ask, is it true that you're opening a girls' school?"

"It is."

Eliza clasped her hands. "And I need a new school, don't I, Mama? I've been at Miss Marsh's, but it's only pretty prattling—you know, music, needlework."

Pearson's daughter, at their school? Even Pearson's book wasn't allowed in their house. This sleek and canny offspring—her face, her skin, her eyes, her words, would all be painful to Samuel anywhere, and unbearable inside his grand new project. Caroline thought about telling Eliza that they planned only pretty prattling too, but just by looking at Caroline the girl would have been able to tell it was a lie.

"I'm not sure . . . ," Caroline said.

"Isn't there room? I can make myself very small, I promise." In her composed face, Eliza's eyes were startling in their hunger.

At home sat Samuel, wrapped warm in blankets and sureness, thinking of his school for girls. He was imagining the girls themselves as a kind of beautiful clay: dense, rich, formless, and waiting for him. He was not thinking about failing, despite Caroline's efforts to remind him, despite the risks of that possibility for her too, the way it would bury both their lives. Had he ever considered her life, really? How its form, her form, was only ever the form he had given her? She the first piece of clay.

Well, perhaps Caroline should give him Eliza now. She was a girl, after all. Let him see what he could make of her. Let him see what it was like to try to make this particular girl into anything.

"There would be room, I think," Caroline said.

David turned to her with a polite smile and lifted eyebrows.

Caroline looked again to the Bells. "You'll of course need to discuss it."

"Oh, Mama and Papa will let me do what I like."

"Hmm," said Mrs. Bell.

"Why don't you talk it over and let us know? Though you'll need to decide quickly, I'm afraid; we do open in a week," Caroline told them.

They parted—Eliza bestowing her hand and showing her white teeth. David and Caroline made their way around the corner.

"Caroline, you saw so quickly," David said. "You understood right away. It took me a moment."

"Understood what?"

"What she could do for us, the word of mouth we'll get from having her."

Caroline looked into the window of the fabric store they were passing—a bolt of plaid, a bolt of black, a bolt of green—because if she looked at David he might see why she'd really done what she'd done. "Nothing will come of it, I'm sure. Why would Miles Pearson's daughter want to come to our school? She must have her pick of schools on two continents."

"Ours will be the best of any. Truly it will." He brushed at his forehead in excitement. "This will make us."

"My father won't see it that way."

"Your father wants this to succeed."

"Though he isn't very well acquainted with success of this sort."

"Caroline," he said sharply.

She met David's eyes. "I'm sorry."

All of this has happened before, she wanted to tell him—*you just weren't here the last time. You didn't see the way it all went, in the end.*

"I think we'd all be wise to remember that it isn't as easy to achieve a thing as to dream it up," she said.

"You think dreaming it up is *easy?*"

"For my father? Easier than considering practicalities. The many different ways of failing."

"We won't fail. And worrying about practicalities, all of that, it's unmaking the dream—anyone can do that."

"Anyone can unmake this one," she said. "We have seven students."

David was shaking his head. "I'm sure you have dreams. What are they, I wonder?"

Smooth red sleeves; her own promising nakedness.

"What I wouldn't give for a glimpse." David caught her gloved hand, then sighed and dropped it. He walked ahead. Behind him in the road, Caroline forgot her breath.

4

SCHOOL BEGINS

❦

She was to other women as a swan to sparrows—silk
to burlap—the finest marble to earth.

—MILES PEARSON, *THE DARKENING GLASS* (P. 72)

Trilling Heart's first morning arrived. Caroline found her
father and David in the barn that would be their classroom. She'd been having nightmares set in this room for the past
week—in the worst, the students weren't students at all but rat-
like creatures that scurried beneath her skirts while she screamed.
This morning she saw the space with fresh horror. Despite the
whitewashing David had done, the window he'd cut into the far
side, it was still unmistakably a barn; the new light only drew
attention to the rough hew of the planks. A wood floor had been
laid but not varnished. The ladder to the old hayloft had been
removed, perhaps so no wayward girl could climb up there, but
the hayloft itself remained. The whole place smelled of sawdust.

Her father sat at the teacher's desk, talking to David over the
heads of the busts of Milton and Plato that he'd carried here from
his study. Behind him stood two cases full of books. Those books
had made dazzling shapes inside Samuel's head, but that didn't
mean the girls would be able to see those shapes. What they'd
see: a barn filled with paper and wood. Caroline wondered if she
was ready to watch what the girls would do to her father.

"Caroline!" Samuel said. He rose and stepped out amongst

the desks and chairs David and Caroline had approved. He still hadn't quite recovered fully from his cold, and she thought he looked a little feverish. "Note the pattern of the desks, the circle. Whoever is giving the current lesson will take the teacher's desk, part of the circle in its own right."

She hadn't told her father about Eliza Pearson Bell until the confirming note had arrived, in handwriting that cupped years of elegant education in the letters' curves. Mama and Papa had indeed decided to let Eliza do as she liked, though that was not, this time, the way Eliza phrased things. Instead she wished to convey that she was beside herself with excitement, would do her best to be an asset to Trilling Heart, &c. When Caroline had carried the note to her father at his desk, he'd read it, then raised his eyes to her face. "Caroline, she makes it sound as if you've already agreed to this."

Her heart hammered. "I only told her there was room. She'd have heard so anyway."

Make of her what you will. Can you?

"What can you have been thinking?" The color of his face had become complicated—too red in places and too white in others.

David, sitting across the room: "Sir, I understand your reservations, but I do think she could be quite a good thing for us."

"It's . . . problematic."

"Does it need to be? Having her here will create new visibility for what we're undertaking."

Caroline and David looked at each other while they waited for her father to decide how he felt. They were united in this. Not for the same reasons, but still, the feeling of mutually assessing, of speaking with their eyes about what they saw—she hummed with it.

Samuel cleared his throat. There was a catch in the sound. "Well. Well, I suppose we should consider ourselves privileged to be touched by at least the fingertips of fame," he'd said, and David had smiled at her.

Now David told Samuel, "The circle is ingenious. One body, neither head nor foot."

"We're all to be like appendages?" said Caroline.

It would be best, she thought, if she could reach a calming verdict within herself about David: that conspiring with him was only a small, inconsequential pleasure, and that the moment on the road from Ashwell could not have meant what she'd at first thought and was only a comradely expression of affection between her father's foot soldiers. This was true even if David himself had thought he meant more by it (because he had sighed, he had walked away, he still didn't seem quite easy with her). He was living in their world now, with its limited cast; if she had his attention, she had it by default. She would be glad later if she kept hold of herself now.

As Caroline left the barn, a blur came at her, then deflected— a trilling heart, perching now above the door behind her as if the building belonged to it, hop, flutter, settle. She'd cried out: she glanced into the dim doorway, but it seemed her father and David hadn't heard. The bird, one of the duller red-brown females, had a tuft of twigs and grasses in its beak. A strong beak, it seemed: one or two of those twigs were thick as finger bones. Wasn't it too late in the season for nest building? The bird seemed to watch her. Had it wanted something, flying at her that way before changing its course? Her fingers curled into her palms, seeking protection.

*

Midmorning, the carriages bearing their students began to reach the farmhouse. One by one they climbed out, into the Hoods' lives, and then their mothers and fathers, all eager to shake Samuel's hand. Caroline tried to read the faces of the girls themselves but found them closed, tipped down in a pantomime of obedience that unnerved her. It screened something she would rather have seen outright. Given how well she knew the names on their list, and how few of them there were, Caroline found it surprisingly difficult to keep the girls straight. Livia had white-blond hair, and Julia a serious, narrow face, but somehow these and every feature seemed shiftable and just as easily attached to different names instead. The girls settled into the farmhouse, two to each subdivided bedroom (the requisite walls had been in place, leaning slightly, since Birch Hill). The parents then drove off again. Their daughters had been delivered efficiently as parcels.

Lessons were supposed to begin immediately—that had been important to Samuel—but Eliza Pearson Bell, final arrival, failed to actually arrive. Caroline watched her father begin to hope she wouldn't. Mrs. Sanders, who had come to cook and clean for them after Mrs. Wilmer died and whom they'd hired now, along with her husband, for expanded duties, led the rest of the girls to the barn. David followed.

Samuel planned to give the only lesson of this first day. He sat in the study, shuffling his notes, and Caroline waited with him because she couldn't bear to leave him alone just now. A woozy nostalgia for this quiet, the sound of sitting in a room alone with her father, swelled in her chest. How could she have considered the number of students small? Eight new faces she'd have to look at over meals, eight new treads going up and down their stairs. Eight pairs of eyes on every shabbiness. Eight notes of laughter that would greet Samuel's kind of words, so beautiful but pitched so high above the girls' heads, and so would the whole scheme crumble into dust, and maybe her father with it.

Or seven, if Eliza did not come, if the universe undid what Caroline had done in inviting her here.

But now, the rattle of an approaching carriage. Samuel flinched, then met Caroline's eyes. "We won't mention she's late," he said, and stood, pinching the seams of his trouser legs.

The dust of their road clung to the carriage's gleaming sides.

The driver tipped his hat, then went around to the back and handed down Eliza in a green traveling suit. Caroline waited for the driver to hand Mrs. Bell down next, or for Mr. Bell to clamber out, but no one else emerged. Eliza scanned her surroundings with the wonder of a child entering a fairy tale—and she was a child, of course.

What else would she turn out to be?

The driver hefted a trunk into their grass.

"Miss Bell? We're very happy you're here," Samuel said. "I'm Samuel Hood."

"An honor to meet you at last."

Caroline's head began to swim: she'd been holding her breath. But if Eliza believed Samuel was the serpent from her father's book, she hid it. She allowed him to press her hand and met Caroline's gaze as none of the other girls had done. "Miss Hood, a pleasure to see you again."

"Your parents aren't with you?" Caroline asked. She couldn't get past the feeling that they must be hidden away somewhere—still in the carriage, or up Eliza's sleeves.

"They're spending a month on the Continent, and it's a scramble to get ready. They thought I might manage. I'm late, I think. I'm sorry. I'll go right in, shall I?"

Without waiting, she followed the sound of the other girls' voices toward the barn, leaving the driver to wrestle the enormous trunk up the farmhouse steps. It seemed very heavy. Caroline imagined the Bells' bodies curled inside.

"She's very like him," Samuel said, in the tone he used to address himself.

Eliza had found an open seat in the circle. The other girls were still talking, still laughing—angled toward one another, not toward the front of the room—but Caroline saw them stealing secret glances at Eliza, drawn by her lateness, her clothes, her way of holding herself. Eliza sat still and faced forward. At the back of the room, David was reading with a suspicious degree of absorption. Caroline wondered if he had failed to stir himself to quiet the students because he feared they might not quiet if he asked, and then what would he do?

Samuel didn't tell the girls to hush either. He strode slowly through the center of the circle as if the noise weren't his concern. When he reached his desk, he put his book down, turned to face them, and waited. His quiet was catching: soon he had all of their eyes. Though of course Eliza hadn't been making noise to begin with.

"Thank you," Samuel said, and lifted his book again.

Caroline sat down beside David, watching her father.

"I thought for a long time about how best to begin with all of you," said Samuel. "How to explain to you the nature of what I hope this school will accomplish. Difficult, to decide the right way to take such a large and dearly loved plan and show it quickly, to best effect. You will certainly encounter this feeling in your own lives, if you haven't already—I have every confidence those lives will be passionate and full."

The girls measured Caroline's father silently.

"In the end, I decided on just a very few prefatory words before we take up our work. Look to your left, please." Coiffed heads turned. "Now look to your right. These are to be your companions. You are now one tribe. Together, you will voyage into extraordinary new territory. I can fix my hopes no higher than to wish that in the end, our experiment might live up to the rarity that already exists within each one of you."

He knew so little about them, rarities or otherwise, but they watched him now with less guarded interest. Who doesn't want to hear that she is as special as she has suspected all along?

"Now onward, my comrades in arms!" Samuel said, jesting and not jesting, and showed them the cover of the book he held. "Who has read *The Pilgrim's Progress?*"

Several said they had, Eliza not among them.

"We'll consider you our resident Bunyan experts. But you might find that on this tour the landscape strikes you differently."

Then he read to them from the beginning, Christian's attempts to convince his family that their city will soon burn. Her father's voice on the old lines: if Caroline had closed her eyes, she might have been eight years old, drowsy by the fire in the study. "'At this his relations were sore amazed; not for that they believed that what he had said to them was true, but because they thought that some frenzy or distemper had got into his head.'" Samuel looked up. "Why do you think Christian's relations didn't believe him?"

No one volunteered an answer. They all seemed to be wondering if this were a trap—if he might reprimand whoever responded for the disobedience of speaking in the classroom.

"Come," Samuel said. "None of you has ever tried to convince someone of something and failed? Raise your hands if you have ever told a truth that was perceived as either a lie or a mistake. Go on, raise them."

Hands, a few at first, then more, crept up. Eliza sat still.

"Why weren't you taken at your word?"

Rebecca Johns, who had tidy braids and a small frown that seemed permanent, said, "Because the truth sounded far-fetched."

"And that's part of the trouble here too, don't you think? Though I doubt, Miss Johns, that your own claim sounded as far-fetched as a prediction that a standing city will be consumed by fire. Yet doesn't it seem that the benefits of belief in this case would outweigh the costs? If there might be a fire or might not be, what does one lose by guarding against it? Think of this in your own lives, in your own homes. Imagine you're told such a thing. Wouldn't you gather your possessions, prepare to leave?"

Felicity Ridell spoke next. "I don't think I'd want to."

As she watched and listened, Caroline found that the girls were coming into focus for her. Felicity was small, sharp-featured—

the bridge of her nose delicate as an ornament—and sharp-eyed. Caroline was starting to feel sure she could never confuse her for any of the others.

"Just so, Miss Ridell, and that's related to the cost, I think. The belief that one's home, everything one has worked for, might be so vulnerable—the fear that occasions is itself a very great cost. Can you all understand that?"

"Yes," said Tabitha Seward, nodding decisively. Samuel waited for Tabitha to continue, but nothing else followed. She only watched him with a dull expectance. Caroline began to have a sense of Tabitha too.

"Well then. Good," Samuel said. "It's too great a cost, perhaps, for poor Christian's relations to face."

Eliza put her hand up.

"Miss Bell?"

"I noticed you didn't raise your own hand, sir," she said.

The room pulled in its breath.

"Pardon me?" Samuel said.

"When you asked who'd told a truth that had been disbelieved, you didn't raise your hand. Can it be the case—excuse me, sir— that you never have? I was just thinking—back when you and my father and the others saw the trilling hearts for the first time. People can't possibly have believed you right away, can they?"

No extra emphasis on *my father* because none was needed. Caroline realized she'd been waiting for this, for Eliza to announce herself, for her to lift her chin—here, where she must feel herself to be standing inside her father's book—and say his name.

"Your father?" Rebecca asked.

"Yes, Miles Pearson," Eliza said.

"Not the author."

"Of course the author." A casual slicing; Eliza hadn't even turned her head. Rebecca sat back in her seat. "Sir, forgive me, but it just seems that people must have thought you were lying."

This perhaps was when Caroline made her first mistake with Eliza—or her first after allowing her out of her carriage, after opening Eliza's letter, after telling Eliza they had space for her here, after stopping, on the street in Ashwell, when she'd heard Eliza call. In this moment she might still have summoned Mr. Sanders to lug Eliza's trunk back down the stairs, put her into their carriage, drive her back into town, and leave her wherever in Ashwell a young girl could safely be left. She might still have lifted every touch of Eliza out of their lives like the lifting of a stain.

But here it was, the test Caroline had wanted. She wanted now to see what her father would do. Now that he had listened to this girl raise a question he had not planned for her, about the father whose name he had banned from his house. Now that he had heard her find a voice and use it to call him a liar.

Samuel's brow knit. "Do you know, Miss Bell, I honestly can't remember. The sure sign, in my long experience, of a thing not worth recollecting." He opened his book again.

*

The next morning, Caroline awoke to a gray sky and the unaccustomed sounds of the girls stirring in the rooms around her: feet on the floorboards, a window opening, a high-pitched laugh. *The second day* was hers and David's—Samuel had bestowed it upon them, biblically, weeks ago. David would teach this morning and she would teach this afternoon. It had seemed a simple enough thing when her father had said it.

The girls arrived for David's lesson well wrapped against the new chill and expecting to be taught by Samuel. David strode through the circle to take his place. Caroline and Samuel watched from the back of the room, and Caroline saw the girls noticing David's height, his breadth, the set of his jaw, his relative youth, and she thought for a moment things might go well for him. Then he began to speak.

"My name is Mr. Moore. I will take the lesson this morning, on natural history." He seemed to peer at the girls from a distance, his face hard. They caught one another's eyes; he was turning himself into something they had to decide about.

David moved from desk to desk, placing a blank journal before each girl. Caroline knew he'd envisioned this bestowing as a joyful ceremony, but there was haste in the motions of his hands. "Part of your education here will concern the inexhaustible variety of creation that surrounds us. We have a duty to study and reflect upon that creation. Our first lesson will therefore take place out of doors. All you will need is a pencil and the book I've just given you."

"Out*side*?" shrieked Livia Bunting, who seemed to speak loudly or not at all. "We'll freeze, sir, truly."

"I've worn my best shoes," said Meg Sawyer. The others laughed.

Eliza cast an eye on Meg's feet. "You don't think you could bear the loss?"

Louder laughter as Meg's expression changed. Caroline wondered how Eliza had already managed to gather in her fist the threads that led to the other girls' hearts. A slight tug there, a repositioning there, and oh, there, a quick, sharp pull.

David worked his mouth while they all waited for his words.

"Miss Bell," Samuel said, from his seat beside Caroline. But this wasn't his classroom, not now, and his speaking didn't help anything.

In a reluctant clump, the girls followed David from the barn toward the crest of the big hill opposite the house. He walked too fast. Caroline and Samuel trailed behind the students.

"Do you think he'll manage it, Caroline?" Samuel said softly.

She'd wanted this, wanted to grow a fear in her father, but now his fear infuriated her. "Early to despair, isn't it? He hasn't even started."

"You're right, of course."

David stopped at the peak of the hill and waited for the girls to reach him. "As you can see, ladies—"

"*I* wouldn't mind being his lady," Livia hissed to Meg, performance-patting her fuzzy halo of hair. Caroline was standing right behind them and could hear, knew this meant she should do something, was unsure what. "Do you think he wants one?"

"—the property of the school consists of both meadow and woods, each with its own flora and fauna. For the next half hour you'll explore these habitats and select a single specimen that interests you. When time is up, bring the specimen you've chosen back to the classroom. I will identify your specimens, and then you'll draw them."

The girls wandered away. David was already striding back toward the barn, desperate, Caroline was sure, for escape.

"I think I'll get a bit of air, just while they're hunting," Samuel said. After all, it was from him that Caroline had learned her habit of walking their fields when most afraid.

Caroline hurried to catch David. She matched his step. She thought of laying her hand on his elbow but didn't. "I'm sure all will be well once they get back," she told him.

"All is perfectly well now." He moved ahead. Back in the barn's dim stillness, he opened a book and didn't look up until the others returned, Samuel first and then the girls. They all took their places again.

And then, a modest miracle: there came a glorious turning. For when the girls loosed their specimens on the desks, they somehow loosed David too. Tabitha had brought back a toad that tried to leap from her desk to the floor, to much squealing; David caught it one-handed and put it in a wooden box. "American toad, *Bufo americanus*," he said.

He grinned at all of them—the same delighted grin he'd given Caroline on the front steps the day she'd met him. Quick as that, they were won.

He knew it too. He fanned out Meg's wood sorrel plant on her desk, pointing out the heart-shaped leaves. He brushed at the fringe of grasses Rebecca had picked. He revolved Felicity's King Bolete mushroom between his thumb and forefinger and pronounced it a fine fat thing.

Samuel laughed with the others, and Caroline could hear his easing.

David reached Eliza. She'd been sitting quietly, her body curled around her hands, which were cupped at her stomach. Now she held one out to show a trilling heart feather like a great red slash across her palm. Looking at it felt like looking at a wound. Caroline's own palm pressed itself to her thigh.

Eliza peered up at David, shyly but intently too, as if she were baring a more private stretch of flesh. "It was so strange," she said. "I saw the bird, not the feather. It flew toward me, and then it waited while I came closer. I got so close I could almost have touched it. When it flew off, the feather was right there in the grass. I swear it, that bird seemed to want me to have this."

Her face shone, of course. Walking her dead father's landscape, she'd found a proof of inheritance, sure as a lock of his hair. Caroline could see it all as clearly as if she'd been present: the bird waiting in the grass, fixing Eliza with its eye that saw in her— what? And then darting up into the air, having left this souvenir of itself for her to lay across her skin.

What, Caroline wondered, would the trilling heart want as payment?

The other girls' eyes were wide.

"Well, the bird probably would have preferred to keep it, given the choice," David said.

"Almost like it *knew*," Meg said. "Who you are. Who your father was."

"That would be a tremendous strain on the avian brain, Miss Sawyer," Samuel said, but his voice seemed thin and slight, a cobweb over what was happening.

"'A place of marvels,'" Eliza said.

Caroline wouldn't place the words until that night, just before sleep. The same words Louisa Blake says to Hammond on the day they first meet in *The Darkening Glass*. "This is a place of marvels." Who was Eliza, to quote them here?

Pearson's daughter, and Caroline had invited her in.

*

Mrs. Sanders served a passable meat pie for dinner, but Caroline would be teaching straight after and found she couldn't swallow any. David, beside her at one end of the long table, wolfed his. "Thank God for all those afternoons I spent out of doors, bored senseless, as a boy," he said.

"I thought you were never worried about how it was going," said Caroline.

"You didn't think that," David said, "for a second."

She'd been planning to ask what he made of Eliza and her feather, but she saw he was too full now of his triumph, of the pride with which Samuel had clapped him on the shoulder when his lesson was done.

Their warm, sated bellies made the girls sluggish, and back in the barn they slumped a little in their seats. From the teacher's desk, Caroline surveyed them. Why did they look so young? At fourteen, fifteen, she'd felt as complete as she did now. The lines of their faces were still cloudy with changing. All but Eliza's, which was clear enough.

"I'm your third instructor, Miss Hood," she told them, "and I'll be directing your study of English literature." She handed around the books while her father and David regarded her from the back wall.

"Miss? Will we read any Miles Pearson?" said Felicity, stealing a glance at Eliza.

"I *loved The Darkening Glass*," Livia chirped.

Eliza watched Caroline. Was that a hint of a smile at the corners of her mouth?

Caroline took a breath. "I'm afraid we won't have time to read contemporary novels here."

"He isn't really contemporary, is he? He's dead," Livia said. Then she flushed—she had skin that mottled—and told Eliza, "Sorry."

"I was aware," Eliza said.

It seemed to Caroline that this was not a place to linger. "We'll be beginning much further in the past. Most of you will have read some Shakespeare, I believe," Caroline said.

Nods around the circle.

"Whatever play you studied, you likely found it at least somewhat difficult." Fewer nods. "Shakespeare is wonderfully rich but also wonderfully demanding, for everyone. Soon we'll be studying *A Midsummer Night's Dream*, but today we'll read some of the sonnets, with the aim of arming ourselves for those difficulties, on a larger scale, by beginning to settle into the rhythms and patterns of Shakespearean language. You may open your books to Sonnet 65, please. Would anyone like to read it for us?"

Sunny-faced Abigail Smith raised her hand. She read smoothly, though with the loaded pauses at the ends of the lines that Caroline had forgotten from her previous schoolroom:

Since brass, nor stone, nor earth, nor boundless sea,
But sad mortality o'ersways their power,
How with this rage shall beauty hold a plea,
Whose action is no stronger than a flower?
O, how shall summer's honey breath hold out
Against the wrackful siege of battering days,
When rocks impregnable are not so stout,
Nor gates of steel so strong, but Time decays?
O fearful meditation! where, alack!

Shall Time's best jewel from Time's chest lie hid?
Or what strong hand can hold his swift foot back?
Or who his spoil of beauty can forbid?
O, none, unless this miracle have might,
That in black ink my love may still shine bright.

Abigail's cheeks were red with risk.

"Thank you," Caroline said. "Let's begin by discussing the *structure* of the poem. You might already be familiar with sonnet form. Like all of Shakespeare's sonnets, this one has three quatrains and a couplet. Each of the quatrains, in this case, elaborates upon the same basic problem, to which the couplet then offers a solution. Let's see if we might determine what that problem is. There's a struggle set up here, a war between two opposing forces, which the speaker fears are unequal—what are they? Can anyone tell?"

"Time," Eliza said, "and beauty."

"Exactly right."

Julia Altman raised her hand and intoned, "Beauty is fleeting. True grace belongs only to the soul."

Caroline hoped never to spend much time with Julia's mother. "Yes, thank you, Miss Altman. Now, everyone, look at the poem again—what clues does the imagery give us about the strength of the two forces in question? What are the images associated with time, or with the things time manages to destroy?"

The girls gave them to her: "brass," "stone," "earth," "boundless sea," "wrackful siege," "battering days," "rocks impregnable," "gates of steel," "swift foot." Then they produced the images associated with the lover's beauty: "a flower," "summer's honey breath," "best jewel." "Note how vastly stronger time is made to appear," Caroline told them. "It isn't until the end of the poem that we arrive at the only possible solution to the problem of beauty's inevitable decay. Which is what?"

"Well, his writing?" Livia said. "Anyone who reads the poem will know how beautiful she was."

"Yes! This grants a sort of immortality." Caroline felt so eloquent suddenly, as if she might have explained anything to anyone. "A perpetuation of the spirit, the immortal thing we all do have."

"It's a comfort, to think there might be ways of compensating for loss," Eliza said. "That's what I've found, anyway, in my own life."

"What do you *mean*?" Meg asked.

Livia elbowed her. "Her father, obviously."

"Oh, both my parents."

Caroline said, "Your mother is living." It was startled out of her.

"Her life doesn't include me, though, really, and so in many ways we're lost to each other, I think."

Caroline watched the girls mull this over in the light that spilled through the barn's new window—watched them begin to wonder if it might be true of their own mothers too. What did it mean that Eliza had aired such a private thing so quickly? Only that she was seeking attention, perhaps. Or that she hoped if she met Trilling Heart with her entire self in her hands, it would give her its entire self in return.

That she wanted, wanted, wanted.

"What about you, Miss Hood?" Eliza said. "Does this poem comfort you too?"

The question was like a specimen pin fastening Caroline to her desk. *Louisa Blake*, they were thinking, the ones who knew. Soon they all would. *Her mother was lost Louisa Blake.*

Comfort? No. She'd never found a record of grief that she recognized. These words did what all beautiful words had always done, more and more the longer the years she spent with them: they inflamed her. They promised and promised, and yet here she still was.

She glanced at the back of the room. David looked stricken. Her father was getting ready to open his mouth and try to save her. Eliza leaned in, and Caroline knew better than to let her draw breath.

"Let's return to the poem, Miss Bell," Caroline said. "It's more interesting than I am." A fruitless wriggle on the pin.

5

COUCHED

❦

Deep, transformative, is a spiritual satisfaction!

—MILES PEARSON, *THE DARKENING GLASS* (P. 93)

Those first weeks, teaching exhausted Caroline. After the long quiet of her previous life, all the words she spoke in front of the girls sapped her, and her throat felt always raw from use. By evening, if she tried to sit and read, her eyes drifted closed. There was satisfaction in this tiredness. She liked using herself up.

They'd started *A Midsummer Night's Dream*, and Caroline had the girls act frequently, entering and exiting the patch of cleared floor in the center of the desks' circle, reading their parts. Felicity was a nimble reader, Eliza delivered lines almost musically, but the real revelation was Livia. The drama of her voice and expressions, overdone for her own life, bore up beautifully under the play's weight. "'How happy some o'er other some can be!'" she read, accusing them all.

"Extraordinary," said Samuel, during one of their teachers' meetings. "It raises the question of what roles she's playing at other times."

In these meetings none of them seemed to know what to say about Eliza. On every one of her days at Trilling Heart so far, Eliza had remade herself. She appeared one morning with her dark hair upswept and tightly coiled, the next with it pinned loose and low. A plain dress that on Tuesday hung modestly was transformed on Friday, by a purple sash and draped lace, into a frothy swirl.

"Such variety!" Caroline said to her.

Eliza smiled, and beneath the smile was that craving for— what? "I'm looking for the right way to be, here," she said.

"The right way to be is of course to be yourself."

"Yes, of course."

That same Friday, three sashes appeared on other girls. Felicity and Meg both came down to breakfast with their hair high on their heads the day after Eliza had; finding that Eliza's hair had changed, Meg re-pinned hers lower by dinnertime, though Felicity's stayed tentatively in place, small wisps escaping to cling to her thin, fragile-looking neck.

The girls seemed drawn together as easily as iron filings. They walked, sat, and ate only in groups. Patterns became clear. Livia and Meg were a set, always talking loudly and always in the same way, with Livia offering some new salaciousness and Meg answering with her noisy toneless laugh. Abigail, Felicity, and Rebecca made their own group, quieter and more deliberate, often echoing the quips and styles of Livia and Meg an hour or a day later. Tabitha and Julia were left a pairing by default, like two spinster aunts seated next to each other at supper. Eliza attached where she wanted. She was most often with Livia and Meg, and rarely with Tabitha and Julia, and never, ever alone.

One day in their third week, Caroline went into Eliza's empty room to deliver a thin letter from Mrs. Bell. Putting the envelope on the girl's pillow, she saw the trilling heart feather from the first day of lessons tacked to the headboard, as if part of some blood ritual.

She ran her fingers over it. So crisp one way—smooth enough to feel almost wet on her fingertips—but the other way, a jaggedness. Those red tines stiff and sharp enough to bury themselves in her skin. What could Eliza want with it? Posted there where she might look up and see it first thing each morning, a promise of what the day ahead would bring. Who would want such a bloodred promise? Caroline smoothed the ruffled edges down before she left, erasing her intrusion.

She hated to bother her father with formless fears when his project seemed in most ways to be succeeding so marvelously. The girls had adapted quickly to their new right to speak, think, question—as if all of it had been ready inside them and waiting only for someone to ask to hear. As Samuel taught, Caroline had the feeling that she was witnessing the creation of one of those great Renaissance paintings of crowds, a monumental sweep in which each face is individual and sharp. He brought the girls, so gently, to see themselves in the mirror of the text and to decide what they might want to change in that reflection: Julia her prizing of rules; Meg her swayability; Felicity her ambition.

Though Eliza did sometimes hoist a piece of the past out of its grave, into the middle of the classroom floor, where it sent up its pervasive odor. "My mother said my father always loved the House of the Interpreter episode. Did you know that, sir?"

"No, Miss Bell, I can't remember that our favorite passages of *Pilgrim's Progress* ever came up."

"What other books did he love, do you know? I've just always wondered."

"Of course you have," Samuel said. "But it was so long ago. I'm sorry."

Eliza nodded. "Did you talk often, I wonder?"

"Certainly."

Eliza nodded again. *If you say so,* that nod said.

Also: *I am doing what you like, for now, but I am not yours.*

*

Apart from one another, David was the girls' main audience. He was the only object for all the feelings they'd brought with them.

They laughed and shrieked louder than usual during David's lessons, and their voices were higher. After the lessons were over they argued about whom he had looked at the longest.

"You've certainly made an impression," Caroline told him, at the end of his lesson on cloud formation. The girls had just disappeared through the door, Livia calling, "Fare*well*, Mr. Moore!"

"Though never on you, despite all my best efforts," he said, smiling, with just a quick glance at her, as if wary of looking too long, as if the sight of her cost him somehow.

Her heart, her heart, surely he could hear it.

"You don't impress easily. Your approval would be a particular triumph," he said.

"You know you have that," she told him. It had a less playful sound than she'd intended.

He stepped toward her, close and then closer, and then reached past for a book left lying on the desk to her side. When he straightened again he looked at her with surprise, because there was a feel in the space that separated them now of a thread being drawn tight.

"Caroline," he said, and put his hand on her upper arm. Her skin beneath her sleeve greeted that weight joyously, and he met her eyes, and his were wide, and his fingers tightened as if to pin that joy between them, at this meeting point of their bodies.

Did he drop his hand first? Did she move her arm first? Impossible, after, for her to know. She reached for her books and took her time stacking them, watching only her own hands, not letting herself look at him again. When she was finished she left.

David's lessons moved into the biology of plants. The girls preened before him as he bounced around the room: to the blackboard to draw the details of a leaf's architecture, to Julia's desk to point out an omission in the labeling of her diagram, to the center of the circle to explain the role of sunlight, rocking a little from heel to toe to heel again. "It's a trade, light for fuel," he said.

Here he caught Caroline staring at him and looked away.

He came to find her that night in the sitting room, where she was sewing an old sheet into a robe for Oberon to wear in the morning. "I saw Miss Ridell leaving," he said. "Is she all right?"

Felicity had come to talk to Caroline about a barbed letter her sister, a year younger, had sent her. That and she'd lost one of her favorite earrings, and no one else would look very hard for it, and the day had become a tragedy. She'd cried a little.

"Only hurt feelings," Caroline said.

The girls often brought their problems to her. Mostly they didn't want help, only to learn they could withstand the speaking of these problems out loud. Caroline was good at giving them this feeling, just as she was good—not great, not her father, but good—at helping them see the meaning of words on a page.

She'd found herself beginning to have a curious feeling, previously unknown to her, of fitting.

"Oh, good," David said. He cleared his throat. "Caroline, might I speak with you?"

She noticed he had his fists balled in his pockets. "You look like you're coming to confess something." She laughed, but he didn't, so she stopped.

He sat in the chair opposite. "There's something I should say, something I probably should have said long ago."

How would it unfold, Caroline wondered, if it did? Would he touch her hands, her face, carefully at first? Or a seizing, her lips to his, the salt-bread-and-heat smell of his throat, the feel of her face caught in his hands? These were scenes she had never played. She neatened the sheet in her lap: creasing and creasing again.

Gesturing to the sheet, David said, "But you're busy."

"Caroline!" Samuel called from the hall. He appeared in the doorway. "Mrs. Sanders is wondering about new bed linens. I find I have no distinct opinion."

David smiled at Caroline. "Another time."

She returned his smile. *Say the rest,* she willed him, as she stood; *Stop me,* as he let her father lead her down the hall.

When she lay down that night beneath her quilts (the nights were growing cold already), she tried letting the rest of the scene play out.

I didn't know such a feeling could exist, he would tell her.

And she would say, *Nor I.*

Nor I.

I.

I.

Hands on her face. Hands on her neck, her breasts, her waist, her hips.

I.

I.

Hands on her central pulse, all the warmth gathered there. Hands. His, hers. Here they were. What words had ever given her hands before?

*

In the back garden, planning her lessons a few days later— sitting in the grass, one palm flat to the swell of the ground, like a hip's curve—Caroline saw a group of trilling hearts fly by. One seemed to have a bundle of something in its beak. Another thieving of some part of their woods or their meadow. Except— was that a circlet of hair? Brown and long and fine, too fine to be grass. At the sight, a queasiness washed over her, a recoiling like what she felt on occasionally discovering the viscera of small animals strewn in their fields, dark and bloody near the hollowed-out skins. She stood for a better look, but the bird was already out of sight, carrying whatever it was to wherever it was going.

Grass after all, probably.

*

The time had come to hold their experiment up to the light, Samuel announced in a meeting at the end of the first month. By *light* he meant the eyes of Thoreson, the educational champion of order and discipline he and Hawkins had discussed. It transpired that Samuel and Thoreson had lately been corresponding.

"Why?" Caroline asked.

"He wrote to me first," Samuel said. "He expressed an interest in seeing our project for himself."

"Papa, doesn't that seem an unnecessary risk? He'll see what we're doing here as a direct challenge to his own work, won't he? And we know he has a propensity for essay writing."

"If it's a challenge, a competition," David said, "we'll win."

And so, one gray and drizzling Thursday, Thoreson arrived. Mrs. Sanders showed him to the study, a young man in a smart coat, with sand-colored hair and a square jaw. "We're so pleased to have you," Samuel said. He shook Thoreson's hand. "It will be an honor to show our project to a fellow educator, a fellow thinker."

"The honor is mine," Thoreson said with a smile. He was probably no older than David. He looked like a person who liked right angles and who would enjoy making rooms of people quieter. "I still remember reading your essays in school." *Long ago*, he wanted Samuel to understand.

Samuel clicked his tongue modestly. "These are our other teachers, David Moore and my daughter, Caroline Hood."

Thoreson pressed Caroline's hand and smiled at her without seeing her, as people tended to do. With David there was a strong gripping on both sides. David said, "Mr. Thoreson, we hear a great deal these days about your own schools."

"Yes, we just opened our sixth, in Boston. So I know this early phase you're in very well. Astonishing how different it all is in practice than in planning, isn't it?"

"As in so many areas of life," Samuel said.

"I'm fascinated by the particulars here. Teaching these girls Greek, and mathematics, and scientific inquiry. I do admire your ambition."

Exactly what Caroline had known he would say—what she'd known the whole world would say—and perhaps because she was so ready to hear it, she surprised herself by speaking before her father did. "Mr. Thoreson, you teach both girls and boys, is that correct?"

"That's right. Almost equal numbers, at least in the earlier grades."

"Have you found that there's any difference in aptitude?"

He squinted consideringly. Perhaps he really had never thought about it before.

"No, you're quite right—there isn't a marked one, anyway, Miss Hood. Though we aren't teaching much Greek at present." He chuckled. "We're more—if you've read anything about our schools, you'll know—we're more interested in teaching the kind of self-control our girls and boys will need when they're women and men, as good, productive members of society."

"Oh, certainly," Samuel said. "But it is an open question, what good and productive members of society most need. Now if you'll come with me, the girls will be almost ready." He walked from the room.

Visibly, Thoreson wanted to answer, but he would have had to answer to Samuel's moving back. He followed.

Samuel settled Thoreson on the visitors' couch, with Caroline and David to either side. Caroline watched him take in the circle of desks and the girls seated at them, who were eyeing the visitor curiously. She glanced at Eliza—innocent looking in light blue and braids—and felt a little twinge of senseless fear. *Please don't*, she thought, *not today*, without even knowing what she would have liked to prohibit.

"Girls, we have a guest, as you can see," Samuel said from the front of the room. "This is Mr. Thoreson. He is interested in our daily work. Let's show it to him, shall we?"

Greek had not been first on the agenda. It was first on the agenda now. The girls opened their Homer and read in turns, Samuel correcting their pronunciation. They wrote in response to brief prompts and read their responses aloud. The room felt charged with their desire to perform well, and they did, though Abigail used an incorrect declension. It would have looked worse if no one had done that, Caroline told herself—less real. And this was real, their high voices making those weighty sounds. Caroline could have sung.

Instead of fearing Thoreson would write about this, she began to hope he would. She looked at David, his forward tilt on the sofa, his eyes on the girls except for quick assessing glances at Thoreson's immobile face.

Next Samuel asked the girls to put their Greek books away and take out their copies of *The Pilgrim's Progress.* "You all began part two yesterday evening," Samuel said. "What are your impressions thus far?"

"Is it really going to be the same story all over again, all the same exact stops, just with Christian's wife and their children instead of Christian this time?" asked Livia. The other girls laughed. "It's just we've already read all that."

Thoreson narrowed his eyes. Caroline wondered what would have happened to a girl in a Thoreson school who said such a thing. Chains in the corner, maybe. An underground chamber in the center of the classroom springing open, the offender fed to the dark mouth of impudence.

"If you'll allow me, Miss Bunting," Samuel said, "I'll answer your question with another. *Is* it the same journey if different people are on it? Girls, do you believe that Christian, alone, experienced this journey in the same way as will his wife and their children?"

"Well, no," said Felicity.

"And why not? Think, please. Imagine yourself as Christian, walking down the road. Then imagine yourself as his wife. How do you see your surroundings in each case? In each case, how do you feel?"

He waited for their girls to imagine themselves men, then imagine themselves women.

"I'm more afraid the second time," Eliza said. "Threats are different when you're a man, I think, since you yourself are more of a threat too. It's all more even."

"Just so," Samuel said. "How then might we anticipate that will affect the experience of this journey?"

"It might be slower," Julia said. "Because they'll be afraid and reluctant to go on. And because everything will take longer too for them to get by."

"Oh, *slower*," Livia said, and groaned, and they all laughed again—Thoreson took in a breath, stirred on the couch—but it was all right, Samuel laughed with them.

"But not necessarily duller, Miss Bunting—fear not!" he said. "Suspense in large part has to do with the scale of obstacles— the *relative* scale—and not with pace. There will be quite enough to command your interest, I assure you. What else, girls? What other differences might you expect?"

"It might be sadder this time," Abigail said quietly.

"Interesting. Why?"

"Well, they're weaker. And *Christian* barely made it to the Celestial City. So it's not a certain thing they'll get there, is it?" she said.

Once the lesson was over, in the study, Thoreson barely let the others get through the door before he started talking. "Impressive," he said. "Thus far their progress with the Greek is clearly passable, and you've certainly got them thinking."

"I certainly hope so," said Samuel.

"I wonder what you make of what that round-faced girl said, though. About Christian's family. How some of them may suffer." Thoreson waited. He seemed to feel he'd said enough to be clear.

"Was she wrong?" Samuel said.

"But she wasn't speaking only of the characters. You can see that, surely."

"No, she wasn't."

"Do you consider it *right*, to make young women think about such things? Weakness, and the difficulties of their lot? The future tragedies that may befall them?"

"I would argue that it is always right to think," Samuel said.

"What good will it do them to dwell on it?" Thoreson said, disconcerted at finding his unanswerable point answered—as if he'd tried to make one of his beloved right angles and discovered the edges would not quite meet. That square jaw hung slightly. "What will it accomplish? Many of the hardships that will confront them are not avoidable. They are inevitable."

Samuel nodded. "Some might be changed, perhaps, if they know about them ahead of time. Others not."

"Giving them that kind of knowledge—encouraging that kind of contemplation—seems to me cruel."

"I don't think so. It's in such contemplation that we foster the enlargement of the soul," Samuel said.

"Oh, souls, souls. We need to worry about the *world*, not souls. *Show* me a soul."

"Didn't we?" Caroline said.

Samuel bid Thoreson farewell and shook his hand at the front door, though he came out onto the stoop to see him off. Caroline and David walked him to the carriage. Four trilling hearts cut across the sky, and Thoreson stopped to watch them. "They are real then," he said.

They were, they were real; perhaps they were the same kind of real as their girls and what their girls were doing. Perhaps, after all, everything was linking together in the way Samuel had designed.

David lingered next to Caroline by the carriage door, after it had closed behind Thoreson. "We rattled him," he whispered, leaning in. Caroline could feel his breath on her neck. She turned toward him and laughed. She looked at her father across the grass as he waved at the carriage, pulling away now, carrying Thoreson and their triumph, like a fellow passenger unwelcome beside him.

6.

A FAINTING

That instant broke upon him in a vast wave.

—MILES PEARSON, *THE DARKENING GLASS* (P. 120)

The feeling of having won was a lingering sweetness perched far back on Caroline's tongue where she was accustomed to tasting dread. They were doing what they'd planned, sweeping even Pearson's daughter up. All of them together were doing it, and David seemed on the point, the very point, of telling Caroline what this meant to him, their togetherness, hers and his, in accomplishing such a thing. Any day now, any moment that felt to him like the right one—it didn't matter which, for here Caroline would be, ready, here where she had always been. She sensed a newness in the air of the house, in its taste, and now even, she thought, in the shape of her own features in the mirror, their somehow lighter set.

The books came, then, souring.

One day Meg had *The Darkening Glass*, that thick black volume Caroline would have known anywhere, tucked between wholesome schoolbooks; the next, Livia had it on her desk, like the black mark of a spreading plague. Natural, Caroline tried to tell herself—not worth worrying over—until she saw Abigail and Felicity too with it.

"New reading?" she asked.

"My doing, Miss Hood," Eliza said. "I had a few sent for the girls who were interested. Some of them hadn't read it. You don't mind, do you?"

She presented to Caroline her adult smile, her calm, inscrutable face.

"It's so *beautiful*," Felicity said. She pressed her palm to the cover.

Samuel wasn't present; Caroline would have liked to see his expression. Those black covers made phrases stir greasily in her memory. If it had been a different bad book, she'd have told Felicity she was smart enough to know better. But as things stood, what could she say in front of Pearson's daughter? She wasn't going to become David's Ohio schoolmaster, prohibiter of reading, especially this reading. She wouldn't prize a poor fatherless girl's remembrance from her fingers. She knew so well what that clutch felt like.

"Only remember it's a work of fiction," she told them. "It might be easy to forget, given where we all are, but it's a product of imagination." She looked not at Eliza but at the others. *What her father wrote of mine was his own invention, nothing more.*

"Oh yes," Eliza said.

And perhaps it would be fine. The girls might simply wade through all Pearson's words and come out clean on the other side. They were receiving something here, after all. If she wanted proof of that, she'd had it in Thoreson's slack mouth.

Before long, though, a certain resistance crept into Samuel's lessons, in small enough ways that at first Caroline couldn't be sure. Her father was still brilliant, and the lessons still went where he wanted them to go, but now Caroline could sometimes feel a moment of drag on the line before he began to pull the girls with him.

"What do you all think of Mercy's behavior here?" Samuel asked.

"What aspect of her behavior in particular?" said Julia.

"Well, her words, I suppose."

"What *about* her words, sir?" said Meg.

Caroline found her father afterward. "They seemed a bit reluctant today."

"Reluctance is the natural province of the student," Samuel said. "We do not blame the sky for being blue."

On a chill Wednesday afternoon, six of the girls, in cloaks and shawls, circled on the grass under the birch by the front step. *The Darkening Glass* lay open on each lap. Caroline spied them from her bedroom window, went down the stairs, out the back door, and around the house. She wasn't creeping up on them—she was going for a walk. They would see her when they saw her.

In the meantime, she could hear Abigail's voice, reading. "'Night approached quickly, but not as quickly as the answering night within.'" Caroline drew nearer. Half of them looked down at their pages, dutiful as if this were a classroom. Livia fidgeted, Tabitha stared up into the leaves—Caroline had yet to see Tabitha attend to any reading, or really any sustained task, without several promptings—and Eliza reclined on one elbow, watching Abigail, whose face, tipped to the words, seemed to glow in the sunlight reflecting off the page. "'A fear, nay, a terror for her grew in him.'" Eliza's eyes on Caroline now.

"Hello," Eliza said.

Abigail stopped, startled.

"Aren't you all a picture of industry."

Had Abigail volunteered, or had Eliza called on her?

"How are you finding your reading?"

"Wonderful," Tabitha said.

"It's the best book I've ever read," Rebecca added. Rebecca who had now read *A Midsummer Night's Dream*, *The Pilgrim's Progress*, and the Bible.

Eliza smiled. "They're so kind to me."

A chorus of protests.

Caroline wondered what the lines sounded like to Eliza, read aloud by these other girls—if she were only making use of every voice available to her, in the hopes that one of them, reading, might happen at last to catch a cadence her bones knew. If she meant to fill her world with the speaking of her father's words, strike and strike herself with them until she could feel their marks. Had she managed it yet?

"I should have said this before, but if any of you have—questions about anything you find—I'll do my best to answer them," Caroline said.

She felt the offer limping from her. They had chosen already. That was why this circle frightened her; she had not formed it, nor had any of the teachers.

The girls looked, every one of them, to Eliza.

"Thank you very much, Miss Hood," Eliza said.

*

The weather warmed again in the second week of October. The leaves flared, filling the air with the spectacle and earthy scent of their dying, but the ground was still soft and alive underfoot, and the sun ripened in a hot blue sky. David moved his lessons back outdoors.

"But I'm *tired*, Mr. Moore!" the girls would cry, each time he announced they were going out. "Couldn't we just talk in here today?" Performing their exhaustion, going limp, draping themselves over their desks and chairs. Their love for him was connected to their bodies in ways most of them didn't yet understand.

"We could not," David told them briskly, and clapped his hands, so up and out they went.

Sometimes Caroline came along on these lessons. As he scaled the hills, David would remove his jacket and roll up his sleeves to show broad forearms, sun-browned against the white of his shirt, a color as rich as promising soil. He had still shown no signs yet of reopening his failed attempt to talk to her, about whatever it was.

He sent the girls one morning to find stones that showed sedimentary layering. He wandered amongst them answering questions, then sprawled on the grass beside Caroline and said, "I give this weather my permission to continue."

His hand was inches from the edge of her skirt. She could feel that edge as if it were an extension of her skin.

"The kind of day that makes it hard to believe in unpleasant things," she said.

"Unpleasant things do happen on days like this."

Caroline stole a glance at his face, which was turned away from her, toward the sky. It had been a stupid thing for her to say. David, of course, had been in the war and would have seen men kill each other in picnic-bright sunshine. The war had been so separate from her own life that she just had trouble remembering. Samuel had been impassioned on the slavery question, if the writing of thunderous essays were proof of passion, though what else he should have done, being too old to fight, she wasn't sure. They'd been too far north to see active soldiers or damage or even many uniforms, and so the only obvious change the war made in their lives was giving them the new ceremony of reading the day's papers solemnly aloud in the evenings by the fire. If the news they read was true—the dead in numbers so large her mind couldn't grasp them concretely; all the chains fallen from all the necks—she wondered how she and Samuel could still be sitting there on the same faded patch of comfortable carpet, in their habitual chairs. How not even the books on their shelves were disarranged.

A friend of Samuel's had mailed him three reproductions of photographs from the aftermath of Antietam. He had gasped when he opened the envelope and retreated with it, watery eyed, to his study, calling to her that this was a thing she must not see. She'd crept to his desk after he slept that night and found them in the main drawer. There in her father's chair, she'd studied the heaped, intimate bodies: the casually bent knees, the flung arms, the hair on a stomach, the open mouth, the strange defenseless repose of so many ruined men.

"It's one of teaching's best gifts, isn't it?" David said to her now. He had moved his hand to his own kneecap. "Your students know nothing yet about unpleasantness. You get to borrow their ignorance while they borrow your knowledge."

"Oh, but of course they know unpleasantness," Caroline said.

He laughed. "Look at them!" David waved at Livia and Meg, traipsing along with interlooped arms. For some reason, Meg had draped a shawl over her head, and Livia was batting at it.

"You think being unhappy has some particular choreography?"

He looked at Caroline more closely. "Fair enough," he said. He rose, then. "Girls! Time!"

They gathered, each bearing her stone. Felicity's and Julia's were both large enough to require two hands to carry. "I don't know if this is right," Felicity said, inspecting hers doubtfully. "I thought I could see layers, but maybe it's just the lines where the dirt hit."

"My hem—I soiled it," Julia said. She put down the stone to pull and brush at the fabric.

"Pity," said Abigail, the only one kind enough to look.

Julia drew out her workbag from a pocket. "I have just the perfect bit of lace to cover the mark."

"You carry that with you all the time?" Livia said. "In case of an urgent sewing matter?"

"Only a few things, so I'm prepared," Julia said, with dignity, still rummaging. "It was here. I know it was. Have any of you seen it?"

"Are you saying one of us took it?" Meg said.

"Well," said Julia, sniffing.

This didn't seem impossible to Caroline. They were all living so close together. One of them could easily have noted and pilfered a beautiful bit of lace from her neighbor's desk in between Latin exercises. Which of them had that covetousness? It would have less to do with what a girl already had than with the intensity of her desire: maybe Livia, with those limber dramatic fingers, or Meg, with her longing to make herself a little lighter and more graceful than she was, or fearless Felicity, or even Eliza, though Caroline couldn't quite imagine her wanting such an uncomplicated thing.

"Really, Julia," Abigail said pacifyingly. "You know we wouldn't. You've just misplaced it."

"I'm *offended*," said Livia. She looked around to judge her effect. Then, "Where's Eliza?" she asked.

They searched one another's faces as if one of them might be hiding her.

"Miss Bell!" David called.

No one had seen her since he'd released them. David called her name again, then said he was sure she'd be along and tried to continue with the lesson, but no one was listening. He set them free to search for her. By this time Caroline could see the tightness at the corners of his eyes.

She was trying to stop her own mind from going to water-logged places, high places, crushed places, places where traveling men with wagons might have spied a girl a bit far from her friends. She walked off. As soon as she was out of the girls' sight, she ran for the high ground, the main hill and its surveyor's view.

So Caroline saw her before anyone else. From a distance Eliza on the grass looked like a piece of discarded clothing, a summer-white wrap thrown off in the warmth or blown from a clothesline. "There!" Caroline shouted. Everyone turned toward the sound of her shout, then followed her pointing finger.

Three or four of the girls reached Eliza first, but only Julia closed in to touch her, shake her shoulder, and call her name; the others hung back, gripping one another's hands. Caroline swallowed the bitterness rising in her throat—still, up close, that cloth-limp look of her—and went down on her knees at Eliza's side. David too. Eliza's hair had fallen over her face; Caroline brushed it away. Was this how her mother had looked when she'd fallen?

"Miss Bell," she said, and patted Eliza's cheek while David felt her pulse. He met Caroline's gaze and nodded, his face relaxing. Caroline felt her shoulders loosen.

Just then Eliza opened her eyes.

"What happened, Miss Bell?" Caroline said. She softened her voice. "Eliza?"

"I'm not sure."

David helped her sit up; pale, she hung on his sleeve.

"I was walking. Then . . ." A pause, in which Caroline felt some next sentence hang. "Then I must have fallen," Eliza finished. Whatever she'd almost said, she'd decided to keep it for herself.

David helped her up. He peered into her face. Had he heard the unsaid thing too? He glanced around the circle of tense waiting faces and put on a smile, which he directed at Eliza. "Please be more careful, all right?" he said.

"I will."

"Let's return to our discussion," David said, but only Livia still had her stone. She opened her fist to show the white hollow it had made in her palm. "I forgot I was holding it," she said, as an apology for not having the decency to lose it in the face of the disaster.

David gave up and dismissed them. He and Caroline began to walk toward the barn.

"Poor thing," David said.

When Caroline looked back, she saw the other girls drawing nearer to Eliza. Closing and closing like a tightening knot.

*

That evening, Caroline knocked on the door of Eliza and Felicity's room. She'd seen Felicity downstairs in the parlor and thought she might catch Eliza inside, alone.

"Come in," Eliza called.

This room had belonged to Hawkins and his wife in the Birch Hill days. Caroline had a faint recollection of a dim place she'd avoided, Mrs. Hawkins often stewing over a table in the far corner. It was very different now. The girls had all decorated their areas with amazing speed, building little nests against homesickness, and the farmhouse bedrooms were bedecked with drawings and nosegays like the ones on Felicity's side. Eliza's was simple in comparison: just a rose-colored swath of fabric draped about the curtain, a bright blue quilt on her bed, that horrible trilling heart feather still on the headboard, and a stack of books atop a slim folding table that she must have brought with her in the depths of that trunk. Also a single picture frame that Caroline hadn't noticed before, with a painting of green hills at sunset—amateurish, the lines convincing but every color slightly false.

Eliza sat on the bed reading. The pink had returned to her cheeks. She'd opened the window, and soft, summerlike air blew in.

"Hello. My, it's nice in here," Caroline said.

"Thank you."

Something about this peaceful room made Caroline feel indecent about her intentions in coming, as if she were about to uncover some concealed, unpleasant part of Eliza's body—a mangled toe, a raised furred birthmark. She searched for something easy to talk about. She pointed to the painting. "Did you do that?"

"Oh no," Eliza said, "I'm not a painter. My father did it. I've been thinking it might be of here."

Caroline sat down in Eliza's desk chair. She squinted at the painting. Its hills might have been theirs, or anyone's. She made a noncommittal noise.

"It's one of the only things of his I have."

"Really?"

"My mother threw most everything away after he died."

"Oh, I'm sorry. She was trying to find her own way of handling things, I'm sure." Caroline knew it wouldn't have helped if there had been more, anyway. There was a drawer in her father's bedroom that held a folded lace ribbon, a volume of Browning, a crumbling flower with the look of old skin, and a bottle of scent that had long dried into a gum on the glass. Caroline visited this drawer sometimes when her father was busy somewhere—not as much now as when she was younger—and found the items had always shifted slightly from the positions she'd remembered, as if they stirred while the drawer was closed. But when she touched them, she felt no life beating. From the neck of the scent bottle she could catch only the smell of dust.

"My mother has trouble believing in things that aren't right in front of her," Eliza said. "You know, when I came home on my very first school break, she'd turned my bedroom into another sitting room. She had to bring my bed back down from the attic so I had a place to sleep." She laughed, saw Caroline's face. "No, it was funny—she'd clearly just forgotten to consider I would still sometimes need a bed there. She went into the hall to whisper for someone to fetch it, as if I might not have noticed yet."

Caroline tried a laugh too.

Eliza was watching her almost timidly. "Can I ask—Miss Hood, what do you remember about him, my father?"

"Not much, I'm afraid." Caroline thought she remembered once being lifted onto the shoulders of a tall man with dark hair, having to bend low over his head so as not to knock her own head on the ceiling, but it didn't seem like enough of a thing to say.

"Nothing at all? Really, nothing?"

"I was so young. Only four, five when he left."

"You were older than that when he died," Eliza said.

"Miss Bell, I'm not keeping anything from you," Caroline said. "Truly. We were not . . . in touch with him, after. I do wish I had something I might tell you."

"Ah. Well. What about your mother?"

That surprised Caroline. She felt herself pull back from the bed. "What about her?"

"I've just always wondered, from the book, you know, what she was like."

"I remember very little about her either," Caroline said.

Eliza hugged her knees. "I think I would give anything to go back, just for a day, and meet him. Do you ever wish that? I find it so hard, not being able to remember."

The trouble with Eliza was that she had a perfect, tragic right to say all that she was saying and had paid dearly for that right— yet Caroline mistrusted her motives in saying it. She could not quite believe Eliza was only voicing her own heartache, could not overcome her suspicions that Eliza had other surreptitious motives. She knew to the core of her that Eliza said little that was not intended to create some certain effect. She wished she knew what that effect was. She seemed almost to feel Eliza's fingers pushing and pushing at her own flesh, looking for the place that would give, like a soft spot on a piece of fruit.

"I do, yes, of course. I know just what you mean." Caroline folded her hands in her lap. "Though actually I wanted to discuss something else."

Eliza sat back again, and her face composed itself. "Yes?"

"Today, when you fainted. Can I ask, what do you think happened?"

Eliza shrugged. Caroline had moved them from the ground she wished to occupy. "I'm not really sure."

"Well, I don't think there's any reason to worry." Caroline was trying to get the words right, but a sense of echoing distracted her: someone must have said just this to her mother once. *Don't worry—but . . .* "I only hoped we might try to understand it a little better. Has that sort of thing happened to you before?"

"Not that I know of." A quick exhaled laugh.

"All right. Would you tell me more about what you remember, from when it happened?"

"Well, I was walking, looking for my stone for the lesson. The sun was very warm, and I remember a tiny snake slid out of my way—a black racer, maybe? Mr. Moore showed us the plates, but I always confuse them—and it startled me. When I looked up again I saw some trilling hearts in the taller grass. I thought I'd see if I could get closer without frightening them off."

"Why?"

"Just to watch them. See what they did, what they looked like. It's hard to get a real sense of them from a distance. So I got closer, quite close. And then—" Eliza stopped. "Miss Hood, do you ever feel just . . . overwhelmed—by things? It sounds silly. But the birds were so *red.* I know that's how everybody describes them, but seeing that color still feels . . ."

"Overpowering," Caroline said.

"Yes. It wasn't just the birds—all of a sudden, everything seemed so bright. The green of the grass, and the blue of the sky. I could feel that color pressing down on me. As if it were all right up against my face. I couldn't seem to breathe." She breathed now, deeply. "And the next instant, Mr. Moore was standing over me. Or that's how it felt."

Caroline wondered if David's face had seemed part of all that thickening color, the gloss of his hair and beard, the deep brown well of his eyes, his lips' red—whether Eliza had tried to breathe these too in. That she could also understand.

Eliza said, "Has anything like that ever happened to you?" and Caroline felt caught, as if the girl had glimpsed recognition stirring.

"No," Caroline said shortly. Heat crept up her neck. She rose from Eliza's chair.

"I thought you might—"

Caroline touched Eliza's knee. "It sounds to me as if you just got too warm, on a warm day," she said. Word for word the explanation her father had given, when Caroline had come with her heart in her throat to tell him about Eliza's fainting that afternoon. She tucked Eliza's chair neatly back under the desk before she left, so that Eliza wouldn't suspect her of flight.

*

Later in the week, Livia and Meg found Caroline in the orchard, where she was gathering the last of the apples from that one fruit-bearing tree. "Yes, girls?" she said.

"We were passing by," Meg said.

"On your way to the market, you mean? The post?"

Meg watched her stolidly. Through the screen of her curled hair and silk ribbons, it was possible to discern the heavy-jawed middle-aged woman she would be some not-too-distant day. Livia shot a glance at Meg and said, "No, we were just out walking, and we saw you and thought, if you have a minute—since you offered, there are some things we've been just dying to ask."

"You look fairly distant from your deathbeds to me," Caroline said.

Their foreheads creased.

"Never mind. Help me with the fruit while we're talking."

They moved to the branches and began to pick, Livia un-discriminating, Meg overcareful, spinning each apple on its stem to look for blemishes first. The sun through the leaves dappled their faces and made them both beautiful.

"Eliza said she tried asking," Livia said, "but she thought you might not want to tell her."

"Asking what?"

"Oh, look!" said Livia.

Caroline turned. A trilling heart paced the ground between the trees, its legs like clumsily animated twigs, the red clot of its body lurching. It was coming toward them, and Caroline's arms tried to extend and make a separation between girls and bird. Foolish, and she stopped, instead reaching up for another apple and hoping it would seem this was all she'd been doing. "I've been expecting they might go south," she said, "or somewhere, soon. When they came before they only stayed for a couple of months, I think."

The bird flew away. Meg set off running, stopped, bent to pluck something from the grass. "It's dropped a feather! Like what happened with Eliza."

"It's nothing like that. Let me see," Livia told her.

"I found it."

"I just want to *look.*"

"Girls?" Caroline said. "What was it you wanted to ask me?"

They turned back to her, Livia holding the feather now. "We wanted to hear more about Louisa," she said.

"Anna was my mother's name."

"Well," said Meg.

"We wondered if you could tell us about her. What it was *like,* having her for a mother," Livia said.

"What is it like having your own mothers as mothers?"

"That's different."

"Not really. My *mother* was real, just like your mothers. *Louisa* is a character in a novel."

"Was she very beautiful?" Meg said. "I love that part in the book, about her face."

"There are many parts in the book about her face," Caroline said.

"How did you stand it when she died?"

"Well, what would not standing it involve?" But she was being unfair, asking them to answer for every careless person who'd

ever asked. She wasn't even sure why their questions were both-
ering her; she had, after all, invited them to ask her things, and
here they were, only asking. Though of course at Eliza's behest.
Caroline gathered herself. "I was far too small to really understand what was happening, which was in many ways a blessing.
It was much harder, I think, for my father."

"Your father," Livia said, pursing her mouth.

"Yes, my father, her husband, who greatly loved her," Caroline
said sharply. "Girls, there isn't much more I can say about this,
I'm afraid. And I'm certain you both have other things to do."

They piled their apples into the sling Caroline had made out of
her skirt and walked off across the grass together. Caroline took
an unthinking step after them, so she could try again, do better
than those storybook words. *Who greatly loved her.* The apples
knocked together like knees. She had no other kind of words,
really, to offer.

The house lay so still. She felt full of so much motion. She
wanted David to emerge, stride toward her, grab her wrists, spill
the apples on the ground.

*

The next day they were reading act 3, scene 2 of *Midsummer*,
Livia as Helena rending their hearts—just Caroline and the girls;
her father and David were busy planning their own lessons—and
sweet, open Abigail cried, "I just feel so awful for her."

"You do?" Eliza said.

"She's so in love with Demetrius, and he can't stop talking
about how much he loves Hermia."

"I'd rather be Helena than Hermia," Eliza said.

"What do you mean?"

"Of course it all hurts her. But pain is . . . I think pain can be so
important. I think it can have such value."

Eliza's voice swooped with inflection. She was performing this, and the performance itself, the golden weight of their attention, was in all likelihood her motive. Unsurprising enough. Yet in substance it was an alarming thing for her to say and to make them all think about: the *value of pain.* Caroline tried to speak lightly. "It depends on the type of pain, Miss Bell, don't you think? I'm not sure the stubbing of one's toe is good for much."

The girls didn't seem to have heard. "What kind of value, Eliza?" Julia asked.

"Of the two of them, who's more interesting? Never mind Demetrius—which one do you think *Shakespeare* loves more?" Eliza held out her hands, as if she were showing them herself.

Caroline imagined Thoreson on the visitors' couch, watching with eyebrows raised. *Was this also a part of your vision, I wonder?*

It was not. It was not a part of hers.

*

Caroline sat at her desk in the fading afternoon light to write a letter to Miss Marsh's, Eliza's old school. A letter of inquiry after Eliza's health; perhaps they might know how to help her. She phrased her question tactfully, delicate words for a delicate girl, though she didn't think that was quite what Eliza was. *Might you know, might you be able to share, might there be anything* . . . The vagueness was polite and let her feel that she was not doing anything so very dramatic in writing this letter, but it was also useful—a wide-open invitation, a prompting that might summon anything at all. She walked into town and sent the letter off.

At their teachers' meeting that evening, Caroline's father told her, "Your work with *Midsummer* has a nice pace to it, Caroline."

"Yes," David said. And then, "I've been wanting to ask both of your opinions—do you think that Abigail is making progress? I still question her grasp of the fundamentals."

"The place that had her before did let her down," Samuel said, "but she's rallying."

So here they were, in the first conversation they'd all had since the fainting episode, bestowing a lukewarm compliment on the lady teacher, worrying about Abigail's arithmetic. Caroline had thought they would try this—it was why she'd written and sent the letter to Miss Marsh's on her own.

"Shouldn't we talk about Eliza?" Caroline said.

Samuel sighed. "We could try."

"It must have been very frightening for her," David said.

"Though people do faint," said Samuel. "She seems quite recovered now. And academically, she's above reproach."

"Academically," Caroline said.

"Caroline, I just don't feel I understand her well enough yet to know how to proceed. She's a somewhat complicated case, isn't she? We will watch carefully and do our best to determine the right course of action." Samuel lifted his shoulders helplessly. "The foreignness of the fifteen-year-old girl! Sophia might have more luck, when she arrives, being a bit closer to that world than the rest of us."

"Sophia?" Caroline said.

A silence.

David watched the floor. He looked cornered, younger than she'd ever seen him.

"You haven't spoken to Caroline about Sophia, David?"

David knew when the corner was too tight.

"Sophia," he said, and raised his eyes to Caroline's, "is my wife."

7

MRS. DAVID MOORE

"I often find that at night I feel freer," she told him.

—MILES PEARSON, *THE DARKENING GLASS* (P. 144)

Sophia would be radiant: a winsome sliver of light put by God in Ohio, now moved by God to Trilling Heart, expressly to illuminate David's life. She would be straight out of every book and song—she would come dripping words and notes, leaving pools of them in her wake, little puddles of grace for others to wander into. She would shape air into loveliness with her hands and arms. Her face would be blinding. David's, turned toward it, would look sun-dazzled.

Sophia was due to arrive the following week and begin teaching fine arts classes, it having been long decided that she should come only once the school had been established, so as to miss any early discombobulation. (So as not to turn the music discordant, mar the shapes, dim the light.) October was soon enough for the girls to begin their arts study.

"Why didn't you tell us you had a wife?" Felicity screeched during David's lesson, while Caroline sat still at the back of the room, wondering if she herself had spoken without her own permission.

No, because if it had been her voice, it wouldn't have held laughter.

"It was unnecessary. I am not the subject of our studies," David said. He didn't seem to know what to do with his arms.

Livia said, "You *kept* it from us."

"She must be very beautiful," said Eliza, no laughter in her voice either.

Just once, prior to Sophia's arrival, Caroline tried to talk to David about her. "She's an artist?" she asked him, while her father was finding a book upstairs. She saw now of course that it was Sophia that David had failed to tell her about, that day with the sheets, and all the days before that and after, the many days on which he'd said many things to her and none of them *wife*. Or it might be that he hadn't failed—that he'd only decided there was no particular reason he should have to tell Caroline anything.

He was wrong about that.

David got up to tend the fire. "She enjoys the arts," he said stiffly.

Sophia, perhaps, was such an artwork herself that no one expected her to learn, produce, practice. She'd breathe on the girls' art and it would bloom.

"You know her from your town back home?"

"There's nothing there that can fairly be called a town. But yes, Sophia is from the next farm over from my father's."

He prodded the coals with his head tipped low. Caroline resented the coziness of the scene—watching David from the settee, across an otherwise empty room, while he added kindling. She hoped a stray spark might ignite his curls and singe them a little. She wouldn't mind hearing him yell.

"You grew up together, then, the two of you." Something like what might have happened with her and William, if she'd let him keep pulling that summer day. If William had been brilliant, and she herself less burdened, more beautiful.

"After a fashion, though Sophia's younger than I am."

Nothing else seemed to be forthcoming—certainly no apology.

He might feel he had nothing to apologize for. Perhaps, after all, he was right. What did Caroline know about the ways men and women usually were together?

"David," she said, meaning to ask if it had all been only friendliness for him, if she'd invented every hesitation and almost-said word. Why not ask now?

David raised his face. He looked at her as if they were strangers passing on the street and she'd pinned his toes beneath her heel.

"Must we discuss this forever?" he said. If she kept making him talk, Caroline understood, he would look for ways never to talk to her again. And he could find them. She had no real claim on him, no ground in which to stake one, nothing that could hold. Losing more was always possible.

She excused herself and went to bed, where she lay in the same darkness that had covered her at twenty-four, eighteen, twelve, eight, the walls and ceiling of her room like a box that fit her, neat as a dead thing, inside.

*

Caroline wanted to talk to her father. She needed some way of tricking help out of him without having to tell him why she needed it. She chose a moment when she knew he'd be in his study to go and get a book there, nodded to him, fetched it, then stopped at the door, turning back as if she'd only just remembered something—the dance around her shame giving her such shame. "Papa, I wondered, do you have any thoughts on disappointment? Just generally? For one of the girls—she's having some trouble, and I'd like to help her. Great, very great disappointment, the kind that feels unbearable."

"Of course not *actually* unbearable," Samuel said, smiling at her above his book.

"I don't see how that helps," Caroline said. She'd come close to Samuel's desk now, though she'd meant to stay at the door like an alighting insect on the brink of detaching. "Telling her that the thing that seems so huge to her ought to seem small. How does that help? It doesn't make her stronger."

"No," Samuel said, closing his book now and giving her his whole gaze. "I'm sorry, dearest. I do think it might be a useful reminder, though—to help her adjust her vision. To help her see that the trial can't be so great." He wasn't asking who the girl was. She'd known he wouldn't force a more specific lie from her. He did not pry, had always believed in their right to keep things from each other.

"If it *is*, though," Caroline said. "If it seems so to her."

Samuel considered. "Then she might be asked to think of the very partial view she has—we all have. To remember and trust in the wisdom of the Father, who sees the whole."

"Thank you," Caroline said. She closed on the sentence and carried it from the room.

But she found that the longer she held the idea, the flimsier it grew as a comfort. She had never really needed reminding that she saw only part of things.

Later that week, coming back from a walk, Caroline spied Eliza walking on her own. Wandering and grieving over the existence of David's wife, perhaps—and Caroline's steps quickened. She thought of what to tell her. *I know it's hard when a silly little dream comes to nothing. But you always knew that's all it was, didn't you? You didn't actually think . . . ?* She loved the prospect of saying these sentences, being a person high enough above to say them, and she chased this excitement across the grass toward Eliza.

Except Eliza, she saw now, was not wandering but circling. Her body always turned toward the house as she moved, as if pulled that way.

"What are you looking at?"

Eliza stopped. "Nothing."

"It did seem you were looking at something."

"Oh, well. It's a mysterious house, don't you think?"

"Is it?" Caroline said. "You've seen all of it, I imagine, except maybe the cellar."

"What's down there?" Eliza said.

"Cellar things. Some preserves, and old broken furniture. Tools we never use. What's this about, Miss Bell?"

"I just want to know everything about this place." Eliza's fingers played at the fringe of her shawl as if weaving.

Uneasily Caroline watched her go. What she was doing now did look more like romantic wandering—but before, that had been a sleuthing circle. Their house had no secrets to yield, but the house in *The Darkening Glass* did, a whole secret room that was the site of Louisa's torments at Abner's hands. Worrisome, the possibility that Eliza had been looking for it, as if the things and people in that book were real and findable.

She wished for some way of making Eliza declare truthfully her reasons for coming here. She suspected those reasons of poison, of creeping rot—tainting the water, eating the foundations, ruining the belowground substance of all their lives in some place none of them could quite see, perhaps not even Eliza herself.

Though for Caroline's own part, it turned out that what she'd been building here needed no undoing to fall down, having never had any soundness.

*

October 25, a Saturday, was sunny but cooler. David, Caroline, and Samuel assembled on the lawn of the farmhouse to meet Sophia's carriage as it drew to a stop. Caroline adjusted the collar of her dress, readying herself to withstand the music, light, and loveliness that would break over her. She wanted the memory of having stayed on her feet.

The driver handed down an inexplicably ordinary girl. A traveling companion, Caroline thought—this broad cream face, with its frame of yellow hair, had been provided to stitch Sophia safely to reality during her journey.

"Here I am!" the girl cried, and ran forward into David's arms, which opened for her.

Then the girl leaned back, still gripping him around the neck, and looked around. "So it *is* real, then," she said. "Mama and Reverend North said I'd get here and find it was all made up, and my husband pacing and talking to some dolls he'd set up for students." An eager spreading of her thick red lips—everything about her so milk-fed.

This girl was David's wife?

"Some common geese dyed scarlet, for the birds."

"Reverend North?" Caroline said, before she'd even said hello, disoriented enough that she couldn't tell what questions needed answering.

"Our minister back home. Very learned. You've never told them about Reverend North?" Sophia said to David.

Somehow Caroline suspected that this Reverend North would not have met her father's standards for *learned*. Where had her father gone? Hanging back behind her, lips a little open as if preparing to speak, but saying nothing—it seemed Samuel didn't know what to do with Sophia as she was turning out to be either. The girls stared from a distance. Tabitha peeked at Sophia through the windows of the farmhouse; a group stole glances at her from the garden across the lawn. They all wanted to try to read what she would mean to them.

"He knows more than anybody. Except maybe this one," Sophia said, and nudged David with her elbow. "Reverend North can quote a Bible verse for anything. He had one for me, just before I left. What was it? Something about a journey, a good journey."

Samuel, sensing his opening, stepped forward. "'Provide neither gold, nor silver, nor brass in your purses, nor scrip for your journey, for the workman is worthy of his meat.'"

Sophia frowned. "That wasn't it. I'd know it if I heard it."

Samuel's smile stayed on his face. "Well. An effort. Welcome, Mrs. Moore. I'm Samuel Hood. We're so pleased you're joining us, and grateful to you for sharing your husband with us all this time."

"I've heard a lot about you," Sophia said crisply. Caroline wondered if David had gone on at too great a length about Samuel when he'd written to her—if his letters had read too much like love letters to someone else. "You too," she said, turning a warmer face on Caroline, stepping forward to take her hands.

David had written, perhaps, of Caroline's library, her tea making. Such a fool Caroline had been.

"A pleasure to meet you," Caroline said, brittle as a schoolmarm. Sophia, to look at her, might almost have been a student. Caroline hadn't imagined that *younger* could mean this face still smooth at all its creases, no years at all gathered in the corners of the eyes.

They began to make the necessary noises about how Sophia must be tired after her journey. They dispersed. Samuel returned to his study, to read in preparation for his upcoming classes, he said. David led Sophia off to their room, where he would lay her down on their bed and wrap himself around her, this earthy girl without any special light, and taste her skin.

It might be the only line that mattered in life: between those who thought about things and those who did them.

The girls were chattering again. Their interest had ebbed for now.

Caroline went to walk until her mind was quiet enough for her to do something else.

*

Sophia at the breakfast table the next morning, looking out the window at all the green: "How far do we have to *go* to get to services Sundays?"

"We attend in Ashwell, when we do attend," Samuel said.

"When you do?"

"Well, Sophia—it is all right if I call you Sophia, I hope?—the distance is a bit of a deterrent." As was Samuel's inability to listen in peace to what he called *the pompous half-musings* of the slow-speaking reverend. "We go periodically, when circumstances allow. The rest of the time we hold a small worship meeting ourselves, right here, Sunday mornings."

"No church," Sophia said.

"Sophia," David whispered, and touched her wrist.

Only the four of them still sat in the dining room; the girls had finished and gone back upstairs, but the teachers had lingered at Samuel's suggestion, so he and Caroline could get to know Sophia. They were getting to know her now.

"You don't pray?"

Samuel extended his arms. "Of course we do. We pray wherever and whenever the Spirit moves us." He wanted to continue, Caroline could tell, but Sophia was neither his student nor his child, so he wasn't sure what voice to use. She herself knew the rest. She remembered hearing it on a snowy Christmas Eve in childhood as they bumped over ice heaves in their warm carriage: *We're quite as well able to know God as any member of an official clergy, Caroline. We need no ordination. Our ordination is our awakening to the world, and to the divine, and to our own role in relation to both.* Pressed against her father's solid shoulder, she'd felt as if they were the only two citizens of a wise country. She'd wanted to live nowhere else. They hadn't returned to church for two years, after.

"But who *leads* the praying?" Sophia said.

The truth was that Samuel did, most of the time.

"It's as I told you, my sweet," David said. "Any thought, any sustained, questing thought, is holy. No third party is necessary to sanctify it."

My sweet. Caroline spoke so that her face might have its motion

91

as a screen: "It's surprisingly busy here, I think you'll find. We're in need of our rest come Sundays."

"I promised about church," Sophia told David. "Mama, and Reverend North."

"Why would they make you promise such a thing?" David said.

Samuel squinted at his own fingertips as if inspecting them for dirt, doing his best not to witness this marital moment.

"They were right to, weren't they? Reverend North told me it was especially important I look after my moral welfare. He senses a lot of the Spirit in me."

"How did he come to sense that?" David said. "You know I think you spend too much time with Reverend North."

"Well, you weren't there," Sophia said, chewing egg, looking as if she might cry.

Under other circumstances Caroline would feel pity for this woman, who had come so far from her home to a place that did not seem to suit her and to a husband who spoke to her as David had just done. Under other circumstances she might have reached out just now and touched Sophia's hand. She watched Sophia's trembling mouth and thought how terrible it was to feel so ungenerous, so unmoved; to have such scant resources remaining to her that she couldn't afford to spend them on anyone else, lest she herself be left with nothing.

"My fault he was away, I'm afraid," Samuel said lightly.

"I'm sure," Sophia said, as if she had barely heard.

*

In the barn, just before his lesson began, Sophia asked her husband, "Duck, aren't you going to sit at the desk?" She was close enough to Caroline on the visitors' couch that Caroline was breathing her flowery, humid smell.

"Duck?" Livia said, seizing on this extravagant gift.

"That's what I've always called him. He just has a duckie sort of look to him sometimes."

Sophia's mood seemed to be lifting, perhaps because David was at the front of the room, and hers.

"Please, Sophia," David said. He was trying to seem amused. This was the opposite of his usual act in the time just before his lessons began, when the girls would pepper him with teasing questions and he would feign offense. *What do you do when class is over, Mr. Moore? Mr. Moore, what's your favorite thing to eat? Do you like mornings or afternoons better? Summer or fall? Blue or green? Walking or riding?* Each question a search for a loose piece of skin they could pry up. David knew better than to answer most of the time, but Caroline had seen the way he relished the search.

"Duckie," Felicity said.

"Duckie duck," Livia said.

"Please, girls."

Samuel wouldn't have said *please*; he would have just stopped it somehow. But Samuel was in his study, reluctant, perhaps, to see any more of Sophia's first full day at Trilling Heart.

David took a breath, adjusted his face, and reached into his pocket for his notes. As he drew them out—just at that moment, as if he were pulling a rope—the section of ceiling over the bookshelves gave, with a wet rotten-voiced splintering. A cascade of something fell to the ground.

Everyone shrieked, then gathered around the column of dusty light that now stood in the room, peering up at a patch of blue sky. A cloud drifted. The boards sagged, lolled like a tongue.

The smell—wet, rich, dark, animal—reached them, and they pulled back, covering their mouths.

"What happened? It's not even raining," Meg said.

Sophia gestured toward the boards' moist, ragged ends and spoke through her fingers. "It didn't have to be. Look at the wood. It's amazing it held this long."

The brown cascade had heaped at their feet. Like the weave of a basket, it was at first one thing—one dun-colored mass—and then, when the gaze lingered, many small bits of things. Slivers of soft wood but also loose twigs, grasses, all of it wet looking. A dirty tuft of reddish-brown feather. Pieces of it still together enough to suggest curvings, cuppings, but of several different circumferences. Caroline tried to assemble the mess into one shape in her imagination.

"A nest?" said Felicity, wrinkling her sharp nose. She toed the feather, closer even than David to the whole mess despite the smell. Felicity, Caroline sometimes suspected, might have a future as an intrepid explorer of some distant region. "A trilling heart nest?"

"I don't know," said David. "It's the wrong time of year. But it does look that way. They must have piled all this on the roof, and then water accumulated in it, and that's the source of the trouble."

Could the others see now that they were being invaded? These birds were not some beautiful, romantic happening, some trans-forming touch to turn life into Pearson's novel or Samuel's essays. They were strange, savage creatures that carried their inscrutable nature with them and sent it raining down on top of other, feebler plans, and could the others smell it?

Caroline peered up through the ceiling hole into the sky, cran-ing for a glimpse of—what? Whatever landscape the birds had made of their roof. Though somebody would have seen, wouldn't they, if there were much more than this, if this weren't all or close to all of it.

"Oh!" said Julia, and pulled something from the jumble, touch-ing only the corner. "Look, the lace bit I was missing!"

"We told you none of us took it," Livia said.

"It's all stained." Julia dangled it so they could see the watery blotch in the middle. "Do you think with washing . . . ?"

From within the layer of brown peeked something else, underbelly-light. Caroline bent and lifted it. A small bit of fraying ribbon, sun and rain bleached to a faint seafoam color, rough between her fingers with grime.

"That's mine!" said Abigail. "I lost it the first week."

"No, I think it might be mine. I've been missing my blue ribbon for ages," said Tabitha.

"It isn't blue, though, it's green—I dropped one just like it somewhere," Eliza said.

"Can I see?" asked Rebecca, taking it from Caroline's hand. "Really, I think it's mine. My sister gave me a pair of them for my birthday. I've only got one left in my box upstairs."

"Girls," said Caroline, taking it back, "it's only a tiny scrap. It could be anybody's, or a tatter of laundry from the next house. Certainly it's good for nothing now anyway."

David used his foot to rake the pile toward the corner, as if in this manner the birds' invasion could be reversed, when the smell still hung, thick with life as the mud at the bottom of a river. He stretched up to push the loose boards back into place, but when he let go they dropped again. "I'll nail it back up for now," he said. "I'll just be a moment—I'll fetch a hammer." This chance to escape a lesson that hadn't been going well was not, perhaps, unwelcome.

The door closed behind him and they all went back to their seats. The shaft of light hovered solidly, like a feature of a holy painting. And in the corner that formless, indecipherable heap.

Slowly, the smell dissipated. Slowly, the room began to shift its attention to Sophia. She had long ago done what they all wanted to do, after all, pried up David's skin and gotten to the meat of him.

"Mrs. Moore, how did you meet Mr. Moore?" Livia asked, leaning her chin into her hands.

This Caroline did know how to stop. She could just stand, go to the blackboard, and copy out a prompt for the girls to answer in their notebooks while they waited. In doing so she would show the girls they were not to ask such questions and show Sophia she was not to refer to her husband as "Duckie" in front of their mutual students—show her that she had, perhaps, much to learn here and that Caroline knew it all already.

But Caroline also wanted to hear the answer to the question Livia had asked.

"Oh, when do you meet the people you've known forever?" Sophia said.

"You were childhood sweethearts?" Rebecca asked.

"*I* was a child, anyway." Sophia laughed.

"What were you wearing when he proposed?"

"My best yellow gown. This was just after church."

Every girl in the room was putting herself into that yellow gown and into the space in front of David. Caroline too could feel the sunshine warmth of its fabric under her own palms, and beneath, her own body, warmer still, and soft.

"He told me, *You look beautiful. You always do. Would you do me the great honor of being my wife?*' Sophia's caricature of David's voice made Caroline flinch. "All stiff, just like that, like he was reading lines." She laughed again, and the sound this time was low and almost secretive.

Eliza said, "Do you think we should be discussing this?"

Sophia stopped.

"I mean, it's very interesting, but I wonder if Mr. Moore would like it. Since he's not here," said Eliza, with one of her best smiles.

Eliza was paler and thinner than she had been, Caroline thought, the skin of her face tightening and drawing back. The look of suffering was on her like gray light—though since she had fainted Caroline hadn't caught her suffering at anything.

This intercession of Eliza's was of course a reprimanding of Caroline too.

"He'd think it's fine." Flustered, Sophia waved a hand. "I'm allowed to talk about him."

But she didn't anymore.

As they listened to the clock tick then, waiting for David's return, Caroline glanced—she tried not to glance—at the ribbon she'd put beside her on the couch, which looked—she tried not to think it looked—like one she'd had as a girl, a beautiful spring-green ribbon she'd tied at the end of her long braid. Whatever happened to that ribbon? Thrown away or lost somewhere. It had probably not been sitting in the soil of their fields for over a decade, waiting for a beak to pluck and carry it. No reason to look at this scrap and read her name. And what if it were hers? There was no special meaning in that. Only that so many years had passed, and the birds had plucked the ribbon straight through those years for some purpose of their own, and here she still was, just the same, to meet that purpose, to have it done to her.

*

While Caroline was walking that afternoon, Sophia waved to her from across the fields: "Miss Hood! Caroline!"

Caroline stopped to wait.

"I'm scouting for places the girls might draw during our first lesson," Sophia said when she reached her. She brushed a tuft of grass off her skirt. "Is there anywhere a bit more manicured?"

"You had more gardens in Ohio?" Caroline revised the great dust-colored tracts of farmland she'd been imagining as the backdrop for the younger David, replacing them with an overwrought spread of flowers. Sophia at the center of the panel, stems and blossoms twined about her as if growing out of her flesh.

"It's just when I pictured this, where David would be taking me, I pictured gardens. He made it all sound so pretty."

"I'm sorry he misrepresented," Caroline said.

"That's not what I meant," Sophia said, checking Caroline's face. "But not even a little rose garden at the back door? Mama had one—I always used to draw there."

This was the woman they had teaching art at their dream of

a school, because as a child she'd liked drawing roses. Of course Caroline's skills too had always been cloistered, but she knew their scale; she'd learned them from her father. Poor Sophia. Nothing she'd taught herself in a rose garden could equal what they would ask of it.

No, not poor Sophia, because all the time she'd had David waiting outside that garden, just there, by the gate.

Caroline gave Sophia her calm face. Calm was what she would always give Sophia, a calm uncrossable distance. "You might have them draw the trees, the leaves, if you want color?" The hillsides still flamed, though they were browning.

"Miss Bell would *love* drawing leaves, I'm sure."

Caroline shrugged. "It's hard to tell ahead of time what Miss Bell will like."

"She's the famous one, isn't she?"

"Her father was famous."

"That writer."

"Miles Pearson."

"That's right," said Sophia. "What sort of a girl is she?"

Sophia's brow bone, Caroline noticed, came to a sort of cliff's edge above her eyes, which gave her an air almost of studiousness. Caroline had to resist pressing her fingertips assessingly to her own forehead. "I don't quite know what you're asking," she said.

"Just, was that—this morning—the way she usually is?"

"That challenge? Certainly it's happened."

"I wouldn't call what she said a *challenge* exactly," Sophia said.

This woman was a feature of the landscape of her life now, Caroline reminded herself. She was a tree or a rock that made unpleasant sounds; she was another new bird, calling. "Eliza enjoys exerting an influence."

"If I knew more about her, for tomorrow, maybe I could make sure I don't get off on the wrong foot," Sophia said.

"She can be . . . difficult to predict," Caroline said. "I'm not sure it would be worthwhile to try to make a plan around her. And of course that's not what we do anyway, plan around one student." Though no mention had ever been made of any previous teaching Sophia had done, and Sophia didn't necessarily know this at all. "You could always ask David for his ideas, about the *right foot*." Caroline might stage a contrast: arrange to walk in right after Sophia asked this question, read a tricky passage aloud, then ask David's opinion on some thorny pedagogical question.

But what was she hoping for? David had talked to Sophia before. He'd known her for a long time before he'd married her. He'd married her anyway.

Sophia laughed. "I doubt he's noticed a thing about her, he's so busy thinking his thoughts. My poor Duckie—he misses things about people. It's just the way he is. The whole time he was courting me, you know, he talked to me mostly about your father's essays."

"Really? What did he say?" asked Caroline.

"*I* don't know. You'd have understood better."

Caroline stared at the trees. Yes, she would have.

"He just started coming around, taking me on long walks, talking about truth and *knowing myself*. I don't remember half of it. I could see what he meant by coming there, though. The rest didn't matter." She stopped. "I don't mean any offense."

"Of course."

"I hope we can be friends."

"Oh yes."

A trilling heart flew past, alaruming. A brighter flame than any of the leaves even at their brightest. Caroline's cheekbones ached with the sound.

Sophia watched it. "Everyone says they're so beautiful, but I don't know. They make my skin creep."

"Mine too," Caroline said, the admission surprised out of her—that of all the people she'd heard talk about the birds, it was Sophia who'd come nearest to articulating her own feeling.

*

At night, Caroline listened for sounds. The Moores' bedroom was just across the hall from her own; she thought she might hear things. It was quiet, but she imagined what she might see just now if she crossed the hall to that door and opened it. David hunched over his wife's body on the bed. The room close and warm. Their faces would turn to her, and what expression would she see?

Imagined humiliation blanketed Caroline, trailing a thrill like a lace hem. She touched its edges, setting off waves and waves of red.

Then came a noise, a real noise.

Caroline stopped moving.

Doors opening and closing softly; the hissing of whispers. The full moon through the windows let her make out the clock: it was twelve thirty. She went quietly to her door, quietly opened it, tiptoed to the top of the stairs. Like peering down the shaft of a well, in the darkness at the bottom she glimpsed a scrap of nightgown, there and gone, cloth floating on the surface before submerging.

Caroline knew which stairs creaked. No one was waiting for her on the landing. She cracked the front door open and saw, in the moon's strange white light, a huddle of girls in their night-clothes, walking away from the house. One warm yellow lantern surrounded by the pale bobbing bits of them.

She followed, through the dark. She left some space, but still, if they looked back they'd see her. They didn't look back. On they all walked, to the faint tin buzz of the season's last insects.

What kind of plans had these girls been making?

They reached the woods' edge and passed under the first trees. First the girls, then Caroline. The night's sounds grew softer, closer, and more muffled, more like sounds in a room. Caroline wasn't sure she'd ever been in these woods at night. She didn't recognize these slim faint lines of trees, this heavy darkness. Every night her woods had been changing into a different country while she'd slept.

A girl, hard to tell in the lantern light which, held up her hand. "Here," she said.

Eliza's voice, of course.

"Just here might have been where Louisa came at night. These are the same trees. The same birds even."

The girls stood still in their clump, waiting. Tabitha said tentatively, "I don't see any birds."

"But we know they're there," Eliza told her. "All around us."

"Yes," someone said.

Somebody else: "Amazing."

"You were right, Eliza. It's marvelous out here."

"I want to do something," Eliza said.

"What kind of thing?" asked Livia.

"We could read. I brought the book," Felicity said.

"Or sing?"

"Sing what, ninny? 'Yankee Doodle'?"

"I want to feel part of it. I want to *do* something," said Eliza.

She seemed to search—the sky, the trees, the ground. Then she lifted a fallen branch, which gave her a strange silhouette, as if one arm had grown long and attenuated.

"Give me that lantern," she said.

She was going to start a fire, thought Caroline. She'd been wrong about the nature of Eliza's subterranean motives—they were not poison or rot, but more direct in their violence, and faster. Eliza was going to burn everything down. She was going to take this fire she held, for someone had handed the lantern to her now, and throw it around herself to watch it eat and blacken everything. The fall had been dry—it would all catch.

Step forward, Caroline willed herself.

Eliza was now the only lit-up thing Caroline could see. The girls had drawn away from her, away from her circle of light, and they were almost invisible in the dark, though their waiting could be sensed there at the circle's edges. Eliza touched the tip of the stick to the lantern. She held the flaming branch close to her face, looking at its orange point. The flame bathed her features and showed but also shadowed them—her cheekbones turning her eyes into dark hollows, her lips casting blackness over her chin, so that the dark seemed part of the substance of her face. Her mouth pursed as if she were trying to understand some difficult problem. And then she was pulling at her nightdress, baring an ankle, and before Caroline knew what was happening Eliza was closing in on herself with the branch.

She was pressing the flame to her skin.

Almost immediately Eliza cried out, pulled the stick back. The flame had gone out, smothered against her. She pressed the blackened tip back in again, cried out again, a sound like surprise.

Had the fainting been this way too? A sighting of a source of pain, and then an invitation.

Caroline's skin rippled. *Step forward.*

"Eliza!" said Abigail, catching her by the shoulder. "What are you doing?"

"I don't know," said Eliza thickly. She brought a fingertip to her ankle, pressed.

"Didn't that hurt?"

"Yes. It feels real—it's a real feeling."

"What do you mean, real?" asked Julia.

"I'll still have this tomorrow. I'll remember what happened. That I was here, really here in these woods. I've marked myself with them."

"A scar?" said Meg.

"Maybe. But even if it goes away"—Eliza's hand pressed her ankle again—"I'll know it was here, and I'll remember."

She looked around the circle. "Does anyone else want to?"

They were all quiet. Everything in Caroline tightened.

"It's not bad. It's really not. It would be a secret we'd all have." Eliza shifted and Caroline couldn't see her face anymore, but her voice was faster, excited. "It would tie us together."

So this was where Eliza wanted to take them. Caroline could sense the girls considering, feeling it before feeling it, that singeing just where their shoes usually nipped.

"I will," said Abigail. Abigail who was above all else compliant, who walked easiest in lines with other people at their heads.

And that was it, Caroline knew; a row of smooth ankles was assembling.

Finally she managed to move. She lifted her foot, then put it down hard, once, twice, three times, four times, until she cracked a branch.

"What was that?"

Caroline held her breath.

"It was something. I heard something."

"An animal, maybe."

They sounded a little afraid now; the spell was breaking.

"We should get back." Julia's voice. Julia was not really the sort of girl who came to the woods at night. "They'll see we're gone."

Now, though she couldn't see their faces, Caroline knew they would all be looking to Eliza for permission. She still needed to step out and speak. Send them back to their beds, bandage Eliza's blister. Most important, she needed to say, *What are you doing?* in just the right voice. But she was somehow sure that if she stood before them, they wouldn't see her, that if she spoke, they wouldn't hear anything. That their eyes and ears and minds were too full of Eliza to hold Caroline at all.

There was obedience here, and it was not to her.

"All right," Eliza said, and then came the rustling sounds of their leaving, chattering, their voices farther and now farther away.

*

The following morning, Caroline buttered her bread, brought it to her mouth, chewed, swallowed. If anyone remarked that she seemed tired, she'd just say she hadn't slept well. Telling her father and David and, heaven forfend, Sophia what she'd found the girls doing would mean explaining why she hadn't stopped them and why, when she finally had, she'd done it in the same way a deer or a loose tree limb might have.

She needed to explain all of this, explain about Eliza—that she was not just some ordinary fainting girl—but the words would need to be the right ones, and she would need to be sure of them.

Samuel said, "What are your plans for your first lesson, Sophia, if I might ask?"

"I thought I might take the girls outdoors to draw."

"Ah, plein air work!" Samuel said.

Sophia laughed. "Instead of fancy air?"

David coughed and began talking in a rapid voice about the weather. It continued warmer than he'd expected at this time of year. Pleasant, very pleasant.

But Samuel was still gazing at Sophia. "You know," he said, "it would be all right if you wanted to wait a bit longer before beginning your teaching. Watch some more lessons, get to know Trilling Heart, see our mission at work for a while. There's no need to toss you right in."

"I might as well get started," Sophia said. She wiped her mouth with her napkin and rose. "If you'll excuse me, I have some things to sort upstairs."

After she'd gone, David took a bite, chewed. Then he sipped from his glass and said, "Her work has always shown talent."

"I'm sure," Samuel said. He pushed his chair back. "At any rate. I look forward to the lesson."

"He'll see," David said to Caroline, once they were the only two left. "He'll see once she begins. She's going to be good."

"You would know best," Caroline said, taking satisfaction where she could find it.

8

RED SPOT

The world, he had long decided, could never deserve her.

—MILES PEARSON, *THE DARKENING GLASS* (P. 187)

Caroline walked with Sophia to the barn before her first lesson that afternoon. Sophia carried two pads of art paper, atop which she had balanced tubes of paint and small bundles of brushes and pencils tied with string, and watercolors in a small japanned box, the corners rubbed down to dull metal.

"Can I help you with those?" Caroline offered.

"I'm able, thank you," Sophia said.

That this was the same path Caroline had walked last night seemed impossible—so recognizable, so mystery-less in the light. Sophia's face had a slight shine. Sophia probably didn't believe in nightmares and would have called to the girls long before they reached the woods.

Caroline thought of the girls' ankles, still smooth and moving unmarked up and down the stairs of the house as they readied themselves for art class. She had kept them that way, all but Eliza's. Did it matter how?

When Sophia reached the teacher's desk she set her supplies down gently. She made small, hopeful adjustments. Everything looked well maintained but well used, and Caroline could picture its history, ordered slowly, a piece at a time, from the store back in Ohio, then stacked in Sophia's room. Sophia's students, even the ones not artistically inclined, would all have three times as many art supplies in their own bedrooms back at home. Caroline felt again a stirring of would-be pity.

Finished, Sophia raised her eyes to Caroline, who'd taken a seat along the back wall. "Where is everyone?"

"They all run a bit late after dinner."

"Not you, though," Sophia said.

She sat at the desk and folded her hands. Her toes tapped beneath, first one foot, then the other, one, then the other, as if she were working the pedals of an invisible machine.

The girls began to arrive—Eliza arm in arm with Abigail, who was likely being rewarded for volunteering last night—and took their seats. Eliza had a bright blue ribbon around her neck, and her hair glowed. That her ankle was invisible beneath her skirts did not change that it was marked, just as her fainting spell's having passed did not change that she had fainted, that some force had made her faint. That she looked like any girl with a friend did not change that she was bestowing a privilege on her subordinate.

Samuel and David sat on opposite sides of Caroline. David was drawn and haughty again, waiting for his wife to teach. Caroline couldn't catch his eye. Her father looked at her and smiled: *Shall we see how this goes?*

She smiled back. This remained to her, at least, the chance to see how Sophia and her teaching would turn out. For a moment she and her father shared again their old high separateness.

Sophia introduced herself brightly, as if she had never met the girls before. She explained that they would begin their first class with portraiture. Ungroomed nature had, it seemed, provided nothing worthy of drawing.

The girls looked a little bored. Sophia wouldn't be talking about her marriage today.

Eliza said, "My first drawing master told me all portraits are lovely lies."

"Did he," Sophia said.

"For what his opinion is worth."

"He must have been a very gifted man, I'm sure, Miss Bell."

"He made everything wooden somehow," Eliza said.

Samuel watched over the tops of his spectacles, his face now less philosophical. He had worked so hard on this room and what it held.

"I'm no good at portraits," said Meg. "Maybe we should draw fruit or something first?"

"Fruit isn't interesting," Sophia said, dismissing whole artistic schools.

Samuel drummed a finger on his closed book, as if hoping Sophia would look in his direction so he could signal to her to become a different person. David stared out the window in a way that Caroline considered cowardly.

Sophia instructed the girls to pair up. Every eye darted to Eliza, who bestowed her hand upon Livia. The jilted others took their partners with disappointment. Caroline looked to Samuel. Was he seeing? But now he was looking at his hands.

The feet of the chairs groaned against the wood floors as the girls bent themselves in half to drag them.

David winced. "Be careful, please. I sanded these floors myself."

"Of *course* you did," said Felicity slyly, the sort of meaningless, weighted thing the girls were always saying to David.

"Oh, Duckie, a few marks on the floor aren't your biggest problem," Sophia said, and the girls laughed, glancing at the ceiling patch from yesterday. There the green ribbon had been, for who knew how long, just above. Woven into all those bits of grass and twigs and sitting over Caroline's head, and she never would have known if the ceiling hadn't dropped it at her feet, a part of the past but reeking of some strange future. The ribbon was tucked into Caroline's desk drawer now. She hadn't been able to surmount her sense of ownership and throw it away, though every one of the girls thought it had been hers, returned to her.

Informed of the ceiling patch and the nest, Samuel hadn't shown much interest, but certainly he didn't want them marshaled as failings of his school by one of that school's teachers. He cleared his throat. The sound seemed to fluster Sophia. She rustled through her papers. "If you're the one being drawn, just sit naturally," she told the girls.

The subjects of course could not. They held themselves rigidly, at carefully chosen angles, the way Caroline had seen them hold themselves before mirrors: here an extended neck to compensate for the little fold of fat that was prodded fearfully every morning, there a downward tilt of the chin to minimize a nose's length. Small, uncomfortable shiftings, as if the eyes of the drawer prickled. Eliza was the only one who sat, subjected to Livia's pencil, much as she always did. She was used to the feel of eyes.

Sophia circled the room. "Remember proportion."

The ones drawing were beginning to prickle now too. "You don't actually look like this, all right? Don't worry," Rebecca said to Meg.

"I'm hopeless," said Livia.

Felicity giggled. "You look a little like my uncle."

"Your uncle?"

"Not *like* him exactly. It's just he has this expression—this sort of pucker to his lips. I did that to your lips here, see?"

"What is that?" Livia said, in a different tone. She had put down her pencil and was stretching her hand across the desk toward Eliza's face. "There's a red spot in your eye, Eliza."

"What?"

"What sort of a red spot?" Samuel asked.

"Come see."

They closed in. Eliza's fingers hung in the air, wondering where to press. "Which eye?" she said. "What does it look like?"

Livia's finger advanced. Instinctively, Caroline batted her hand away.

"I was just *showing*," Livia said.

Caroline could see it. The red dot began in the gray of Eliza's iris and stretched into the white. It was the size of a ladybug or a very small button, darker in the middle, fading to a haze at its edges.

"Does it hurt?" Sophia asked.

"Who has a mirror?" Eliza said.

Julia, of course, produced one. Eliza held it before her face, widening her eyes at herself in the glass. Here was the posing that had been missing before as she tilted herself for the best view. She touched the outer corner of the afflicted eye, then stared at her fingertip, as if she thought it might come away bloody.

One of the trilling hearts has pecked her there, Caroline thought nonsensically.

Eliza looked afraid, as she had not when burning her ankle or poking afterward at the blister that lay concealed now beneath her skirts, when she had commanded the lantern's one circle of light. Her hand, held out with finger extended, trembled a little, and her lips. The difference between what you chose and what happened to you. Caroline almost told her she might just have walked into a branch in the dark, before remembering that her knowledge of last night was something she'd stolen.

"It looks like a little red sun," Rebecca said.

"No," Samuel said. "No, it looks like what it is: a bit of a hurt place. You must have bumped your eye, Miss Bell, that's all."

"I didn't. I really didn't."

"Come, you can't possibly remember all the discomforts you feel in a given day," Samuel said briskly. "And the eye is unusual territory. It has its own way of registering complaints, quite apart from the nerves."

"A simple broken blood vessel, probably," David said.

Eliza's fingers tented over the skin just to the side of her eye, then flew away. "I can't see!" she said wildly. Her eyes fluttered. "I can't!"

"Miss Bell, of course you can. Let us remain ourselves." Though Caroline could hear the effort in Samuel's voice, she doubted any of the others could. "You saw perfectly well until Miss Bunting pointed this little injury out, didn't you? A problem so feeble as that isn't a problem at all. And I can tell you can see; you're looking at me."

Let us remain ourselves. Yes, let us. One constant in Caroline's life: how much better she could feel when her father was talking.

Eliza's hands flapped. "There's a place—a place where I can't see. A hole," she gasped.

"Shouldn't we fetch the physician? She's saying there's something wrong," said Sophia. "Wouldn't she know?"

There was a pause at this violation of the teachers' unspoken understanding never to contradict one another openly in front of their students. This public assertion that Eliza's damage required reckoning. Caroline had wanted to assert the same herself, but she resented that Sophia had done it, and done it in this way.

"Once a suggestion enters the mind it can be difficult to know what we usually know," said Samuel, collecting himself, smoothing this particular circumstance into a feature of human nature.

Caroline stepped forward and touched Eliza's hand. "We'll keep watch on it." She'd almost said *keep an eye*. "We'll do next whatever is needed."

Samuel clapped briskly, trying to force a different rhythm on the room. "But for now, girls, portraiture awaits you."

"You want me to pretend this isn't happening?" cried Eliza.

"Very little has actually happened. But no, I only meant to suggest that there are questions at hand worthier of your talents and energies, Miss Bell. The question of proportion, as you rightly suggested, Mrs. Moore. Among other artistic matters, I'm sure. Tell us, what else should the girls attend to?"

Sophia hesitated. "Well, shading," she said. "And line."

The girls were sitting back down in their places. After a moment, even Eliza, the hollows beneath her eyes wet with tears.

"Shading and line," Samuel said.

Quiet fell as they drew. Caroline watched Livia's pencil, waiting to see it bore into Eliza's eye on the page. Her own eye watered.

*

That night, the four teachers sat before the fire in the sitting room, pretending to read while they watched one another and listened to the sounds of the girls' feet on the upstairs floorboards, tapping into and out of their rooms.

Sophia was reading her Bible, which had a recitation-prize look to it, all crisp gilt edges. Caroline could imagine the letter she might write tonight, if David would let her, to Mama or maybe Reverend North. *This is a cruel place.*

Broken blood vessel, broken blood vessel, Caroline silently repeated, instead of reading the page she had open. The reasonable words David had uttered. Blood vessels could break, like glass, like hearts, without their breaking meaning anything.

The way the spot looked there, though, against the gray and white of Eliza's eye. Another splash of red where it didn't belong. Or perhaps not a splash but a welling-up from somewhere deep inside Eliza that all their lessons and words couldn't touch. Perhaps part of some plan her body had for itself. Hadn't Caroline spent her whole life understanding that bodies could make such plans?

They read on. Caroline was more aware than usual of her own blinking. Sophia adjusted the weight of her Bible in her lap.

David rose: "I need a book from upstairs."

Caroline waited, turning a page, turning another. *No plant now knew the stock from which it came; / He grafts upon the wild the tame* . . . Then she shut her book and stood, saying, "That reminds me."

David had left the door to the Moores' room ajar. Caroline ducked inside, feeling too late the heavy stillness of the room, seeing too late Sophia's dress splayed across David's desk chair as if it had fainted away with passion. David whirled; she'd startled him.

Her own discomfort made her angry. This was her house, even if David and Sophia and all these other people were living in it. She had played with her doll on this carpet.

"What your wife said to my father was surprising," she said. "Don't you think? Questioning him in front of the girls."

Sophia might overhear, if that Bible wasn't holding her attention. Let her.

David reddened. "Sophia is . . ." He paused, lowered his voice. "She's still learning the way things work here."

He shifted on his feet. Caroline saw that he wasn't going to ask her to sit down. After all, to sit in the desk chair she would have had to sit in the lap of the dress, unless he moved it.

"How *is* she at learning?" Caroline said.

He flinched. "Sophia left school when she was eight, did you know that? Her mother needed her to help with the littler ones. I'm not sure she'd ever read a book, a whole book, before—"

"Before you." Caroline was starting to see. "So you were saving her."

"Not *saving*. *Showing* her, maybe. All anyone else ever gave her to think about was dresses and chores and camp meetings."

David in the corner while the preacher screamed and the people flailed, just as Caroline had imagined, but it seemed his eyes had been on one particular body in that moving crowd.

Those eyes were on her now, and his brow furrowed. "I wish there were some way to make you understand that place, what it's like to be from there. Growing up here—there's really no way for you to grasp it. Since you were a girl your father's been clearing away all the dimness. Teaching you, just the way we're now teaching all of these girls. You don't even realize why you are the way you are."

"What way is that?" Caroline said.

"So clear of sight."

She considered telling him she might be happier if her sight were a little dimmer. She considered asking if he really thought it was true that she was the way she was only because it was how her father had made her. How would she know? (And how would he?) Instead she said, "I didn't see Sophia. I had no idea at all about her. You never mentioned her, not once."

He closed his eyes for a moment. "I should have, I know. I meant to. But somehow we were talking so much about other things that I didn't happen to say anything for so long, and then I just couldn't quite think what the words should be. I couldn't think how to explain her to you."

That hung in the room.

David turned abruptly to search for his book again.

Caroline looked at the dress. The neck had been left turned out just a bit, and so at the collar she could see a glimpse of the lining, pink silk, a pretty secret for tucking against Sophia's skin. She reached out, lifted the dress, pulled the neck straight, watching David watch her holding it. She draped it neatly over the arm of the chair.

His wife. Her house.

"It would be better if Sophia didn't speak to my father again that way in front of the students. We may be teaching them to question, but we don't want them to think we're questioning ourselves."

"Caroline, I—"

"You can tell her, or I can." She turned and left, knocking her hip against the bedpost, but not letting him see the ache of it anywhere in her stride.

*

Three days after, Caroline walked to the post office. Partway to town her footsteps raised a flock of trilling hearts from the grass beside the road, and they wheeled and flew toward town. Maybe they had other nests there, on other roofs. She eyed the lines of each house and building she passed but spotted no shaggy bundles.

Two letters were waiting for her, both from Miss Marsh's. One fat and one thin, addressed to Caroline in different hands. Caroline opened the thin one first:

Dear Miss Hood,

Thank you for your letter. We enjoyed teaching Miss Bell and are always happy to hear word of her. We found her to be an exemplary student in all respects, however, and do not have anything to report in response to your inquiries. We send to her and to you our best wishes.

Yours sincerely,
Miss Lucille Marsh
Headmistress

Then the fat:

Dear Miss Hood,

Our headmistress has undertaken to respond to you already, but I heard of your letter—you will understand the way everyone hears of everything here—and felt I should write one of my own. I have the utmost respect for Miss Marsh's judgment, but fear she may on this occasion be erring on the side of forbearance.

I have been the sewing instructor here for some years. It is not in my official capacity to form opinions on the character of my pupils; but such opinions nevertheless play a daily role in my life and in my teaching, as, I believe, they ought (this too I am sure you will understand). I taught Miss Bell for the whole two years she was with us, and in that time I had ample opportunity to observe her. I found her to have many of the important womanly gifts: her turns of phrase, her needlework, naturally beautiful. There were occasional instances in which her behavior toward her educators overstepped, but that is not unusual in girls of her age, and she was mostly tractable. She was well-liked by her fellow pupils.

There was, though, at times a strange quality in that liking. The examples I have to disclose are small: imitations of Miss Bell's dress, or gestures, or manner of speaking, things of that unremarkable order. But one episode did frighten me, when Miss Bell began to control her own consumption of food such that she became quite thin, and several of the other girls followed her example. I recall on one occasion looking around my classroom and noting how slight, how very slight, all their wrists had grown—so slight I felt cruel asking them to complete the tasks I had set them. None would give us any reason for what she was doing. Each only said she hadn't much appetite.

This passed, after a month or two, with no great consequence. Now that I have recorded it on the page it does not strike me as so very dramatic.

I only felt I ought to write, because your letter seemed perhaps to suggest that this pattern has not abated, as I had hoped it would, when Miss Bell departed from us. I hope that I am mistaken, and hope too that you understand that my motive is a true desire to help you and help Miss Bell. Please forgive me if this letter seems to you unnecessary, and please believe that I have no salacious wish to spread tales for the spreading's own sake.

With all my best wishes, from our school to yours.

Most sincerely,
Miss Gloria Sterne

Miss Gloria Sterne. She had a plump hand, stuffed full of those *womanly virtues*. Samuel, Caroline knew, would only huff if Caroline brought this to him. *Of course Eliza undertook her own projects, if what they were giving her was needlework*, he would say.

But it was not every girl who would decide to turn herself into a needle in response.

Caroline herself had stopped eating once. When she'd read *Lives of the Saints*, at twelve, for three days after she'd eaten only crusts of bread. To achieve this she'd cut the crusts from their doughy, inviting centers, there at the table with her father, and pushed the soft goodness to the side of her plate to be resisted.

"I'm not hungry," she said.

"All right," her father told her on the first day. "We should all allow ourselves to be invaded by our reading from time to time."

"That's not what I'm doing." Caroline felt cheated that he'd guessed.

"All right," he said again, and returned to his book.

The second day, her father paused in his eating, when she refused the plate of roast, and said, "I'm not sure Saint Boniface and Saint Philippa and the rest would want you to slight Mrs. Wilmer in this way, Caroline. She started cooking this supper at two o'clock this afternoon."

Actually, Saint Catherine was the one who had caught Caroline: the bedridden girl afflicted with her vision of the crucifixion, her white-hot blisters. When Caroline read about Saint Catherine it was her mother she was picturing in the bed.

"You don't really know what they'd want, though," she said to her father.

He set down his knife and fork. "You're right," he said calmly. "I don't. It's at least worth considering, though, that neither do you, dearest."

She had always wondered what *dearest* really meant, when she was the only one left.

On the third night he was waiting for her when she came to the dining room for supper. "Let's take a walk before we eat."

It had been a lovely summer evening, the air gentle and delicious. Her father had walked quickly. She had to hurry, her empty insides cramping, and still she couldn't catch him. He finally stopped just before the woods to wait for her.

"Here," he said. "Look and listen, please."

"What?"

He only shook his head. So Caroline looked. So she listened to birds making soft, contented sounds, and insects chirping, and the wind rustling thick, thriving leaves. Those leaves flickered their undersides. A wren flew from one branch to another.

She looked back at her father.

"God created this plenty and set you down right in the middle, Caroline. His intent can't be for you to turn your back on it. Since you're interested in proofs just now, you can tell because turning your back is impossible. Where could you look without seeing something beautiful? The saints are important figures in the history of faith, but you, dearest, are not a saint, and that is a wonderful thing."

By the time they got back to the dining room, and her father took his plate into his study and left her alone with the fragrant roast chicken, her plan had felt far away from her, somehow. She'd piled her plate high.

Now Caroline needed to find the equal of that walk and those words for Eliza. To show her it was foolish to read too much into the body, its failings, its needs, its capacities for withstanding.

While she considered, the spot in Eliza's eye didn't grow and didn't shrink, but just stayed there. A small red fact. There was a wince in that half of Eliza's face, and she led with the other when she entered a room or conversed, so that her attention seemed perpetually turned to the side. The other girls spoke to her reverently and only from her good angle.

"Pay it no mind and it will pass," said Samuel, said David.

Sophia said to Caroline, as they walked from the house to the barn one chilly afternoon, "I still don't understand why we aren't doing anything about it."

Outward agreement with Sophia was too much for Caroline to expect of herself. "What, like a poultice? Do you know one for a small red dot in the eye?"

"We should be doing *something*."

"What Miss Bell needs," Caroline said, "is for all of us to stop paying so much attention to her."

Sophia looked incredulous. "What person has ever needed that?"

Caroline walked a little faster.

But of course there was no leaving Sophia behind, not really. That evening when Caroline came around the corner of the house—walking again, she was always walking now; she wondered if this was what spinsters did with all their unfillable old age—she discovered Sophia and David. They sat with their backs to her on the bench beneath the maple, whose last dull brown leaves had mostly fallen, covering the bench seat to either side of them and the ground. They hadn't heard Caroline coming. She stopped.

"I've been praying for her," Sophia was saying. "That's all I said. I can't do that?"

"Oh, love," David said, with her hands closed in his.

Caroline closed her teeth on her lip.

"Your prayers are, of course, your own province."

"Duck, so serious." Sophia reached up to his face and moved his mouth with her fingers. *"Province."*

He dodged away from her hand, laughing. Sophia grabbed him by the back of the neck to pull his face toward her.

"Not here."

"You don't want to?"

"You know what I want," he said, his voice very soft. Caroline's face flamed. "But we need to talk about this."

"Why?" Sophia said. "What else is there to say? For some reason you wish I wouldn't pray for Miss Bell. Or say too much about her, or to her. Or read that book."

"I didn't say any of that, love. But we should be helping her forward in every way we can and encouraging her not to dwell."

"That's what *Samuel* thinks."

"He does, and what he thinks carries weight—can you see that?"

"It's a different kind of place here," Sophia said. "People thinking they're better than everybody else, thinking they know everything."

"No one here feels that way."

"You know, Mama always thought that about you," Sophia said. "She'd say things. 'He's just a farmer. All very well to feel tenderly, but don't forget there are twenty other farmers a stone's throw from here.'"

"I knew she wasn't fond of me, of course." Caroline could hear David's hurt. "I thought it was because of church."

"She didn't love that either."

"If you feel that way too . . . ," David began.

"Duckie. I always told her, every time—I said I had eyes and I could tell what was what."

He kissed her hand.

"I'm praying for Eliza is all. Nobody can tell me that's wrong, not even your Samuel, or your Caroline."

Caroline's fingertips prickled: *your Caroline.*

"Why would you call her that?" David said.

"I'm praying for your Caroline too," Sophia told him.

*

For Thanksgiving, Mrs. Sanders heaped the china that had been Caroline's mother's with potatoes and roast onions and cranberry sauce and a turkey that spilled stuffing from its neck. "We don't use that china often," Caroline said, when she saw Mrs. Sanders bearing the platter, with its prim, intricate blue rim, to the table. By *often* she meant *ever:* those dishes had sat enshrined in the cabinet in the corner since she could remember, too holy to eat from.

Mrs. Sanders set the platter down and dabbed her sweating face. She said, "It's the only set with enough pieces."

This made sense, certainly, though it had taken Mrs. Sanders to see so.

Samuel gave Caroline a nod and a brave smile when he saw the food on the dishes, the new flesh on those brittle, flowery bones. He sat down at the table and surveyed the girls.

"Before I say the blessing," Samuel began, "I encourage each of you to take a moment to give thanks silently. Each of our souls has different debts. Let's remember them now."

They sat with their eyes closed or on their plates. Caroline watched her mother's still, blue roses. *Gratitude* was one of her father's favorite words. She herself had never had any trouble thinking of what she loved: their hillsides, their library, her father's abstracted face while he read. But gratitude seemed to require a stationary accounting, and she'd never wanted to consider her position fixed enough to survey from.

After a few breaths, Samuel began the general grace: "Our truest Father and friend, on this day of thanksgiving, we are ever grateful for the gifts You have bestowed on our hearts and heads, and grateful too to have this day set apart to remember them. We are grateful to be taking part in the project You have enabled us to begin here. We are grateful that we are becoming, each of us, daily, wiser and stronger. We are grateful for the company of one another. Your gifts have made us rich, beyond measure rich."

He looked up, then, and lifted his fork and knife.

Sophia said, "That was a different kind of grace."

"Thank you, Mrs. Moore," Samuel said.

The girls began buzzing to one another as they always did at mealtimes. Caroline caught indecipherable snippets. "Just like that pink thing you had on yesterday." "The cruelest!" "*She* could have sniffed it out."

"A noble act on Lincoln's part, marking this day off," Samuel said to David. "Smaller than his other noble acts, of course."

"Yes," David said, a little flatly. In response to Samuel's questioning look he added, "Oh, nothing. Today certainly isn't the day."

Samuel laughed. "Now I think you *must* say it."

"Well, Lincoln was a hero, of course. A great man. A tragedy. But the fighting, the actual living through the fighting—there wasn't much about it that felt noble." David's voice came slowly, as if he wished he weren't speaking at all.

"But what cause could have been nobler? You fought to free your fellow—"

David held up a hand. Something Caroline had never thought she'd see, David asking her father to stop talking. "I do know all of that," David said. "I know all of the reasons."

"You should be proud of what you did," Sophia told him. "I've never understood why you won't talk about it."

"Really, the reasons can't seem unimportant to you, David," Samuel said.

"Only they seemed very removed from what we were actually doing. That's what I love about this, our school." David gestured around the table, at the oblivious girls. "We have noble reasons, and what we're *doing* is noble."

"I abhor violence, you know that. But you were helping to end a terrible, a godless tyranny," Samuel said. David was injuring him with this refusal to take what he wanted to bestow.

"Yes, I know how terrible enslavement was. I saw it. The fighting was terrible too."

"That's *different*," Sophia said.

"And do you know, that wasn't even the worst of it," said David, looking at his plate, speaking softly, though the girls weren't listening anyway. "The worst was that it was so dull most of the time—these big empty periods of waiting, in the heat or the cold—and there was no distinct margin between the waiting and the fighting. Nothing set off the one as more important than the other. It all happened at the same pace, in the same colors. It made you start to wonder whether everything in the world counted the same after all—whether the value you'd always ascribed to certain things, certain ideas, was an invention. What the purpose was of any of it."

"The *purpose*—" Samuel began.

"I'm only saying it makes me peaceful, here, being able to stand to look at both the motives and the acts."

Horror might have fueled devotion; David might have polished his idea of Caroline's father with more and more vigor each time he saw a new terror. Samuel's ideas might have seemed all that could make some things actually matter more than others, the way David had always assumed they would. Coming here, then, and meeting the Hoods, building this school, might have felt like the answer to every question the war had given him.

Caroline looked at the faces of the girls, who were giving her so many new questions, as they twisted and laughed.

9.

PERFORMANCE

❧

He wrestled mightily with a mad jealousy of her pain—
for its exclusion of him he could not bear.

—MILES PEARSON, *THE DARKENING GLASS* (P. 212)

Caroline first read *The Darkening Glass* when she was six-teen. Her father had never outright forbidden her from doing this, but only because he believed the prohibition went without saying. Miles Pearson had been famous for a decade by then, and dead for a year or two. Dying had not won him Samuel's forgiveness.

At that age, Caroline was learning Greek and Hebrew in Samuel's study, and frequenting Ashwell parlors on the social calls he kept arranging for her, and trying to understand how she was supposed to be one person in those two so different surroundings. One afternoon, she'd been visiting Miss Philomena Cuttman, eighteen years old, daughter of Samuel's attorney. Philomena patted at the rows of curls that framed her face and talked about her younger sister's recent engagement. "I'm very happy for them," she said, fear in her eyes.

"Yes, how lovely."

"I already know the sort of dress I want for the wedding. I want it to be simple, the sort of thing Louisa Blake might have worn. Oh." Philomena pressed her fingers to her mouth, as if she'd let slip an embarrassing noise.

"It's all right," Caroline said, the way she always did when people accidentally mentioned *The Darkening Glass* or its people in her presence.

But that day she wondered: Was it? She didn't know enough about the book to evaluate her own grounds for offense. She'd always understood that *The Darkening Glass* was a bruise on her father that she must not press, no matter how she wanted to.

Her father who'd sent her to spend this time in Philomena's parlor.

"I'm sorry," Philomena said. "Will you help me decide on the sash?"

On Caroline's way home, she paid a boy she passed on the street to go into the bookshop and buy her a copy of the novel.

She hadn't needed long to see that *The Darkening Glass* was ridiculous. It filled her quiet bedroom with its moaning. Samuel would have hated it even if it had been about another place, other people. She could hear him: *Everyone certainly seems to have a great many gusty feelings.*

But of course *The Darkening Glass* wasn't about anywhere or anyone else. It was a lurid, smeary picture of something Caroline desperately wanted to see, and when she flipped to each new page, she scoured it for Louisa's name. Louisa seemed often to give of herself, or cower in fear, or suffer, while being—Caroline learned over and over again—very beautiful. She did not say very much. Hammond, the main character, on the other hand, liked long words. So did Abner, in giving voice to his terrible plans from his dark corners.

Caroline read the book for longer stretches. She became less careful about choosing her moments. She began to want her father to find out.

Yet when the evening came that Samuel knocked at her door and entered too fast for her to haul herself up out of the book and hide it, she was filled with visceral horror to be caught with it in her hands.

"Papa, don't look," she blurted out.

He stopped in the doorway. An issue of *The Compass* was clutched in one hand; he'd been coming to tell her about something he'd read. That was why he hadn't waited after knocking—he'd been too eager to share it with her. Meanwhile she'd shut herself away in secrecy to do a thing she knew would hurt him as much as anything she could think of.

"Where possible in life, we should avoid practices that cannot bear the eyes of others." His voice broke.

"I don't *like* it." Her eyes stung. "I only wanted to see."

He nodded. "You wanted to see."

Then he left, closing the door behind him so softly it made no sound she could hear.

*

At Trilling Heart, fall was now turning to winter. The leaves had gone. The air thinned; the remaining grass dried to straw. Silent too on Caroline's walks, where before there had been buzzing and chirping. So many small deaths.

The woods drew her. She might understand something about that night with the girls and the branding if she could return to the precise place where it had happened, if she could find the stick with its burned end, and then—she wasn't sure. Hold it? Break it? Throw it as far as she could, bury it, convince a tree to take it back onto itself? It didn't matter; she couldn't find it. Each day she was certain that she was just there, that she recognized the shape of a copse or the bend of a trunk, but the next day she was just as sure about a different place. Each time she scuffed up leaves, searching—burrowing through the dry top layer to the wet beneath, and then to the depth where leaf began to turn to dirt and fleshy white earthworms writhed frantically for new cover. With the leaves mostly fallen, the woods were becoming a place of exposure, and while she walked she sometimes saw a red trilling heart cutting across the sky. The birds seemed quieter in the cold. She could not understand why they hadn't left. It had already snowed. Their continued presence, as if following some rhythm more powerful than seasons, unsettled her.

Caroline had often felt a desperation arrive with the fall—worse this year than usual, with the promise of more time in rooms with David and Sophia, but not new. Winter had sealed Birch Hill's ruin. Not the first winter but the second. The group had survived the first on momentum and food they'd brought with them from their previous lives, and when it warmed again, their planting went promisingly enough—what doesn't seem promising in spring? But that second fall, the little grove of birches after which they'd named the settlement caught a mysterious rotting blight and fell, and set the tone for what followed. The harvest faltered. The animals sickened. None of those men was a farmer, really, and they didn't know what to do with so physical a disaster.

Before the second spring everyone else had fled to reassembled lives or new ones: two solicitors to reopen their old businesses, Dr. Hawkins to resume his practice in Boston, a newspaperman to start a new paper out west, and Miles Pearson, unbeknownst to them, to write *The Darkening Glass*. The three Hoods, left behind, went back to hiring out their farming and buying what they needed instead of trying to make and grow it all. Samuel went back to writing about his ideas instead of trying to live them. And then one September day Anna died of a fit, and there were two.

Caroline wondered how the Birch Hill failure had looked to the women as it was happening. It hadn't been their dream, probably. One or two had been professional writers and thinkers, but most had only been married to them. It seemed to her that they might have seen the coming end more clearly, and sooner, than their men had seen it. Had they talked, as they patched and plugged and repaired, about how they'd come to be tending this dying vision? How early had they known it was beyond their ministrations? Anna, how early had she known?

Returning to her room after failing again to find the stick, Caroline passed Eliza in the upstairs hall. "I've noticed your eye is improving," she told the girl.

Eliza stopped and put a hand to the wall as if she required its support. "Somewhat, yes."

Afternoon light streamed through the windows on this side of the house, and Caroline could see that spot perfectly well, shrunk to a pinprick now. From inside, its slow dissolving might have looked to Eliza like the burning off of a red fog. "More than somewhat, from appearances."

"I suppose. I've been a little afraid to believe it."

"I think it's especially important to believe in good developments and cling to them. Those kinds of slow daily miracles—like healing, like spring—you know."

"It's almost winter now," Eliza said.

"I'm doing you the credit of imagining you might still remember springtime."

Eliza tilted her head, and the light caught that pinprick of red, small as it was. "You sounded very like your father just then. You often do."

The words made Caroline's tongue lie heavy in her mouth—though any of the boys who'd tromped to the Hoods' door through the years to pay homage would have given, for that compliment, an eye, a toe, a finger.

Eliza knew her effect. Caroline could tell she knew.

"I'm nearly done with the reading for tomorrow," Eliza said. They'd finished *Midsummer* and begun *Romeo and Juliet;* Caroline hoped to show the girls the resonances between the two. "Romeo *is* absurd."

"Well, he's very young."

"He makes that very obvious," Eliza said.

As it turned out, all the girls relished mocking Romeo. They read aloud his overelaborate faux despair over Rosalind gleefully, their arms clapped to their foreheads. Juliet, on the other hand, they loved. "She's too good for him," Felicity pronounced.

Eliza was as perceptive as ever in their discussions, if sometimes quieter and preoccupied seeming. Caroline called on her frequently but avoided giving her certain roles in their acting. Needing no extra wit or new adoration from the others, she couldn't be Juliet. And never Romeo, with his dramatics and his celebration of pain. Not Mercutio, irresistible and doomed. Not even the Prince, who called all action to a halt when he chose.

She would have liked for Eliza just to sit and watch every day, but the others would have noticed. So Caroline made her various servingmen, or sometimes Lady Capulet or Benvolio.

*

Samuel wrote a letter to the parents suggesting the girls might remain at Trilling Heart for the Christmas holiday. He managed to imply that there would be something important and transformative about the experience.

"Why do you want to keep them?" Caroline asked him.

"I was hoping to avoid the interruption. So much lost time!"

She suspected he also hoped to prevent word of the Eliza-related dramatics he refused to acknowledge from reaching the parents. Tabitha's, Livia's, and Rebecca's sent for them anyway, but all the other girls stayed.

There had been a bit of snow cover since early December, but Christmas Eve day was warm enough to melt it. By Christmas morning the ground was wet, brown, and bereft looking, like something hatched too early from its egg. The scene in the sitting room was cheerful as a picture book, though, with a fire pleasantly popping and hissing, and a garland of pine boughs on the mantel giving off its fresh, spicy smell, and bright stockings hung below. The Hoods' life had grown so many new feet.

The girls squealed as they went to collect their stockings. Eliza too. This morning she seemed just like the others, all of them sitting together on the sofas and opening their bundles with the excitement of younger children. Their treasures accumulated in sweet troves in their laps. The girls had given one another new ribbons and peppermints and butterscotches. Caroline had given each of them a scrap of fabric, out of which something small but pretty might be made: green paisley for Meg, madder stripes for Felicity, purple flowers for Eliza, chintz on white for Abigail, gray jacquard for Julia. Samuel gave them all lexicons. David gave them unusual, lovely bits of rock he'd collected from the fields in warmer days, and these they pocketed like secrets. Sophia gave them each three new colored pencils.

They'd also all contributed, even the girls, to the Society for Poor Relief in Ashwell, and Samuel reminded them of this now. "Because of you this day is warmer for someone than it might have been."

The teachers had agreed ahead of time not to give one another presents, but this agreement did not extend to presents between fathers and daughters or husbands and wives. As always, Caroline had given Samuel a book he'd said he wanted: a new translation of a French essayist he liked. And as always, Samuel had given Caroline a book she wanted but hadn't known she wanted ahead of time: Goethe's *Egmont*.

David gave Sophia some fine new drawing paper. She stroked the surface of a sheet. Sophia gave David a magnifying glass with a pewter rim. "For your rambles," she said.

He laughed and lifted her and spun her around once before setting her down on her feet again. Caroline acknowledged to herself that they looked like an illustration of love. The girls giggled. Meg, who seemed a little easier and gentler in Livia's absence, clapped.

Four days later, Tabitha, Rebecca, and Livia returned, right on schedule. They went into exaggerated raptures about their Christmases at home, trying to make the others jealous and heal their own jealousies over what they'd missed. Nothing much was said about their parents, what they had or hadn't told them about life at school. Lessons resumed.

On a gray, cold day in January, Caroline cast Eliza as Tybalt. They were reading act 3, scene 1, so it was the last chance for anyone to be Tybalt, or Mercutio, about to doom all the others with their deaths.

Samuel, David, and Sophia sat at the back wall. "An audience!" Rebecca said, as the girls wrapped themselves in sheets—why sheets were any better than dresses to attire Verona's gentlemen, Caroline didn't know, but the girls had protested against their retirement after *Midsummer*—and picked up the branches they'd gathered outside months ago to be their swords. Leaves, now turned brown, still clung to a few.

"You'll be kind to us, won't you, Mrs. Moore?" Meg called.

"*Mr.* Moore is never kind," Livia said.

"I am," David said.

"You always have a lot of criticism." Livia shook the hem of her sheet into place.

"Kindly meant, Miss Bunting."

They adjusted themselves, tucking at their hair, smiling.

Caroline clapped, and they assumed their places. Benvolio and Mercutio bantered, then Tybalt arrived, then Romeo; the fight began. From the beginning, the girls had taken to swordplay. Today they set their jaws and violently swished their branches, playful and also serious as death. The aging leaves wafted a mossy smell, detached, floated to the floor.

Eliza jabbed at Livia, who threw up her hands and toppled.

But then Eliza also fell, though it was too early in the scene for her scripted wounding, though Julia, as Romeo, hadn't yet come anywhere near her.

She'd tripped, Caroline thought. Then her body began to jerk. Her back arched, relaxed, arched again. Her hands batted.

Her open eyes moved from face to face to face.

"What's happening?" she screamed.

Caroline crouched beside her. Samuel came forward and collapsed to his knees. "Miss Bell!" he shouted, his voice loud and strong. "Miss Bell, stop!"

"Can't! I can't!" Her movements garbled the words.

Samuel grabbed her by the shoulders. "You must."

Those stirring limbs were the shape of Caroline's oldest fears. She could not get air.

Samuel also gasped. "Stop it, Miss Bell!"

"She can't help it. *Look* at her," said Sophia.

A spasm, another spasm. Lessening now.

Eliza's hands calmed. She began to cry.

Sophia pushed close, gathered her in, making *shh* sounds and smoothing.

"This is cruel, Miss Bell," said Samuel.

The motion of Sophia's hands pushed the drapery of the sheet aside, baring Eliza's arm up past the elbow, showing them all a vivid mottling of red on the skin, tucked into the crook of her elbow and extending both up and down. Like a dappling of thumbprints, as if someone had seized her over and over.

"Look," someone whispered.

"Look," someone else.

Look at the red, red, red.

Everyone was very quiet then, except for Eliza, still crying, still with that rippling moving through her, a shiver, a pause, a shiver, a pause, a rhythm like breath.

*

They sent to Ashwell for Dr. Burgess. He came and examined Eliza. "No immediate crisis, anyway," he told them after, in Samuel's study. "It seems to have passed. No physical trouble that I can find, other than the rash, which could be anything really." He was a weak-chinned man who'd spent decades stitching up his patients' mowing wounds and delivering their babies. Here he was out of his depth.

They put Eliza to bed and stationed Mrs. Sanders to watch while she slept.

When Caroline went to talk to her father that night, he was writing and didn't hear her enter. She wondered how his own words could transfix him even now. "Papa," she said sharply.

"One moment."

She stood there—she actually stood there—and waited. Furious with herself, her own biddability, she ran her eyes over the rows of books, the rich reds and browns and greens of their spines. She looked down at her feet on the Turkey carpet. She remembered when her whole foot had fit inside a single swirl of its pattern, and she would leap around the room from one to the next in a dance she had felt sure the carpet's weaver had mapped out for her. Her foot was large enough to hide the swirl now.

The Moores had retired for the night. Caroline listened to the quality of the silence above her head. They would be talking about Eliza, surely. What would each be saying?

"All right," her father said, setting his pen down. "What is it, Caroline?"

"You must know."

He pushed his fingers back behind his spectacles and rubbed his eyes. "Such a frightening moment."

"More than a moment. All the moments. We need to send her home, Papa. I know it's my fault she's here, I know it will cause trouble—"

"That isn't what matters now," Samuel said. "You're right, of course."

She felt such relief at his reasonableness and his forgiveness.

Eliza was ill, that was all, and they would send her back to the people whose job it was to take care of her. They would all recover; the school would survive; there was no need for them to take Eliza's collapse as their own failure.

She sat down opposite her father. "Did Mama have many fits in a row?" she asked. She wasn't sure she could stand to watch another.

Samuel started. "But Caroline, this isn't like what happened with your mother."

"What do you mean? Didn't she fall down and shudder?"

"Whatever we're dealing with here, it's not that. Miss Bell never lost consciousness, for one thing. And your mother never had any—any skin ailments."

So that was what they would be calling those fearsome splotches.

"It was different with Mama? What was it like?" Her father had never agreed before to talk about this.

Samuel sighed. "Often it began with a suspicion. She'd sense one was coming. Though not always."

Caroline imagined that, waiting for a vast hand to paw her clumsily, pin her to the ground.

"There was one morning I recall when she told me she thought she'd best stay home that day. Would I mind staying with her."

Would you mind? As if politely requesting that he close a window or repair a rotted shingle. What kind of a woman could give fear such a dainty voice? Though perhaps Anna had been too accustomed to her sickness to be afraid, and of course she hadn't known it could kill her, and perhaps Samuel wasn't remembering exactly how she'd phrased her request or couldn't bear to say the words as she'd actually said them. "Did you stay?" Caroline asked him.

"Of course! I would have given up anything to be there."

"Of course."

"It wasn't painful, she told me. Just a strange sensation. Something like electricity."

More internal than the vast hand, then. The first time it might have felt like the arrival of some impressive new power, sudden grace or speed. Had it left its mark on Anna in other ways, this unusualness? This being a person whom strange sensations visited? She had known, as people rarely have to know, what she could sustain. The knowledge might change the way a person walked and spoke and wore her own face.

Samuel played with the page of the book he'd been writing in, flipping it first one way and then the other. His fingertip whispered against the paper. "Sometimes there wasn't any warning."

"Perhaps she didn't always tell you. Not wanting to worry you, in case she was wrong."

Samuel shook his head. "When she suspected, she always told me."

Marriage mystified Caroline in its attending certainties about the actions and intentions of someone else. She had spent more time with her father's habits and words than with her own (he had more of them), and still she sensed hidden, quiet rooms she'd never entered, with heavy curtains pulled. But the contract itself, the formal decision to live all the days of the rest of your life with a person, might make it impossible to believe any thought could be kept from you on every one of those days. So her father could say, *She always told me;* David could say, *I was showing her;* Sophia could say, *He misses things about people.* Caroline knew less of the country of marriage than she knew of ancient Greece or Shakespearean England, yet it did seem to her that Sophia didn't see things quite the way David wanted, and David from time to time did trot out a small, surprising observation about the subtext of a remark or the expression on someone's face. And her mother could not have told her father everything.

"She understood it was better for me if I knew it was coming.

She never would have kept it from me willingly," Samuel continued. His voice caught. Caroline wanted to go and comfort him, kiss the top of his head, but the words seemed slightly wrong.

"I wonder if making it better for you was always the first thing she considered," she said.

Her father's face sharpened. "Suffering isn't a winner-take-all game, Caroline."

"Thank you for the lesson. Tell me what it was *like*."

"You want me to describe the fits for you? How they looked and sounded, and how I felt, watching that, nothing at all I could do?"

Yes, she was about to say, when he went on.

"Dearest, you can't ask that of me."

He had always been so ample with what he did want to say: tidbits of Anna's preferences, habits, sayings. Tiny pieces of her surface. Caroline had taken each of these shards into her open palm to try to assemble later if it turned out there were enough, not wanting to ask for more when he worked so hard to seem happy, and when she'd always known this work was for her benefit.

"The last time, did she know?" Caroline asked.

"No. That last time was . . . unforeseen. You were sleeping, and I was reading. Your mother had gone for a walk."

Her mother dying while out on a walk was one of the facts Caroline had been given long ago to hold in her hand. Now it felt strange there, improbably angled. Caroline took many walks, but Anna, wife and mother, must have had enough to do without solitary wandering. "But where was she going?"

"These questions!" Samuel barked. "Where does anybody walk to? I don't know. I wasn't able to ask her after, was I?"

They watched each other.

"It's upsetting to remember it," he said.

"I'm sorry."

She was. Still, *where?* Nowhere, maybe. Anna had just liked walking. She'd liked walking right up until she died walking, that was all. Or away from the fullness of her life. From Samuel telling her about his latest essay, or talking too loud to someone in the study, another of those conversations that unfolded as parallel performances. Away from Caroline's yells, laughter, and tantrums, her small clutching fingers. Birch Hill that had lately rotted on the vine. Anna liked to get as free as she could, and one day the escape had become more permanent than she had planned on.

Her father's expression gentled. "I know it must have been . . . terrible for you to watch that today, Caroline. Please trust me, though, that this is quite different from your mother's illness. Miss Bell has, I think, only allowed some suggestion to take hold of her."

"You think she shuddered like that on purpose? What about her skin?" Picturing even as she said it the way it might have happened: Eliza, at night, or beneath her desk, or as she walked from one place to another, thumbing up inside her own sleeves and bearing down.

"I don't pretend I understand it. But you heard Dr. Burgess— this doesn't seem to be some straightforward physical malady."

"I don't see—"

He held up a hand. "In any case I do think you're right. It's best, now that things have reached such a pitch, to send her home. Tomorrow morning I'll have David and Mrs. Sanders bring her into town and arrange it, and telegraph to tell them she's coming."

"Won't they blame us?"

"They may. But an ill girl—it isn't so unusual. Everyone knows one. And anyway, I don't care for the trajectory here. We'll have to face it. We've faced worse."

"We have."

He smiled in a tired way.

Upstairs the hall was still, but as Caroline walked toward her bedroom Sophia emerged from hers, still dressed—she must have been waiting inside for sounds. Her eyes and cheeks were puffy.

"Any news?" she whispered.

"We'll send her home tomorrow."

Sophia nodded. She glanced sideways at Caroline's face, seeming to gauge something. "You know what it looked like?"

Like my mother.

"Like what happened in the camp meeting once," Sophia said, "when God came to a girl and pitched her over, and moved her."

Caroline looked at her. "You think—"

"I didn't say that, did I?" Sophia said quickly. "I just said what it looked like." The Moores must have had a tense discussion about this already. "I'll tell David, about tomorrow."

Inside her bedroom, Caroline found that the skin of her inner arms itched. Her sleeves were too tight to push up and see, and when she unbuttoned her dress, she held her breath in the moment before the cloth came away. But there was her skin, same as ever. She took in a breath, blew it out. She'd been letting her panic run with her—the skin markings weren't even the part of this visitation that was familiar, that she had long practice fearing. She raked her fingernails gently over the place until the itch left.

10.

CARRIAGE

Like a tempest in the distance,
trepidation amassed and brewed.

—MILES PEARSON, *THE DARKENING GLASS* (P. 288)

I n the morning, Eliza, informed of the plan, informed them she
did not want to leave.

"I'm feeling much better," she said.

That was excellent, the very most welcome news, but did not
change the necessity of sending her home, as she herself must
see. And once recovered she might come back again.

Eliza said, "I'll tell everyone."

A question, a quite natural question, was: *Tell them what?*

"That I'm ill. That I fell ill here."

Of course she might say as she liked, as ever. And of course
people fell ill in all kinds of places, and was it really true, really,
that she'd never been ill before, elsewhere?

"You can't make me leave," she said, and clutched the arms of
the chair she was sitting in (they'd told her after breakfast, wanting her fed at least).

It seemed, though, that they could. In the end David had to
carry her to the carriage, where her possessions and Mrs. Sanders were already stowed, Mrs. Sanders having packed everything expeditiously during breakfast. Eliza would not walk,
though she did not kick or scream either. She lay like a rolled

carpet in David's arms. Participating in this farewell in which the leave-taker seemed already absent felt like acting a scene with the key player missing. Caroline stood with the blood thrumming in her throat while they drove away.

Samuel waited until the carriage was almost out of sight, then turned to the girls. "We are all concerned about Miss Bell, but she goes now to attend to the duty of getting well again. While she does, we'll all be thinking of her."

The girls were quiet and unsettled looking. Sophia gazed out over the grounds, searching for God, maybe. There was a feeling in the air like a death had happened.

"Our other duty, meanwhile, lies in the classroom," Samuel finished, and sent them inside to ready themselves for a lesson in thirty minutes' time.

But the lesson never began, because it took only twenty minutes for the carriage to drive back, for David to leap out and yell, "I think she's breathing," for them all to see Eliza with her eyes closed and head lolling, huddled on Mrs. Sanders's lap like a child.

*

David fetched Dr. Burgess again, who administered smelling salts and some sort of draught and left once more. The teachers sent the girls to their rooms and met in Samuel's study.

"I thought she was dying," David said. "I thought she was going to die right there in front of me." He was looking at his hands as if newly understanding all they could not do. Sophia covered them with hers.

"What happened?" Samuel said.

"We started, and she told us she thought she needed to stay, that it wouldn't be good for her, leaving. I thought it was just more of what she'd been saying all morning. I thought she was only . . . you know."

"Lying," Caroline said.

"Then she started saying she felt light-headed. She couldn't breathe. She started gasping, and she turned red, and then she slumped over."

Sophia gasped too, as if somehow, even though she'd seen Eliza there in the carriage herself, the conclusion of the story were a surprise.

Samuel was tapping his second and third fingers in alternation on his desktop, making them sound the wood like tiny marching feet, the way he did sometimes when stuck on a thorny bit of phrasing. "Well. In light of this, we may need to reconsider our approach. Clearly just now Miss Bell is in no condition to be moved."

"Her parents will need to come then," Caroline said. "Collect her, decide how best to take her home."

"My concern there," said Samuel slowly, "is that she's taken it into her head that leaving makes her worse. Sometimes a belief like that—believing it may make it true, I fear. Her condition may worsen no matter how the moving is accomplished."

"What are you saying?" Caroline asked.

"What do we do?" Sophia said.

"Let's think. Let's think about this carefully. Dr. Burgess still finds no physical source of Miss Bell's distress. It would seem to follow that the source—it would seem clear to me—must somehow lie in her ideas."

"Then if we could fix the ideas—" David said.

"Yes, I think so," Samuel said. "I think if we can do that, if we can find whatever mistaken view is troubling her, she might improve."

They were sitting in the same room where for all of Caroline's life she'd been taught to see her problems clearly, to name them while her father listened and adjusted her naming—to find them, after, smaller. But this—no one knew the name for this.

"Papa, we can't. You know we can't keep her," Caroline said.

Samuel sighed. "In removing her we put her at risk. Do you want to try that again? Given the result? I think, I truly do think, there's something in her thoughts or in her soul that's made her sick. And I think with care and attention we might be able to figure out how to make her well."

"How?" Sophia said. "What's wrong with her?"

"Of course I don't have all of the answers just yet, Sophia. But we can search for them—we *will*—as no one else can." Samuel looked at Caroline again. "If we did get her home somehow, her family doctor, what do you think he'd do with her? He'd lock her up in her bedroom. Give her draughts upon draughts that would do nothing to reach this trouble where it lives. Miss Bell wouldn't see the sun for a year."

"That's true," David said, and his voice held a kind of awe. "That is what would happen."

"In good conscience I don't think we can let it," Samuel said. "We'll write to Hawkins and seek his advice."

"Hawkins?" Caroline said.

"Hawkins has been an active physician for thirty years."

"Why do we need one, if you're so certain the trouble isn't physical?"

"Its manifestations of course are, and Hawkins is a different breed than whomever Miss Bell's parents would employ, with a wide and varied practice, and a deep and current and active reading in the professional literature. Hawkins will be able to tell us what it would be best to do next."

Caroline thought she saw. "And, of course, you trust him not to say anything."

Tightly, her father said, "I won't pretend that isn't a consideration, though of course not the primary one. He will have information for us, and we ourselves will read too. We'll read, and look for answers, and we'll find them, and when we do we'll use them to the best of our abilities."

He was still hoping they could be saviors, just as they'd imagined from the start.

"Then this scheme has nothing to do with what it would look like to the world at large if Miles Pearson's daughter were to collapse in her parents' coach on the way home, just like a character in his book?" Caroline asked.

"Caroline, I think I needn't remind you that you are the one who decided she should come here, dearest," her father said. "Perhaps you might allow me to decide when she should leave."

That knocked her silent.

*

Eliza had her next fit that afternoon, in her bedroom. She had come down for dinner, eaten a little, then gone up to rest. Felicity screamed, and everyone came running, but by the time they reached her Eliza was already finding her feet.

"It's all right, I'm all right." She patted her hair and her sleeves, gray-faced.

"Miss Bell," Caroline said. "Really, I don't understand—why would you want to stay here? Surely you can see that you need to be at home, under a physician's care."

"I don't," Eliza said desperately. "I need to be here. I need this place, what's here for me in this place. Please, there's nothing at home for me."

Felicity stroked her arm.

"And anyway, leaving would harm me. You all saw that."

Samuel cleared his throat. "Well, Dr. Burgess did say that this might happen," he informed all of them. "He said there can be several attacks in close succession at first. I'll send word to him. See what he advises."

Caroline followed him out into the hall. She waited till they were out of earshot of the rest. "Papa—"

"I'm going to write to Hawkins right now too, so we might begin to get a clearer picture of what next steps to take." Was he avoiding her eyes, or only not looking at her? He walked down the stairs.

Caroline went to her room to dry her sweating face. Then she went to look for David. She found him in the study, hunched miserably over a medical book.

"You heard?" she said.

"Sophia told me. I was in the barn, checking the ceiling patch. I'd wanted to think about an easier problem, I suppose. Sophia said Eliza was recovering for now, so I came in here, to try to pin it down," he told her. "Anemia, maybe, paired with the sort of suggestibility we were discussing. You see?" He swiveled the book toward Caroline, stabbing at the margin with his finger. "That would explain the paleness and lethargy."

"Anemia doesn't cause red markings on the skin, does it? Twitching, jerking?"

He squinted at the page. "No, those I'm thinking must arise from whatever's amiss in her thinking. Or perhaps even unrelated, coincidental secondary problems."

"What was it someone said about the role of coincidence in explanation?"

"I'm sure something damning." David rubbed his face. Caroline wanted to lay soft fingers over his eyelids to make darkness.

"Where's your wife?" she said.

"She said she wanted a walk. I think this is frightening her."

So Sophia was walking now too.

"And you?" he said softly. "Caroline, this must be horrible. The parallels must seem . . ."

He took her hand. The skin of his palm was warm, rough, much as she'd always imagined it. The air went soft around her. She tightened her grip.

He squeezed back but then pulled away. He turned a page of the book.

To let him hear how unaffected her voice was, Caroline asked, "What will Hawkins say, I wonder?"

"He'll have some insight. This kind of thing can't be entirely unprecedented." He looked at her. "I know it seems like a risk to you, keeping her."

"Not a risk. A mistake."

"But your father's right about what they'll do to her if we send her away. And us? We'd have to close. This, all of this, all of us, we'd be ruined."

They would. The school would close, the girls would go home, and who would ever give them any others? David and Sophia would go home too.

"Your father, Caroline," David said softly.

Yes, none would be ruined more than Samuel. He'd had two chances now. There would be no third. After all the beautiful words, all the beautiful ideas, he would die a failure, and no one would look at anything he'd done or written, forever after, without seeing how he'd failed. The result would be a new smallness and poverty, and a new depth of aloneness in her own life, with so many years of it left, still, to get through. She took a breath, then said, "I know. But I think we must, must now take the actions that are best, without considering the effects on ourselves."

"I'm not thinking only of us, though. Think what they'll say."

It didn't take her long to understand. He watched her face as she saw his meaning. Trilling Heart's closing would be used to prove a point: that all of them here had been wrong about girls. *They thought they could pack them full.* Thoreson would have his pen out as soon as he heard the news. *Perhaps now we can see that what individual students require, regardless of sex, is practical preparation for their likely social positions and tasks. As for the rest? Needless weight.* Even the headmistresses of some of the traditional long-standing girls' schools might feel moved to write. *The inherent differences in robustness between male and female, and the differences in the proper roles of each, must, it is clear, be taken into account.* Then those women would resume teaching their posture classes, embroidery, elocution, reassured in the rightness of their elegant miniature worlds—after all, look what happened when those worlds got larger. Thoreson would resume producing well-behaved, adequate citizens who understood how to establish orderly homes.

Caroline wanted more than that for their girls, for every one of them.

David was watching her. "We can resolve this," he said.

As a boy he had lifted her father's book out of the dust of the road. She could see now his expression in that moment, when he'd decided that the force that had thrown it to him would also throw him whatever else was necessary for the rest of his life, and the look of that young, sure face enraged her.

They had trapped her in their plans, these men.

"I admire your faith," she told him. "You and your wife have that in common."

He flinched. "Was that necessary?"

"It felt necessary."

David bent low over the book again. "If that's all, I'd like to get back to this."

*

Caroline sat down at her desk that evening to write the letter to the Bells herself. She would write it and walk into Ashwell in the morning to post it.

Her lamp cast a glow over only the paper and her arms; the rest of the room, even her own lap, was in darkness. There was enough moon to see the branches of the tree just outside the window. At this time of the year they always looked to her like crabbed, crippled hands.

She wrote *Dear Mr. and Mrs. Bell* very slowly, in her largest and most confident script. If she shaped the letters well enough, her pen might carry right into the next, and she might manage to write the words that would stir the Bells to come and fetch Eliza so they could bring her home and properly address the problem of her. Only she wished she'd never met Eliza's parents. It wasn't helpful to her now, picturing the woman who would open this letter and take it to her sofa to read. No, to glance at. With those darty, distracted eyes, Mrs. Bell might not get to the end, no matter what Caroline wrote; Caroline doubted she'd ever read anything whole. (Where had Miles Pearson found her? Why had he married her? Maybe he'd only wanted someone who would never make it far enough into *The Darkening Glass* to worry about Louisa and Miles's feelings where she was concerned.) Or Mr. Bell might be the one to open the letter, decide not to wade into this mess, for fear of griming his nice clean trouser cuffs, and put it by, somewhere, for his wife to read—somewhere she would never find it. Go on thinking about safes or steel.

Or Caroline might be wrong. They might read, and get to the end, and call the papers—no matter how calmly Caroline phrased it all—before they even arranged to bring Eliza home. "He has disturbed her," Mrs. Bell might say, and her eyes, whatever else could be said of them, would be appropriately teary. "Samuel Hood has undone our daughter." Mr. Bell standing beside her, giving the accusations ballast. People would believe them. The ending, for all of them, would be the one David had made Caroline envision.

Caroline shook her right hand: just a few quick shakes. She thought, but was not sure, that it had tingled, and now she could tell herself that was because of the shaking. Then she did the same with her left.

She wished she could write to Miles Pearson himself. *I don't understand your daughter. If we have undone her, she seemed very ready to be undone. Whatever drives her, it is too large for us; it frightens us here. It's changing us. This must be your fault. Please come collect her.*

And if she were writing impossible letters, she could write one to her mother too. *Dear Anna. Dear Louisa. Dear Anna. Dear Louisa.*

Tell me who you were.

The tree branches scrabbled at the sky outside her window—she felt she should actually have been able to hear the scratching.

She made herself practice living through the ending. The Moores would leave if Trilling Heart closed. David would go with Sophia, forever and ever, amen. Caroline and Samuel would resume reading their books in front of the fire in the evenings together—fewer books, older favorites, as they would need to spend less, as there would be less new income from Samuel's reprinted essays, growing daily dustier and more forgotten. Most days neither Hood would mention the Moores or Trilling Heart at all. *Listen to this, Caroline,* Samuel would say, and give his dry chuckle, and read her a line he'd read her three times before, pinching and pinching at his earlobe the way he always had. The skin of Caroline's face every day a little heavier. And elsewhere, all these girls would be preparing for their own domestic firesides, where they would mend clothes and prepare dinner invitations, and no one would ever know how Livia acted Shakespeare, how Abigail's mathematical reasoning had improved, how much they all could do.

Caroline put her pen away.

*

She stayed in her bedroom during supper. Later, she went down to the kitchen to make tea. Sophia was standing at the corner window, looking out, eating a piece of bread with jam.

Caroline put the kettle on. She hoped Sophia would leave the room when she finished the bread.

"I do love sweet things," Sophia said. "I can stand most anything if I have a sweet taste in my mouth. It's a little treat you can always give yourself." Another slight, frivolous insulation, like the pink silk inside her dress.

Sophia hadn't made that jam—Caroline had, last summer, before anyone had said a word to her about a school. On one of the hottest days of the year, because the strawberries were starting to turn and couldn't be wasted, she'd filled this kitchen with sugary steam, boiling them to pulp. Her clothes had smelled of it for days. Her hands had looked bloodstained. All, it turned out, so David's wife could have something sweet in her mouth.

Sophia dusted crumbs from her fingers onto the floor. She took up her jam knife again. "I think I'll bring Miss Bell a piece."

"Is that wise?"

Sophia spread the jam, then looked up at Caroline. "We don't any of us know what's wise regarding her, do we? It must be strange for all of you, not knowing." She carried the plate from the room.

Going to the cupboard to take out her favorite cup and saucer, Caroline felt her fingers tingling again. The last three on her right hand. A buzzing feeling, as if insects with vibrating wings had hatched in the pads. She paused mid-reach and shook her hand in the air, but the buzzing's pitch raised.

It seemed important suddenly to leave the house, so Caroline went outside and sat down on the bench on the back porch. The air was bitingly cold. She laid her buzzing hand in her lap.

The house was too full, that was all. Too much sharing of its air. She wondered if her mother had felt the same about the Birch Hill men and their wives.

Best not to wonder if this was how her mother had felt, though; if, just a little later than expected, she was finally going to feel all of it for herself.

A red flapping, and a trilling heart landed on the lawn, twenty feet or so from where Caroline sat. It stalked, pecked, stalked, pecked, each motion so predatory. How the thin membrane of its throat rippled and pulsed—thin enough, it looked, to give under a fingernail. The bird rustled its wings and bobbed its head and fixed Caroline with its sightless-looking eye. Novels and novels could be written about this thing's beauty, crowds could will themselves into raptures, and Caroline would never see it. She watched it step across the grass and swore she could feel its talons on the skin of her stomach.

She leapt up from the bench. She ran onto the lawn, waving her arms. "Get!" she yelled.

The bird squawked and rose briefly into the air, landed again, and watched her to see what she might do next.

"Get!" Caroline swept her arms up and down, as if she were trying to signal to someone in the distance.

The bird squawked again and flew off, still calling. In response, perhaps, another emerged to join it—flew from where she hadn't seen it, from the branches of the big tree at the edge of the lawn.

Flew from within something that sat amongst those branches, a lump shape nestled in that tree.

Caroline advanced. The nest wasn't high, perhaps four feet above her head, spread between and below two branches the way the meat of a hand fills the space between finger bones. She'd climbed this tree many times as a child; her feet knew the toeholds. A step up, another, and she could reach and see. A small hunched cave of a nest, the hole still, nothing inside moving. She rebalanced with her elbows against the trunk, put her hands on either side of it, like gripping a face, and tugged. Nothing happened. She tugged harder, and it gave.

She cradled it, climbing down, though really she didn't want to touch it, wanted it far from her own body. She could smell it, the same fetidly rich smell from the ceiling collapse—a smell of secret folds full of old food and old birth.

On the ground again, she held the nest upside down, cupping its strange, irregular rounded top, to examine it. The outside was shaggy, its lines bulging as if something inside had pushed at randomly chosen places. In its side, near the base, that small dark entrance. She made herself pull the hole open wider with her fingers to let light inside. The inner weave was tighter than the outer, and denser, a thick knotted curving wall of twigs coated in the grimy residue of feedings and hatchings. Some hay too, and a tangle of rough horsehair. A patch of cloth, brown, with a pattern faded past deciphering. She reached within and pulled the cloth from under, over, in between the twigs, rolled her fingers across it, and was filled with the memory of a dress she'd had at eight or so—wearing it to play, ripping open seedpods while she ran and scattering them behind her, pretending she was a queen sowing a magical forest. Her hem could have caught and left this scrap. It should have rotted by now, but maybe it had lodged somewhere that had provided shelter.

Any of the girls she showed it to would have a memory of the cloth as hers, Caroline understood.

Farther along the curve, closer to the nest's ceiling, was another tangle of hair, finer than the horsehair. She tugged it loose. A small tangled clump, like something from a locket. The color was a deep dark brown. She knew the grain. Her scalp prickled, right at the back, where she wouldn't have been able to see if something had plucked it from her head.

She'd have felt it, though. Many people have dark brown hair.

Caroline would bring David to see the nest, so she could see what he thought, so he could say something rational to lessen her fear. She set it down on its side at the base of the tree trunk, on the far side, where no one went, and laid the cloth and the hair down next to it, weighted with a small stone so they wouldn't blow away.

But coming through the front door, she heard David and Sophia in the sitting room. David said something. Sophia laughed. David laughed too, the sound of a man enjoying what the universe has tossed his way. She did not want to bring the two of them together to see what she'd found. She didn't think she had it in her to stand and talk to Sophia just now, to hear calmly whatever Sophia would have to say about the nest.

If her fingertips prickled as she went up the stairs, well, she'd been rubbing them against that cloth, and fingertips on cloth always prickled.

*

While the teachers read about ailments, and thought, and waited for Hawkins's reply and whatever absolutions and repairs it might contain, they also went on teaching. And so *Romeo and Juliet* continued to progress toward its usual end. The lovers' only night together, the plan set in motion, each chance at happiness once again missed, just as nearly—that tyrannical lack of surprise. David's lessons had moved into chemical compounds, properties of acids and bases.

Eliza raised her hand in class, not infrequently.

On Thursday, Tabitha went upstairs to fetch her shawl before the afternoon lesson and shrieked. Some of the girls were already in the barn—and David and Sophia—but Caroline and Samuel and the girls present ran toward the sound. Instead of Eliza inside writhing, they found Tabitha hovering at the door of the room, flapping her hands, and a trilling heart inside erratically circling the ceiling.

"I must have left the window open," she said. "The room felt close. When I came down I forgot . . ." Tabitha was more apt than any of the others to forget such a thing. She seemed now to forget she was talking in the midst of her own sentence, trailing off to watch the bird with the others.

It wheeled, brushing the windowpane. It struck the wall and careened off again. Wild motions too large and fast for this space, tracing jagged shapes like symbols from a vast, unknown language. Once the bird had gone, Caroline would have to find someplace else for Tabitha and Julia to sleep, away from the feral air it had spread through this room.

The bird veered toward the door. Samuel shrank back, and the girls screamed. It veered away again.

"Sanders!" Samuel called down the stairs. "There's a bird! A bird, caught in the house!"

But it was Mrs. Sanders who came up a moment later, carrying a blanket and a broom. "He went into town," she said, then brushed past them, inside.

"Oh, be careful!" said Abigail.

"Of what?" Mrs. Sanders said. She raised the broom and knocked the bird to the floor. She threw the blanket over it. Before Caroline knew what had happened Mrs. Sanders had it pinned in her hand: a small, unfrightening blanketed lump.

"Thank you," Caroline said, to this woman who cooked their meals, cleaned their house, caught a trilling heart as if it could do nothing to any of them.

"Of course, Miss Hood," Mrs. Sanders said, and went down the stairs to dispose of the bird—living or dead, none of them asked—somewhere outside.

*

On Friday morning, Samuel began his lesson on the Book of John. He asked the girls to open their Testaments. Beside Caroline against the back wall, Sophia sniffed. Caroline had heard her telling David, at breakfast, that the Lord should be worshipped and not studied.

" 'Nicodemus saith unto Him, How can a man be born when he is old?' " Samuel read. " 'Can he enter the second time into his mother's womb, and be born?' "

He surveyed his students with the pensive expression of a man who wanted nothing more than to hear what they might say.

Eliza said, "Of course he can. Nothing's impossible."

"Nothing?" Samuel said.

"Nothing," Livia said, following Eliza's lead so confidently she didn't even need to check her face for approval.

"You believe it to be possible, say, for a twenty-foot man to come walking down the street toward you? For a sea to rise high enough to swallow this barn where we sit?"

"Possible," Meg said.

Caroline knew Samuel had intended for them to end up at this acceptance, but not in this dismissive way.

"If I were to tell you that an enormous python had slithered down the trunk of the tree out front, you would believe me."

"If you convinced us," Felicity said.

"And how might I go about doing that, Miss Ridell? What would be convincing enough as proof?"

Then Meg said, "I don't believe it."

She was peering at her own hands, turning them back and forth in the air before her. She turned toward Livia and then Eliza, arms outstretched. Her face was afraid, wondering.

"Look."

So they did, all of them. They looked at the red round spots making their way up Meg's arms, like the marks of mouths.

11.

SPREAD

～↝↜～

*When he thought of her he thought first of her graceful
hands and, ah, their indescribably delicate motions.*

—MILES PEARSON, *THE DARKENING GLASS* (P. 292)

After Meg, it happened quickly. Rebecca collapsed in the
garden. When she came in to report this there was a
streak of dirt across her cheek.

Felicity lowered her collar to show her red-pocked neck.

Julia shifted her skirts to show a rope-burn of red circling her
ankles.

Abigail's sentences began to tumble into *hmm*s, as if she were
questioning or had not heard herself.

Tabitha buckled at the knee with each step, though she kept
taking them, saying, "I can't make them *hold.*"

Last was Livia, whose fingers began twitching. They spidered
beside her plate at breakfast. "I can't control it," she said, looking
down.

They all said, *I can't control it. I'm not doing it. I don't know how
to make it stop.*

*

"It isn't an illness, whatever it is," said Samuel. "We can feel even
surer of that than before. So many maladies? There can't be one

physical cause." Though he was not overly familiar with physical causes. He went into Ashwell and sent Hawkins a telegram this time. "He'll be here in a matter of days." He fixed his eyes on Caroline's. "Days, Caroline."

"We can still send them home." She pictured even as she said this a string of coaches bearing a string of limp, white-faced girls back to their families, like a funeral procession.

"We will, if it comes to that," Samuel said.

He made this coming-to sound like some state clearly distinct from the one they were in. Caroline didn't see the telegram itself. She wondered how he'd worded it.

She went to find Eliza, because she feared talking to Eliza and she wanted the feeling of doing something she was afraid of. Eliza had returned them all to that night in the woods somehow, she knew. She had found, lifted, lit the stick again, another version of the stick, burning in some cryptic form, and this time Eliza had put it in all the girls' hands, and every one of them had used it.

Eliza was spread on the parlor sofa in a violet dress, reclined and reading. *Romeo and Juliet*, Caroline saw, and she felt as if she might cry, but that wasn't the right sort of feeling.

She sat at the end of the sofa by Eliza's feet. Eliza lowered her book across her chest. She left her hand pressed to its covers as if she were shocked, though her face was calm enough.

"Miss Bell, I don't quite know what to say."

Eliza waited.

"Tell me, do you have any insight into all this? I'm wondering if you can help us, tell us what you think of it. How it seems to you."

Eliza, so still, looked to Caroline like part of the sofa. The thick purple fabric of her dress, so heavy; the thick dark of her hair and lips—as if the pale girl inside all that had been brocaded into place.

"Really, I don't know," Eliza said.

Hidden between her back and the sofa cushion, Caroline's thumb touched each fingertip of her left hand (today it was the left), trying to pinpoint where the numbness started from.

"Well, what are your thoughts? You must see that you can't have all caught a twitching-rash-fainting-fit illness."

Eliza ruffled her book's pages. She was back in act 2. "I've been too busy feeling it to be able to think about it much," she said.

What does it feel like? Does it feel like what I feel?

"You haven't been indulging the feeling, have you? Encouraging the others to indulge it?"

Eliza's gaze sharpened. "You think we're making it up? How could we, even?"

"I just wanted to be certain you weren't taking it in some romantic way. You know, being a tribe of Louisas. All of you thinking yourselves doomed heroines, imagining the birds might land all over you"—Caroline smiled a little here to show she knew she was being absurd, and couldn't Eliza see when she herself was absurd too?—"and carry you off somewhere."

Eliza shifted back on her elbows, and her body in motion was a surprise, that she wasn't sewn still after all.

"What would you know about going anywhere?" she said.

*

Snow fell that night. Since Christmas it had been cold but dry, and the new snow coated the bare ground and the trees in a thin gray layer, making them look sawdusted, half finished.

The girls didn't come into the dining room for breakfast. Instead they went down the stairs and outside, still in their white nightgowns and bare feet, and—as straightforwardly as sleepwalkers, nothing in their bearing acknowledging their own strangeness—sat in a circle on the front lawn.

Caroline didn't move for a moment, though she did let loose a sound, a very soft but wild-sounding gasp. Flesh pressed to snow. The bone ache of it. Their girls were punishing themselves and performing the punishment, there on that bright background like a lit stage.

Caroline went out after and stood before them without speaking for a moment. It was a trick that worked well sometimes in the classroom: letting her wordlessness show them to themselves. Their faces were wretched and pinched. Their nightgowned bodies and feet had already melted away the snow beneath them, and these prints in the grass had the dark wet look of holes in which they were all levitating. Though no one spoke, it wasn't completely quiet because of the *hmm-hmm* that Abigail couldn't stop—and not quite still, because Livia's hands crawled on her lap, and Tabitha's legs bounced beneath her, a slight wave bobbing the rest of her body. Behind them, Caroline saw two trilling hearts on the stretch of dry ground under a pine tree. The birds had folded their legs up and tucked their heads into their wings for warmth. Missing their nest, perhaps.

She should have called for the other teachers before coming out here. It hadn't even occurred to her, she'd moved with such panic, but it didn't work well to have no plans when standing in front of one's students. The derangement of all this skin on snow made her dizzy. This was a thing only diseased girls would do.

At last she said, "Really, what is this? Look, even the birds know to keep out of the snow."

Now the other teachers had seen. Samuel was running down the front steps and across the grass, David and Sophia behind. "Girls!" Samuel was shouting. "Girls, what are you doing?"

Less than ideal that all the teachers were outfitted in their heavy brown and black day clothes, their good warm boots, when there sat the barefoot girls in their thin nightgowns. Julia tried to tug the hem of hers over her toes. Where it had gone damp it clung, almost transparent, to the pink domes of her knees.

"We felt too warm," said Meg.

"We thought the cold, some air, might help," said Rebecca, hugging her arms, showing the backs of her hands, raw and bitten looking.

"How could it?" said David.

Caroline stepped forward to lay a hand on Rebecca's forehead. The skin there did have a hectic heat, more like heat from running than like a fever, as if inside her, unseen muscles worked.

"All of us just felt all of a sudden that we were choking," Eliza said. "We thought out here we might breathe easier."

"But it isn't helping," Felicity said. She looked around at the other girls, and fear pulled her mouth wide. "Is it? Does anybody feel like it's helping?"

"I can't breathe!" cried Rebecca. "I still can't breathe!"

Caroline was still standing close enough to touch Rebecca— she put her hand to her shoulder and gripped, because she had the idea Rebecca and then the rest might spring into terrified flight.

Samuel gathered himself and stood straighter. "Girls, this is foolishness. You'll make yourselves ill."

Eliza laughed. "We aren't ill already?"

"I meant—"

"Do you think we're *choosing* this?"

"Of course not," Samuel told her. "Of course you wouldn't. But it can't be healthy out here for you. I'm sure you must understand that now. It can't feel the way you'd hoped."

Under his gaze they shifted, changing the places where, against the snow, their flesh would be screaming.

"Oh, girls, let us bring you back in," Samuel said.

"It's too warm, all the bedclothes, the fires," said Livia.

"We don't want to be put back to bed," Eliza said. "We want the snow." She sounded unsure now, and so heartbreakingly young.

"Well, we could take off the heavy quilts," David said.

"Tamp the fires," Caroline added, watching them waver.

"You can even have the snow," Samuel said. "We'll bring you some, with water, in cups. Why not? For the most cooling, lovely drink."

Eliza sighed. Then she nodded and extended her arms so David could lift her. He bent and scooped her up as if the problem she posed were only one of relocation: *Let me put this here.* The other girls got to their feet, wincing, hopping from foot to foot, and followed them back in. Beneath the tree, the birds slept on—if sleeping was in fact what they were doing.

After the girls were settled in their beds Samuel sent Mrs. Sanders upstairs, bearing to each her own cup. He sat at his desk to work but kept his door open, listening, Caroline knew, for the arrival of Hawkins's return telegram. In their separate rooms, the teachers read the medical textbooks he'd given them, searching for descriptions of conditions that might apply. "Mental disarrangement," "menstrual hysteria," "migraine," Caroline read. Tapping her fingers on the page, again trying to determine that origin point. Her fifth finger, she thought. The tingling seemed to begin there, spread from there.

Samuel appeared in the kitchen that afternoon, where Caroline was drinking tea and Mrs. Sanders was working. "If you would," he said to Mrs. Sanders, "please go up and make certain they're dressed enough for visitors."

"*What* visitors?" Mrs. Sanders asked.

"Their teachers."

"Why?" asked Caroline, as Mrs. Sanders left to do as requested, as always, her face closed as a stone.

"Oh good, come, listen," Samuel said when David and Sophia entered the room. "I'm starting to see what the trouble is. Or rather the trouble with *finding* the trouble. We're looking in the wrong places. We need, I think, to look first, quite thoroughly, to the girls themselves, since the difficulty lies somewhere in their own minds. It's only in sounding those minds that we'll begin to understand. Perhaps we can help them to inspect their thinking for themselves, find its flaws."

"You think they'll contain their own cures, somehow," said David.

"Likely, don't you think?"

Caroline expected them to begin pacing, as if it were August again and they were still only dreaming about this school.

"Both of you—this isn't teaching," she said.

"It might prove not to be so different," said Samuel.

"If you think that, I still don't see why we need Hawkins at all."

"Well, we aren't physicians, of course, Caroline," her father said, with irritation. "He'll be able to help us know we've found the right way."

"Who *is* he, this Hawkins?" said Sophia.

"I told you," said David.

"But why are you all so sure he can fix this?"

"He is an impeccably educated—an *excellent*—" Samuel sputtered.

"You'd prefer we sent for Reverend North, I know," said David, his voice rising.

So Sophia was not present but lying down when the teachers made their first visit, to Meg and Livia in their room.

Samuel sat on Livia's desk chair, and David on Meg's. They pulled them toward the girls, closing in. They were determined to miss nothing. This left Caroline to the foot of Meg's bed.

"We're trying to understand how best to help you," Samuel said patiently. Caroline placed his posture—the slight lean forward, the tip of the head, the calmness—from the scenes of her disciplining as a child: after she'd once thrown a beloved book of his to the floor in a fit of pique, after she'd spoken rudely to Mrs. Wilmer. "We need to know, first, exactly how you were feeling when all of this began."

Livia said, "Oh, dreadful. I've never felt worse." Her twining fingers, at her hairline, seemed to be signaling something. *Listen* or *Stop*, *Leave* or *Stay*.

"Dreadful how?" said David.

"It's as if my hands aren't mine somehow."

A cold thread slipped down Caroline's throat. She rubbed that fifth finger with the pad of her thumb.

"And there's a weakness at the very center of me. That came first. If you asked me to stand right now I'd fall at your feet, I swear I would. So even before my hands started I knew something terrible was coming."

Samuel wrote something in the notebook on his knees. "And you, Miss Sawyer? How did you feel just before?"

Meg seemed to weigh her words. "For me it was different," she said. "I felt just the same as always, until I looked down at my arms."

She held them up now: that angry red, not raised, its pattern like lichen.

David leaned closer. "What does the rash feel like? Does it hurt? Itch?"

Meg shrugged. "A little."

Samuel wrote some more. The motion of his hand was jerkier than when he wrote his own words. He looked up. "Girls, this is very important. I would like you to consider how the appearance of your symptoms has made you feel. What particular mental attitude toward them you have been taking."

"Mental attitude?" Meg said.

"Just so. As you saw with the struggles of Christian to comprehend the trials of his journey, the view we take of our obstacles often shapes our path more, even, than those obstacles themselves."

"*I* don't know," said Meg.

"This isn't like a book," Livia said.

"Of course not. But books do reflect our lives back to us."

Caroline herself had said that sentence and meant it at other times, but this did not seem like its moment. Even Samuel felt the thud of its landing. "At any rate," he said, and stood. "If there's anything more you can tell us about what's happening to you, tell us, please. We want to be able to help you as best we can."

"Only that you can't know how terrible it is," Livia said.

In the next room Abigail told them, with *hmms* breaking the joints of her speech, that she felt so afraid every time she couldn't say what she wanted to. "Like I'm drowning and yelling and I can't make anybody hear."

Rebecca had a rash too now on her wrists—different from Meg's, a stamping of individual, slightly puffy welts. The teachers gathered close to peer, but none of them was sure whether to touch.

"Excuse me for a moment," Caroline said, and went to her room. Her hand sung out its tingling. She could not, could not, bear the ancient fear that feeling carried with it.

She tried asking herself her father's question: What could she tell about what was happening to her?

Well, now she could tell for certain that it all came from that one finger. From tip to root and from there across her left palm, spreading.

Caroline simply wouldn't allow the spread, then. She'd keep what was hers. She had not asked for this late visit, if that was what this was, would do all she could to thwart it. She plucked a hair from her scalp and felt the small nip of its give—she would certainly have felt it, she thought, had the birds plucked that whole clump of hair from her—and wound it, tight, tight, around and around her fifth finger's base. The thin dark ring dimpled her skin. Her finger, above, began already to flush. She imagined the tingling caught there, behind the tourniquet.

Day gloves, before she rejoined the others. When her father glanced at her hands as they prepared to enter Tabitha and Julia's room, she said she had a slight chill.

"I can't stand the touch of shoes," Julia said, "and my mother always told me I must never walk barefoot. What am I supposed to do?" She wiped her nose with her hand, which surely her mother would never have countenanced either.

"You can *walk*, though," said Tabitha.

Caroline's finger pounded beneath the glove while she took notes. To begin with, the throbbing was worst right at the line of the hair, but soon it took up the whole finger. Harder and harder, so that it became difficult for her to believe her finger didn't actually contain her heart.

Her right hand slid smooth and merciless across the page, completing its work.

"It's not a competition, girls," said Samuel. "We know you are all suffering. What would help us most is to understand what it feels like, precisely what it feels like, and in particular what your inner reactions were at the moment you first realized you were becoming ill." That moment, it seemed, would solve everything, in his mind. That threshold each of them had passed: this moment well, the next moment sick. Caroline could forgive him—she had imagined it that way too—but she was beginning to think sickness might work differently, less like crossing a border than like entering, slowly, a fog that didn't announce itself in any clear leading edge.

Her hand seemed now to be following the waves of pounding forward—though she looked down and could see that it was still, falsely collected beneath that glove.

"I got up from my chair just as usual," Tabitha told him. "I hadn't any idea anything was wrong until I tried walking."

"*I* did feel a bit strange," said Julia.

Forward and forward crept Caroline's still hand. The space it moved through, feeling its way, was of a different kind from the space around the rest of her.

And without her volition, she felt her hand make its way up to her mother's hand. Slide inside her mother's hand, like sliding into another glove.

What would their hands do now?

"Strange in what sense?" David asked Julia.

Caroline was fighting the urge to tear the glove off right where she sat and pull at the hair until it gave. She couldn't, couldn't, because that would let the numbness out. She must remember she was keeping it there, in that finger.

Julia's forehead wrinkled. "I don't know, quite. A little off, and then my feet felt warm. When I looked at them I saw the rash."

Her mother's hand—Caroline's inside it—reached for something.

For Samuel? Miles? For the crown of Caroline's own small head? For roses or paper or a bedpost or a ribbon, a spring-green ribbon to tie in her daughter's hair?

Caroline could hear the throbbing of her finger. Hear, feel, see, smell it.

"I'm sorry, one moment," she said, and rose, and went into the hallway, and tore off the glove to reveal her finger, which screamed its red. She broke the hair.

Oh, the relief of its release. Not numb now; probably it had never been numb.

She turned at the sound of the door opening. David came toward her. "Caroline, are you all right? You seemed—"

Caroline clasped her hands behind her back. "I'm fine. I'm just anxious, I think. Did anyone else notice?"

"No. I said I was stepping out, but they were too preoccupied even to hear." He laughed. "We're all anxious."

"You noticed I'd gone, though."

"I did," he said, more softly.

She sighed. "What are we going to do?"

"I'm not sure we can say yet. None of the girls has told us much that's very revealing—I don't have a clearer sense yet of how to move forward."

She wondered if he knew this wasn't what she'd really meant.

"Your father may be noticing more, though. Having ideas."

"He usually does," she said. And then, "David, might I show you something?"

The nest was where she'd left it, though it had slumped a little into the ground and frozen there. It stuck for a moment, when she pulled, before giving. Caroline moved the rock from beside it and found that the cloth remained, but not the hair—blown away, probably, too light to be pinned firmly and left too long. She would have liked to show that tangle to David, to see if he also recognized it. And she felt uneasy about its absence. Just one hair had been enough to change her hand; who knew what effect a whole tangle might have, on what things.

She held the nest out to David, tipped so he could see inside as she had. "When I saw it first there was a trilling heart in it. A full nest this time. I don't know that anyone's seen their nests before. I don't think they stayed long enough to build them when they came last time."

"Fascinating." He didn't take it from her but instead began to explore it with his fingers while she held it, shifting twigs, testing its firmness. The small motions of this investigation pressed into her palms. "An unusual kind of nest."

"Isn't it?"

"I've never seen one constructed in quite this way. It's not at all uniform in shape."

"Why would they be doing this now?" she said.

"Maybe they were here earlier, in the spring, and we just didn't see them."

"Maybe," Caroline said. "Look at the cloth. I pulled that from the weave of it."

"Such scavengers."

That he could say this so lightly surprised her. "Don't you find it unsettling?"

"Well, I don't know. Magpies do the same, don't they?"

The sound of a carriage coming up the drive made them turn. The front door opened, and Samuel flew out. "It'll be the telegram!" he shouted. "From Hawkins!"

So it was.

Curious. There tomorrow. Keep them quiet. Save dinner.

12.

CORRESPONDENCE

*She seemed suddenly transformed into the most
desperate of wild wounded prey.*

—MILES PEARSON, *THE DARKENING GLASS* (P. 301)

Dear Miss Sterne,

*I ought to have replied before now to thank you for your letter, which
was very helpful and which must have cost some courage to send. I
can sympathize with the difficulties of diverting from official position
in this sort of matter. I kept your letter in strictest confidence, and
if I might, I would ask now the same of you. As I am sure you will
understand, this is a matter of some delicacy.*

*The patterns from Miss Bell's past that your letter laid out have
in fact continued here and actually seem to have intensified, perhaps
under the personal pressures of being at our school, which of course
played a role in her father's life. Whatever the cause, she is finding her
way into unsettling new territory—and evidently leading some of our
other students with her. I apologize for the imprecision of my account
but am not certain it would be right to disclose more until more is
known, and until we have had a chance to take certain steps we have
planned.*

*At this point I did wish, however, to consult you, as Miss Bell's
previous educator and as the possessor of a longer history with her.*

When she limited her consumption of food as you described, did you find that any particular actions, on your part or on the part of Miss Bell's other teachers, helped to move you all onto safer ground? Was there any special tone or emphasis that seemed effective in reaching the students under her sway? Or perhaps in reaching Miss Bell herself, and helping her to understand the prudence of altering her path? Your letter did seem to convey that the episode passed of its own accord, but I wonder if, in retrospect, you can think of any words or actions that seemed to assist its passing.

I care deeply for Miss Bell and for her welfare, as I do for the welfare of all our students. Any insight you can give that might help us to nurture her more wisely would be most welcome.

Sincerely,
Caroline Hood

Since childhood, writing had calmed Caroline, the effect perhaps of all her Samuel-led journaling. *Here this still is, this still works.* She wrote the letter before sleep—they'd retired early—and was comforted by her reasonable, concerned but distant self on the page, a self like Caroline but lacquered smooth. She liked the idea of sending this Caroline Hood to meet plump and pleasant Miss Sterne. With the opening of the envelope, Miss Sterne would feel, across the miles, the touch of this Caroline's sleek hand, a hand that did not tingle, and had not been punished for its tingling, and certainly had not slid inside the hand of any dead mother. The letter helped Caroline to find all that impossible too. She slept heavily after writing it.

In the morning, she folded and sealed the letter. She would do without breakfast until she walked it into town to post.

Who better at foiling a plan than Sophia? She called to Caroline from inside the kitchen as Caroline passed the doorway. "Where are you off to? Have you eaten?"

"I have a letter to send," Caroline said, hovering.

Sophia raised her eyebrows. "An urgent letter."

"Oh no, not really."

To prove this lack of urgency, Caroline came in and took a piece of cornbread from the sideboard. She sat down across from Sophia to eat it. Chew, chew, swallow. Smile. "You're up early," she said.

"I couldn't seem to sleep," Sophia said. Yet her face, in the weak winter light, was marked the way a child's would be after sleeping, with furrows where the folds of the pillowcase had pressed themselves into her moist skin.

"Is something troubling you?" Caroline said without thinking. Then she heard herself and laughed. Sophia laughed with her. The moment was companionable until they caught it being that way.

"Everything feels backward," Sophia said. "All of this. It doesn't feel quite real somehow, does it?"

"It's happening no matter how we feel about it."

Sophia looked at her. "Isn't that a useful sentiment." She rubbed her arms as if chilled. "We need more places to go. If we could see more people, everything might be more ordinary."

"*Ordinary* was never really what my father wanted." When Caroline dabbed at her mouth with her napkin, her fingertips crackled. "Anyway, we have more people now than I ever did before."

"At home I'd wake up, and I'd help my mother awhile, and then I might go down the road and call on my friend or my cousin, and then David would call . . ."

"Here we've always filled the time up with books."

"How did you bear it?" Sophia grimaced to make a joke of the question, but Caroline knew she was really asking.

"It was never lonely, exactly," Caroline said. "There was a certain way of seeing that the words could give me. A certain taste and sound and color of them. Not usually a whole book, but a phrase, a line. It's hard to explain how much I loved it."

"Your father's words, you mean?"

"Sometimes. Sometimes others. Like the 'vegetable gold' of Eden in *Paradise Lost.* Or the green of that vine that enthralled Lucia in the Herrick poem. Does that make any sense? I suppose not." She was surprised at herself, saying all this to Sophia, who watched with her lips pursed. "And I had other things that made me happy. I've roamed where I wanted. I was always very free."

"Where?"

"Oh, the stream, the woods, you know. This place feels to me like a kind of person. A third, to complete us."

"But there *were* others too, like this doctor who's coming. They all lived here once."

"He did, they did. A long time ago."

Sophia peered at her. "You don't like him, do you?"

Caroline would have to remember to be more careful with her face. "Whether I like him doesn't matter."

Sophia gave her head a frustrated little shake. "You're very good at not answering the question."

"I just feel an answer should matter before I give it."

"That's what your father taught you?"

Caroline considered. "I taught myself, I think."

They ate for another moment. Sophia spoke of the cold, and Caroline said it wasn't so unusual for this time of year. Winter. Sophia stood then, saying that she had things to attend to upstairs (David, perhaps), and Caroline at last left the house.

The surface of the road was frozen into fantastical shapes where it had been churned up before going solid. Caroline shattered thin skins of ice with her boots as she walked, making a slight fragile music in the quiet. She slid her gloves along the rich stock of the envelope. Her father believed in good paper.

She hadn't been to Ashwell for weeks. When she reached it, all was shuttered and silent. The pavement felt uncomfortable somehow beneath the soles of her boots, as if she and the town did not join properly where they met, a stiffness at their hinge. She had the feeling she wouldn't see another person at all before arriving at the post office and then it too would be shuttered, and nowhere in this whole town would there be anyone accessible to her.

But the post office was lit. Its door did open when she pushed, and there was Mr. Perkins, as ever, behind the counter, where he probably slept—a plucked-looking man with almost lashless round eyes and a bald head. After the cold the post office had the feel of a hibernation space, warm with the smell of cooking chicken. His dinner, probably.

"Miss Hood!" he said. "Good morning."

"Good morning."

"We haven't been seeing you."

"Oh, we've been busy."

"How are things going out at the school?"

What if she told him? What would he do?

"Well, thank you," she said.

He rapped the counter purposefully, and she smiled—she thought she was smiling; she hoped she still knew what her face did—and fumbled for coins in her purse. The letter left her hands to begin its journey. Miss Sterne wouldn't know she was waiting for it, sewing beside her sitting-room fire, thinking which stitches to cover next lesson with the young ladies whose stitches had been entrusted to her. Warm and well cosseted in flesh and fabric.

Caroline was aware suddenly that she was also warm—too warm. Her sweat prickled. It coated.

The sensation was like the laying on of a new, oily skin, much too small. Intensely, she wanted it off.

She dropped coins into Mr. Perkins's palm and pushed toward the door, out onto the street, into the very center of the pavement of the still town, trying to escape the certainty filling her. This was her mother's skin, here now on her skin. Over her skin, closing over her. Coming at last, late but certainly coming now. That skin craved things it had not gotten, and it carried the electricity of its wanting in itself, and now that electricity was passing into Caroline.

She unbuttoned her coat to let the cold air down her clothes. She raked her hair off her neck. A shimmer was stealing over her surroundings—she could see it out of the corners of her eyes, but it disappeared when she turned to look. The heat, it was from the heat. Why was she wearing a coat? If she took it off she would feel right again.

Her mother's skin, heavy and decorous but sparking all down her arms and legs. It wanted her to move it, as it had not been moved the first time. It had grown impatient with only twitching in place in the rooms where Samuel had placed it.

The shimmer bore down on her now, descending over her head and shoulders like a slick, hot prickling veil, clinging to her mouth and nostrils, stopping her breath, driving her to her knees.

*

"Miss Hood?"

Jeffers loomed. He took up her whole field of vision. From this close his mustache was like a double tail, so substantial it seemed impossible there wasn't some anchoring structure inside, small bone after small bone tapering to those points. Caroline sat up and the street leaned away from her, but she leaned with it, righting herself. Her right arm was wet all down the side from the slush on the ground.

Why was Jeffers here? She hadn't been at the furniture store.

Had he been here in the street before she fell? Jeffers didn't seem to know whether he should touch her. His palm neared her shoulder. The ends of his mustache trembled and she expected them to sweep like the tail of a cat.

"I'm all right, thank you," Caroline said, and stood, and kept her feet.

Jeffers stood too, his hands still outstretched toward her. "I saw you fall. I was at my desk and I saw you through the window."

Mr. Perkins watched from the steps of the post office. Mrs. Thomas from the front porch of her house.

"The heat, that's all." Caroline smiled: *On hot days we all of us faint.*

"Heat?" Jeffers's forehead creased.

She remembered the snow. "I meant I overbundled myself."

His eyes on her naked throat.

"Well, I ought to get back," she said.

"You're red as a new baby. Come in and sit down a minute."

Caroline had to move—the skin might find her again. "Really, I'm all right now."

"Your father would never forgive me if I let you leave like this. I'd feel much better if you'd just come back and rest, and later I can drive you. Why rush off? What disaster, if you wait a moment?"

Caroline had visions of Eliza setting bedclothes on fire, Livia poisoning the well, Rebecca turning the horses loose, a great tidal wave of the earth of their hills gathering itself to bury them all. A laugh escaped her. She could tell from Jeffers's face that the laugh hadn't helped her cause. "Thank you, but I'm quite well," she said again. Before he could catch her wrist and make her stay, she turned and began walking. Her legs felt less responsive to her than usual, as if they were weighing their considerations.

"Miss Hood."

If she turned again to answer him she might fall. She kept walking. Jeffers did not pursue.

There was still no one else on the road. She forded iced-over puddles. She wished she knew what her feet, legs, arms, hands had been doing while her mind was dark, but if there had been flailing, Jeffers would have said, or she would have known it from his face.

Time, though, to tell.

The thought came simply and brought a simple relief. She could do it, tell. Not her father—that she could not imagine; she couldn't stand to imagine his face, hearing this from her. She suspected her mother had only barely told her father—*Another one today, but not so bad, don't worry*—reports short enough to be delivered quickly while he was working, with a dry brushing kiss to the forehead. There was some fragility to Samuel that demanded protection, at least if one loved him. If her mother had turned to Miles Pearson, the need to really say it might have been part of what prompted the turning: *Find me next time. Next time I don't want to be alone.* The idea of being alone when you weren't even there yourself was terrible.

But David, maybe. Caroline might be able to make herself less alone by telling David. His face she would be interested to see.

She walked faster, closing the distance. And suddenly there David was, walking away from Trilling Heart as she was walking toward it; her mind might have made him for her. Her heart beat hard, thickly. She thought she might faint again right in his path and take away the need for telling at all.

A strange thing just happened, she would say.

From his face she would see what it meant to him, her falling like that, into a place none of them could see.

David called to her before she reached him. "Have you seen Meg?"

She saw that he wasn't strolling but hurrying, almost running.

"No, why?"

"She went somewhere, we don't know where, while Livia was asleep." He stopped in front of her, but his need to keep moving was visible in the way he stood.

Somewhere, ominous word. "Eliza—"

"Knows nothing, or claims to know nothing. Your father is talking to her right now."

"And I'm sure she'll just tell him every last thing she knows." Caroline wheeled in the road, dizzy, disregarding the dizziness, scanning the gray-green frozen hills. "Meg can't have gone far. She won't have made much of a plan."

Though this only used to be true of Meg—before the illness and the new boldness it seemed to have given her and all of them. She could have gone far enough now.

David's hands raked his hair.

Caroline stepped off the road into the snow. "Shout if you find her," she said. She'd try the main hill first—it had worked before, given her the view of Eliza limp and tossed down that had made her begin to see what was coming.

The land as she crossed it had never looked emptier. The hills might have opened up and closed over Meg again; she might lie beneath them now, a plain, drowned maiden faceup under the surface of an opaque sea. Above her the red bobbing undersides of birds.

Caroline hadn't even begun to climb the main hill when she heard David shouting. And now here he was, coming back, running. "Caroline, we've found her!"

And Hawkins. Hawkins, not hurrying, walking with his arm around Meg's shoulders.

"I found this one," he called, "going down the road with a basket, as if she were on a summer's picnic."

Meg sniffled. Had she been crying already when Hawkins found her?

"I had a dream some of us were picking berries," she said. "In the dream they tasted wonderful. I wanted them, when I woke up, so I came out to see."

"But Miss Sawyer, it's winter," Caroline said.

"Berries?" said Hawkins. "Even if you could find them—and Miss Hood is right, of course, none to be had in winter—berries will often kill you, miss. I'm surprised at you, a big girl like you, not knowing that."

He smiled, baring his teeth.

13

DR. HAWKINS

Over his mind, her illness hung like a black curtain.

—MILES PEARSON, *THE DARKENING GLASS* (P. 310)

Hawkins wanted an assembly for his introduction. "It will be better if they meet me all at once," he told the teachers, in Samuel's study. Caroline thought of the bridegroom in a fairy tale, his many choices for a bride arrayed before him.

"You don't want to examine them individually?" Samuel asked.

"Oh, I will. But this should come first," Hawkins explained. He seemed to be enjoying explaining things to Samuel. "For me to creep amongst them like a rumor—that's the wrong approach. I suspect their secret connections to one another may be part of what's fueling this. We have to avoid giving those connections more to do and thickening them up."

Hawkins's voice vibrated in the fleshy parts of Caroline's arms, her legs, her belly. *Connections.* She pictured the girls in a circle, their wrists ensnared by interwoven bracelets of hair.

"You know, that's along the lines of what we were thinking too. That their minds—something about the content of their minds . . ." Samuel was relieved to have Hawkins here—he sagged with this relief—but still, he was unused to being taught.

Hawkins said, "In these cases one is really treating the group as well as the individual."

"*What* cases?" Caroline asked, from her chair in the corner.

"Well, I won't know for certain until I've done the examinations—so far I only have conjectures, though I must say I'm fairly confident in them, from what Sam's told me. And if it does turn out I'm correct, it will be important to address the sum along with the parts."

He seemed more robust and even redder than usual, holding forth, and this made Caroline angry. She knew she should want him to be right about all this—for it to be fixable, for him to fix it. Yet what she wanted just now was to send him upstairs into the mouths of all their slight lions, so that he could come back down pale from a fine bloodletting.

Sophia said, "What does that mean—parts, sums?" She leaned forward, attentive as a hostess, but her face was uncertain.

"Oh, Mrs. Moore," Hawkins said, with another smile, "spoken just like a part." He clapped. "Let's round them up, shall we, Sam? Where are they? What have you done with them? I've never in my life seen a school so quiet."

Mrs. Sanders was sent up to ready them, and the teachers went to the barn for Hawkins's unveiling. But the barn did not smell like a place where anything new could happen. Days had passed since anyone had been in here, and the air had a stale earthiness even with the fire going, a scent that suggested animals had died in here and only lately been removed. Perhaps the lingering scent of the ceiling collapse and what the birds had heaped above. Or maybe the barn itself had a memory and was recalling previous disasters; during that last terrible winter at Birch Hill, Caroline remembered the bodies of three dead calves, bony and distended with bloat, piled against one outer corner of the building because the ground was frozen too hard to bury them. They were the first substantial dead things she'd ever seen. Their locked-stiff legs had seemed to her about to pop the bubbles of one another's stomachs.

She must not faint during this meeting. She couldn't bear the idea of anyone having to carry her out.

Her father and Sophia and David all sat against the back wall too. Hawkins stood before the teacher's desk, as if he were only another teacher and this were only a new kind of lesson. The girls eyed him as they appeared, unsteadily, and took their seats. Still in that circle, that *one body* the teachers had been so proud of—forgetting to consider all the things that bodies could do. They rubbed their hands together to warm them.

"Young ladies, hello," Hawkins said.

Now, when they should have been going still and silent, the girls revealed themselves. Most of each girl, each body, settled down, but a part of each was otherwise occupied. *"Hmm-hmm,"* Abigail said. Livia jerked her head slightly, as if an insect nibbled her earlobe. Meg rubbed at the skin of her arms—perhaps they did itch her now. Tabitha's legs bounced beneath her desk. And Eliza teetered in her seat, leaned to one side a little before catching herself, then leaned again, though her gaze stayed fixed on Hawkins.

Would all this happen to Caroline next? Her secret would tell itself to everyone.

Hawkins planted his feet a little apart. The bridegroom displayed. "I'm Dr. Hawkins, and I will be overseeing your medical treatment."

The girls glanced at one another. "What treatment, sir?" Eliza asked.

"Well, Miss—?"

"Bell."

"Ah, Miss Bell. I knew your father, of course. Very nice to meet you."

Eliza inclined her head. Her whole torso slipped forward after it, then straightened.

"Whoops, there," Hawkins said.

Eliza's expression admitted nothing.

"What I began to say, Miss Bell, was that I of course can't tell you precisely what the treatment will be before I have examined you."

"What's the purpose of this meeting then, sir?" Eliza said. "Pardon the question. It's just that none of us is feeling well, and it's taxing to gather like this."

The rest of them nodded. It *was* taxing; what a relief to have Eliza to say so.

"I'm sure," Hawkins said. "And I do appreciate the effort you've all made. It just seemed that an effective way for us to get started would be for me to meet all of you at the same time." His eyes skipped around the circle. "May I have the rest of your names, please, girls?"

Softly, they spoke them. Abigail's *hmm* interrupted between her first and last.

"And you, sir?" Eliza said, when they'd finished.

"I've told you my name."

"Yes, so we know that, and we know you're a physician. Why did he send for you, though?" She nodded to Samuel, along the back wall. "Dr. Burgess has been attending us."

"You, anyway," Livia said to Eliza.

"And have you found yourself much improved, Miss Bell, since Dr. Burgess began his course of treatment?" said Hawkins.

"He hasn't really *done* anything. Just checked on her," said Felicity.

Hawkins widened his eyes and nodded.

"Do you have some additional qualification that better suits you for our care?" Eliza asked.

Samuel said, "Miss Bell."

"No, it's all right, Sam. Well, I've been a practicing physician for just about three times the length of your lives, girls. Not longer, probably, than Richard Burgess—but the bulk of my work has been in Boston, and I think it's safe to say my experience will have been a bit wider, a bit deeper than his. I've seen almost everything there is to see. Mr. Hood called me for that reason."

"You think you've seen this, what's happening to us, before?"

"Do you know how to stop it?" said Meg, with hope in her voice. She looked at Eliza, read that she'd judged wrong, and drew back in her chair.

"Really, ladies, you mustn't worry," Hawkins said.

But Samuel had taught them to know an answer that wasn't really an answer. They sat without speaking, to let Hawkins see this.

He said, "Of course much more information will have to wait until after I've had a chance to make my examination. But if my suspicions are correct, yes, I've treated many young ladies in your situation before, with a great deal of success. I must have treated four in the past month."

"What situation?" Abigail said.

"What is it? What's wrong with us?" said Julia.

"The place to begin is often to ask if you yourselves have any theories. It can be quite useful, quite enlightening, to hear them in cases such as these. What do you suspect is making you ill, girls?"

"Are we expected to know?" Eliza said.

In spite of herself a tremendous pride in Eliza was rising in Caroline.

"Well, we might start with your reading habits, Miss Bell. I hear that your father's book has taken on a particular fascination for the whole group."

The girls looked at Samuel, surreptitious reporter.

"I gave Dr. Hawkins some background, in case it should prove relevant," Samuel said.

"It's certainly a very exciting book," Hawkins went on. "Full of all sorts of alarming occurrences, and of course a physical languishing too. In combination with the return of the birds and with your own presence here now, I could see how such a book might seem . . . suggestive to all of you. I wondered if perhaps you might have had any ideas about the story seeping over into life. You know, ghosts, visitations, things of that nature, perhaps being part of your affliction."

"*Ghosts?*" said Eliza bitingly.

Hawkins bristled. "As it happens, your father didn't find the idea so ridiculous. He loved the whole notion, in the book of course but in his real life too. 'Celestial guests,' he called them. He was always wandering around searching for likely sites of hauntings, saying he'd felt spirits in the forest, spirits in the house." Hawkins fluttered his fingers.

Caroline watched Eliza swallow questions: *What did he say? What were the words, the actual words, every last one?*

"It was never exactly clear whether he thought they were the spirits of the dead, or some sort of spirits of the earth, or what, precisely. You might have noticed that vagueness in the novel too. Logical consistency was never Miles's strong suit, if you'll excuse my saying so, Miss Bell."

"Dr. Hawkins, perhaps we might continue," said Caroline. She didn't want to watch Hawkins dance Eliza along this edge.

"Certainly, Miss Hood—I only thought Miss Bell might be interested in hearing. Then if you aren't similarly mystical, girls, what *are* your theories? It's hard for me to believe you have none. Especially given where you sit, what you've been doing here all these months. You must have theories about everything now."

Tabitha's jouncing knee knocked into her desk. Hawkins winced theatrically. "Careful."

"I can't stop it," Tabitha said.

"Of course. But to continue, I think you must see that this is not some run-of-the-mill fever or cough that's passed from one to the other of you through ordinary contagion."

"Ordinary? No," said Eliza.

"Ah, good," Hawkins said, taking a step forward. "Now perhaps we're beginning to get at something. Tell me, Miss Bell, do you and your friends feel yourselves to be . . . *special* in some way?"

Here in this room, on their first day at Trilling Heart, Samuel had told them that they all were. Caroline glanced at him, beside her on the bench. His eyes were full of tears.

Eliza pulled in a breath. "I think we'd best let you decide, sir."

Caroline feared Eliza, resented her, wanted her cured, bested, gone from their lives, but just then—the little smile on Eliza's tilting face—she would have given anything to see Eliza win at whatever this was. No matter the cost to any of them.

*

"Unstable," said Hawkins, back in Samuel's study. "Visibly, markedly. Small wonder, given what she comes from. Sam, she thinks she's inside that book, and you're summoning spirits to torment her, I'd wager on it."

"Perhaps we might table the question of wagers for now," Caroline said. "I think you'll find that whatever else she is, Eliza isn't silly. And she isn't the only one who's ill." She kept her hands behind her. She worried Hawkins would somehow see the tingling on her skin. It hadn't been so bad earlier, faint and distant, but it was present now, so present she felt she was actually listening to it speak.

"You think the rest of them would be sick if she weren't?" Hawkins said.

No, Caroline didn't, of course.

"To be clear—you're saying the others are only imitating her?" David asked.

"Oh, not intentionally. But in a manner of speaking, yes, without their even realizing. In cases such as this there's often an identifiable ringleader."

Ringleaders, rings of girls in the woods, rings of girls in the snow, a ring of hair around a finger.

"Hawkins," Samuel said, from his desk. "I know you're mostly jesting about the book. But as I began to say before, we *have* been thinking the trouble might lie somehow in the girls' thinking. And perhaps after all part of it is their exposure to that—that story—and its atmosphere. It might have disarranged them in some way their previous lives haven't equipped them to handle."

"Yes. It's what seems to make the most sense," David said.

"Our suspicion that it's their minds that are somehow injured is actually why we decided to keep them here," Samuel added. "Instead of sending them all home, where the physicians who'd treat them wouldn't have the first idea what they were even seeing. We thought that here, where we could find the true trouble, we might be better able to help them."

"*Is* that why," Hawkins said.

"What if it isn't their minds?" Sophia said. She flushed, but having begun to speak, she seemed to decide to finish, and instead of shrinking she stood. She lifted her chin. "What if it's—"

David made a small involuntary-looking movement, as if he'd almost put out a hand to tug her back down and only just stopped himself. "Sophia, please."

"What if it's spiritual?" she insisted.

"Whatever do you mean by that?" said Samuel.

David strode away to the window. Sophia's body reoriented itself toward him, but she turned her face to Hawkins and kept talking. "I've seen God visit people before. I have. And when Miss Bell had her fit, it looked like—"

Hawkins barked a laugh.

Samuel squinted at her. "Sophia, why would God ever want to do this to these girls?" he said.

"We aren't meant to understand His plans."

"I don't think this situation is quite what that sentiment refers to."

Hawkins held up a hand. "Let's just proceed with the examinations, shall we? And we'll see, Mrs. Moore, if I can discern any signs of divine visitation. Or if it's some obscure physical malady or—what did you say, gentlemen?—their *thinking* that's doing this to them. Or if it's as I'm expecting." He turned to go, taking pleasure in his withholding. Samuel followed him.

The two men climbed the stairs: the familiar sound of Samuel's tread, broken by Hawkins's heavier one.

"Why did you say that," David said, low-voiced, to Sophia, "after I'd asked you not to?"

Sophia fixed teary eyes on his face. "I'll say what I want."

Caroline's fingers felt full of wires. She rose from her chair. She didn't have to listen to this argument. She had no particular joy, it turned out, in hearing it.

Sophia watched her leave the room with reproach.

After Caroline closed the study door behind her, she lingered in the entryway, at the base of the staircase. She heard footsteps, the opening of a door. *Creak, creak*. Hawkins was in one of the girls' rooms now, and whoever it was, he was peering into her mouth, pulling back her eyelids, while Samuel sat on the desk chair and looked at the wall. Hawkins pressing the girl's belly, lifting her arms at the wrists, assessing parts and sums.

Caroline hadn't really thought before about what it meant that Hawkins was a doctor. She'd been aware of his profession only in how it supplied him with impressive dense texts to trot out in discussions with Samuel, who was not scientific in his reading habits, and with fine food and expensive jackets in the years after Birch Hill. But now she considered: Hawkins as a physician, with patients. Hawkins as healer. Hawkins tending to flesh with the round, warm pads of his fingers.

She couldn't believe those thick fingers would be able to feel the pulse of what ailed these girls. His eyes were so full of what he expected to see that he wouldn't really look at them. It would seem impossible to him that such small bodies might contain depths.

Caroline sat down on the bottom step, guard on her battlement, to listen to the sounds of the progress through the rooms. She let her fingers patter atop her knees because somehow they felt more usual, more her own, when she wasn't trying to keep them still.

(This perhaps was how every girl felt too. All just alike. Herein the question that attended what her father had told them about themselves, and told Caroline first of all—if he thought they were all special, did he think they were therefore all the same?)

A few more minutes and a door above her opened, and the tread this time progressed toward her. She turned to find Hawkins coming down the stairs.

"Not done already?" she said, rising.

"No, I need something from my bag."

Caroline backed against the wall to let him pass, imagining some metal tool he could want for setting to work on the girls. "What are you finding so far?" she asked. Her hands she put behind her again.

He tsked. "So impatient, Caroline!"

She boiled at that reprimanding finger held aloft in her face. "Dr. Hawkins, this isn't a joke," she said.

"Did I call it a joke?"

"Everything about you has been calling it that since you arrived."

Hawkins leaned back against the opposite wall and regarded her. "I must say, you seem . . . different, somehow, Caroline, than when I was here last."

"I don't know what you mean." She thought her hands might ignite.

"Back in the summer you wouldn't have said such a thing. The influence of becoming a *teacher*, perhaps."

"It isn't so uncommon a profession." *For a woman*, she meant.

"You must be making very fine use now of that mind he gave you."

"Just as you always have."

This seemed to irritate him. "All right, there's something to that, I suppose. Sam always did see further than the rest of us. I must say, though, sometimes I have wondered what he's about. With you, for instance. You interest me, Caroline—wouldn't you rather be doing other things? All these years here with him. You and now all these girls."

"You think we'd all rather have husbands, children."

"Of course you would," he said. "But then that's never been Sam's strongest suit, the wants of women. Take your mother." A pause he let linger. "She had a husband and child and yet still felt a need to look . . . elsewhere."

"That's only a vile rumor."

"You might ask your father."

She stared at him. "He's always told me there was no truth to it."

"Has he?"

Caroline's legs shook; she rested a hand on the wall. She understood now that for all her considering of the possibility of her mother and Miles Pearson, she'd never fully believed it could have happened. Not truly. Imagining it had been an exercise, a restless pushing out of the walls of her world to see how different and new she could make it. To hear that the flesh-and-blood Anna had actually entangled herself with the flesh-and-blood Miles Pearson did not feel like a changing of her world. It felt like a collapse.

Her mother had been a mother and a wife—the gilded, glorious wife-mother of Samuel's every story. Who had Anna been, to think she could do such a thing?

Who had she been?

And there was Hawkins, watching Caroline, wearing openly his happiness at what he'd done. She was close enough to him to see the heavy dents of his pores.

There had been a dark well here once, right where they were standing. She had seen the girls floating on it before she followed them into the woods. In retaliation now she wanted to show Hawkins dark water. She wanted to submerge him.

"Do you know—this is about something quite different," Caroline said, "but I've been meaning to tell you—the birds. I know we thought we'd figured everything out about them." She emphasized the *we*.

"I never claimed that. No one knows what they're doing here, still."

"At any rate, the mystery has deepened, did you know?" She waited now as he had, making him crane forward.

"If you aren't going to tell me, Caroline, I need to get back," Hawkins said.

"We've discovered that they seem to be building nests."

Hawkins shrugged. "Birds do."

"*Now.* In winter. And they're strange nests, a very odd shape. Indescribable. Something for you to put in your next letter when you write to your friend at the Society of Natural History, perhaps. It's perfectly all right with me if you make it sound as if this is information you discovered yourself." She pushed off the wall. "I think I'll go have a cup of tea, while I'm waiting for you to be finished."

Let him have one question at least, however small, that he knew he couldn't answer. Let him hold it too while he held the girls' fingers, feet.

Caroline sipped her tea without tasting it. She couldn't unsee the gleeful look Hawkins had given her as he told her about her mother. He seemed to think he'd bested her in some final way, opened the fingers of one of her hands to show her the sharp humiliation she'd always been clenching there, without her knowledge.

And she had. The shards of Anna that Samuel had given her

to hold—they hadn't been jagged only because they were partial. Whole, Anna had been jagged too. That jaggedness was Caroline's inheritance.

The examinations took another half an hour. The men tromped down. Samuel gathered the others to wait in the study.

"Papa, what—" Caroline began to ask.

But Samuel shook his head. "He hasn't told me anything yet."

When Hawkins came in, he took his time. He sat down; he propped one foot on the hassock in front of him. The others arranged themselves in a standing half circle around him, all of them too anxious to sit, a small court fanned out around their king. Hawkins looked delighted, nothing at all like a submerged man. He settled in.

Then: "It's as I thought," he said.

Was there any line they all loved more to say?

"This is no sudden plague—not in the customary physical sense, anyway. Nor, Mrs. Moore, is it divine possession. What it is: a case of hysteria. Nervous constitutions foundering under strain and under a certain collective atmosphere."

"All the rashes, the muscle spasms—" David said.

"Hysteria is an astonishingly varied ailment, and often very dramatic in its physical manifestations. But its origins are not directly, simply physical."

"All of them? They're *all* hysterics?" Caroline said.

"The phenomenon can be curiously contagious. For it to strike a group is not at all unusual. You get one influential and susceptible girl in the pack—we all know who that is here—and she sets the others off. There's a substantial history."

"We were right then, about what's causing this. About its origins in strain, mental strain, from that terrible book," Samuel said.

Hawkins lifted his palms. "Perhaps. Who can say? The strain can come from many directions."

"You aren't suggesting there's something about the school itself—"

"Oh, no particular reason to suspect so," Hawkins said. "This is common in all kinds of environments. I've seen it amongst schoolgirls, old married ladies. In any case, regardless of the cause, the treatment is the same."

"What does this treatment involve?" Caroline said. It was a magical word coming from the mouth of a doctor, even this doctor. Somewhere in his medical bag existed a solution.

"It's very straightforward. The girls' affliction is caused by an accumulation of nervous tension. Picture a river blocked by a dam." Hawkins's fingers drew a river for them in the air and then rammed into his other palm. "Too much feeling, nowhere for it to go."

Nowhere. That was something Caroline understood.

"To relieve the tension, therefore, we create a release. Simple pelvic manipulation leading to hysterical paroxysm."

The rhythm of the word hit Caroline's ear: *par-ox-ysm.*

"What on earth does that mean?" Sophia said.

"I brought some literature with me on the subject—case histories, accounts of the long development of the treatment—if you'd like to take a look," Hawkins said. He went behind Samuel's desk for his bag, opened it, and began taking out books and piling them.

"Ah," Samuel said, greeting the familiar sight of books on his desk. How neatly contained they looked, those books, what precise rectangles.

"You'll see," Hawkins told them. "These girls will soon be quite healthy again. Good as new."

As if the only way to be good were to be new, despite all the same flesh, bones, loves, will you had ever had. As if to be healthy meant having no history.

14

AN ANIMAL WITHIN AN ANIMAL

᠅

*"You can't imagine how I feel," she said, and her
mournful eyes implored him for . . . what?*

—MILES PEARSON, *THE DARKENING GLASS* (P. 343)

T he teachers took the books, and they began to read.

The books divided into two camps.

Large, and old, the body camp:

Plato and Aretseus knew the womb for "an animal within an animal."

Within this camp of physical cause, authors exulted in the
ancientness of their precedent but also sought to distinguish
themselves.

*While the literature of hysteria dates back thousands of years, few
modern physicians would argue that the disease is caused by an actual
wandering of the womb. Instead, the modern view is that the symptoms
stem from a pelvic congestion.*

Newer, vaguer, and thinner in rank, the mind camp:

*Modern life, with its industry, its bustling streets, its rail travel, its
wealth of dramatic incidents, moves at great and startling speed. In
such extremity there is strain, and to this strain, the feminine nature,
being frailer, proves more vulnerable than the male.*

Both camps offered lists upon lists of symptoms: *nervousness,
fainting, weeping, painful menstruation, cessation of menstruation,
headache, sleeplessness, markings of the skin, muscle spasms, absent-
mindedness, itching, nausea, ticklishness, worry, anemia, abdominal*

*heaviness, flushing, shortness of breath, coughing, overindulgence in
food, refusal to eat.*

They were in agreement upon the treatment: *marriage, child-
birth.*

They differed, though, in their explanations of why this treatment was effective. Because, said the body camp, *the relations of
marital life and the ensuing production of offspring serve to relieve the
pelvic congestion that produces the distress. Hence the susceptibility of
the maiden and the widow.*

Because, said the mind camp, *matrimony and motherhood provide
the patient with a sure tether amidst the stirrings of the world which
proves protective against nervous strain. Hence the susceptibility of the
maiden and the widow.*

But these were medical texts, not spiritual ones, and they had
more immediate relief to prescribe than matrimony. Both pre-
scribed it the same.

The tissues may be massaged.

So as to relieve the tensions, offered one.

Another: *So as to achieve paroxysm.*

*The method of this massage is complicated and difficult to learn, and
involves a level of detail cumbersome to explicate here: please refer to
Galen, Celsus, Boerhaave, Villanova, &c.*

*

The final book Caroline read was a volume of Hawkins's own
medical case notes. He had flagged the relevant entry, but still
she thumbed through what preceded it: old men with congestion
of the heart, old men with gout, old men with rheumatism.

On the scrap of paper he had tucked into the appropriate page,
Hawkins had written, *A representative case.*

*The patient, a woman of twenty-one years, presented with initial
complaints of fainting spells and odd sensations in the extremities.
Her father had been a patient of mine for some years for pleurisy,*

*and I had treated the girl in her childhood for catarrh and
rheumatic fever, but she had been otherwise healthy until some
months before this visit.*

*The sensations, she said, had been intermittent to begin with,
but were becoming more frequent, and were beginning to interfere
with ambulation and to distract her during daily tasks (writing,
sewing, and so forth). The fainting appeared to cause still greater
distress, as she claimed she never knew when a fit would strike,
and in a particularly upsetting instance one had come upon
her quite suddenly in the midst of a dinner party, making her
overturn her plate and raising quite a furor. These attacks were
also occurring more often. She denied any particular change in
her circumstances or occupations around the outset of this period
of increased frequency.*

*I examined the patient. Fine tremors in the hands, a rapid
heartbeat, and brisk reflexes bilaterally were observed, along with
some weakness in the legs.*

All findings were consistent with hysteria.

*I discussed her condition with the patient, informing her of the
nature of her ailment and of the usual course of treatment.*

The patient appeared to understand.

*On three separate occasions over the course of a month,
manipulation leading to paroxysm was employed. After the third
treatment, the patient became busy with her new engagement, and
though we had planned treatments for after her marriage, she did
not appear for them.*

*A year and a half later, I heard that she had been delivered of
the couple's first child, a boy.*

*

The teachers read and skimmed and passed the books one to
another without speaking. People left the room and returned to
it, bearing books. Caroline walked as she read, into the kitchen,

into the alcove of the dining room; she couldn't seem to stay seated. At one point it seemed to her that she should check on the girls, but when she went up into the hallway there was Mrs. Sanders, sitting in a rocking chair and presiding over the quiet. She gave Caroline a reprimanding look. Caroline considered how they must all seem to Mrs. Sanders—reading and talking downstairs while up here the girls lay on their beds. She felt like an intruder. She returned to the study and read some more, and time passed.

When she looked up after closing Hawkins's medical journal, the last book, her father was watching her as if he'd been waiting for a fever to break. Hawkins was smoking by the fire.

"Where are the Moores?" she asked.

"They went walking, don't you remember?" Hawkins said. "You were very absorbed."

Caroline folded her hands. "I don't think I quite understand all this."

Hawkins seemed to find what she'd said very funny. He made a show of trying to swallow his laughter. Caroline waited with her cheeks burning, though she couldn't have said exactly why. She looked at her father. *Are you just going to let him laugh?*

"Hawkins," Samuel said.

Hawkins regained possession. "Forgive me. Forgive me. It's just that of course you don't understand, Caroline."

"What does that mean?"

A pause in which he let meanings echo above her head. She felt furious at the life that had put those meanings out of her reach.

Then, "Oh, only that you've been reading very dense medical texts. They aren't written for a lay audience."

"It *does* all seem fairly full of contradiction," Samuel said. "Some of these physicians are so certain the cause is physical, and some so certain the cause lies in the psyche, but there doesn't seem to be much clarity or real specificity in either case."

"It's a complex disorder, still poorly understood."

"Which camp are you in?" Caroline said. "I couldn't tell, from your notes."

Hawkins stood and cracked his knuckles—broad, thick knuckles, hair below them and above too, all the way up to those blunt square fingertips. "I'm in the camp of it doesn't matter. Quite a popular camp in practical medicine."

"But that's—that's just like something Thoreson would write," Samuel said. "That contradicts everything we've ever—"

Hawkins sighed. "Oh, Sam, calm down. I'm not making a philosophical argument. Medicine doesn't deal in souls. We deal in bodies. If a treatment is effective and we don't know for certain why, that doesn't mean we don't use the treatment."

We deal in bodies.

"The treatment, though," Caroline said. "This massage, this *paroxysm.* Is it—what part of the anatomy—"

She did not want to be stammering.

"All quite proper, of course," Hawkins said. He turned to Samuel. "Of course, Sam. This is a treatment that in one way or another goes back hundreds of years, thousands."

"As does slavery," Caroline said.

Her father's lips pinched together.

She was seeing before her the girls' open, mutable faces on her first day of teaching them. When she had stood before them and talked to them about beauty and loss.

"They're so young, Papa," Caroline said. "So, so young."

Hawkins said, "That's why we need to decide for them. The trick is not to tell them too much about it ahead of time, not to give any sort of resistance time to take hold. It's best for everyone that way."

"I don't know," said Samuel.

"Sam, really, there's nothing at all to worry about. This has been done so many times before, and here it's clearly indicated."

Caroline said, "It seems, Papa, that had we sent them home, their doctors would have been able to treat them after all, if this is all so well established. No life of draughts and darkness."

"I wouldn't be so sure," Hawkins said. "Many practitioners misdiagnose, or implement the treatment unskillfully, or are too squeamish to attempt it. And I do think in this case there's a special suggestibility that's set in—if we were to send them home now, each of them would still be thinking of herself as an ill girl, and that's an idea that can take root and persist, despite treatment, even proper treatment. I've seen it happen. You're doing what's best."

Par-ox-ysm. Caroline tapped her fingers to the pulse of the word.

She stood. "I'm going for a walk. While you discuss what's *best.*"

*

Outside the earth was hard beneath her feet, her steps dully percussive in the cold. The ground of Trilling Heart had gone to sleep on her, frozen with its back turned.

Her mind spun and her hands and feet buzzed. It seemed the consensus was that one of those things might be making the other happen. Tricking the other. As if her mind and her body were two different beings, only clumsily attached.

An animal within an animal. But which inside which?

That twitching word *paroxysm*, and their girls, and Hawkins's big, blunt hands.

She heard shouting then. She turned the corner from the near field into the far one, and there were David and Sophia, arguing. "But *you* don't—" Sophia was yelling. She stopped and took a step back from David when she saw Caroline, and resettled her scarf around her neck.

"My apologies," Caroline said.

"No, we must apologize," David said. His cheeks were flushed.

"I was just explaining to Sophia that she shouldn't meddle where her understanding is imperfect."

Caroline had waited for so long to hear David say something like this about Sophia's understanding; she couldn't have imagined she would find the words so unsatisfying. "None of us has perfect understanding here, I think," she said.

"Hawkins does. Hawkins does understand it; he's seen it, he knows what steps to take," David said.

"*He* certainly thinks so," said Sophia.

"We're still deciding what to do," Caroline said. "I wanted a walk to clear my head. When you get back, tell them I'll be just another minute."

David took Sophia's elbow and turned her back toward the house, as if corralling a child.

Caroline went on. She thought about her mother walking these same fields, dying eventually in these fields, and wondered—but no, the best doctors in Boston had called her epileptic and had never once mentioned the word *hysteria*, not that Caroline had heard. She had been an epileptic and an adulteress but not a hysteric, and thus had no place in current concerns. Her mother was not the point; Caroline's own mind was not the point, her own hands, her own feet. The point was the girls lined up in their beds upstairs and what those girls would have done to them.

Caroline would have liked to ask someone who was not Hawkins and who was not her father about how to proceed. Talk to someone who could help her understand what they were deciding before they decided it on the girls' behalf.

The fine society girl from Hawkins's journal, perhaps. Hawkins's representative patient. She would have things to say.

Caroline imagined this girl walking beside her, stride for stride, her skirts rustling dryly.

He says you're better now, Caroline might say. *Are you?*

The girl would lift her narrow shoulders. Pearls would roll across her collarbones. *I don't fall as often.*

Why did you fall?

I don't know. I couldn't understand how everyone else stayed stand-ing up.

Had your pelvis felt heavy? Had you felt too full of something?
Another lift.

Was it because you wanted things you couldn't have? Had you read about things, and that made you want them?

I never much cared for reading.

The treatment—was it all right? Did it help?

It wasn't too terrible. I tried not to pay much attention. Afterward I barely remembered anything.

And now your life is better, now that you're married, and you have your child? You're fine now?

I nearly died, having him. Everything seems different.

You must love him very much.

I must.

Caroline imagined the girl back to her dinner parties and her new health, her son's nursery; back to the pages of Hawkins's case notes. A representative, recovered patient. Who was Caroline to question the fact of a recovery?

Yet Hawkins's hands.

She was walking now by the tree where she'd discovered the trilling heart nest. There it was, still at the base of the tree, where she'd set it again when her father had come out for Hawkins's telegram. It still held its shape. As she passed, three birds, two females and a male, flew from the woods behind the tree to land on the lawn, to pace and peck.

Caroline's eye caught in the dark of the woods. Something about its depth, about the way the birds had flown as if coming from somewhere.

She changed course, stepping toward the woods, toward the birds.

She expected them to fly off—scatter before her as they had always done. And they did bounce and lift into the air, but then they landed again, just a bit back from where they'd been before. Arrayed themselves, almost, so she'd have to cross through the line of them to get to what was behind. She walked on, pulled now by a curiosity about how close they might let her get. Just as Eliza claimed to have been pulled, the day of her fainting. Fifteen feet. Slower now. Ten feet. Seven. She hadn't been this close to any birds except the one that Hawkins had killed back in the summer.

Then the larger female let forth its high, piercing call, and lifted into the air, and flew at Caroline's head.

It was coming for her eyes. Caroline ducked her face low and shielded it with her hands. It would pluck her eyes from her and stud its nest with them, wet twin trophies, weave them right into its fabric, entwine them in branches, twigs, hair, until they were dim and buried, and forever after Caroline would see not black but red, because this blindness would be a red, red sea.

She crouched, her body trying to sink itself into the ground. She felt a breath of wind from the bird's wings on the nape of her neck. She flinched farther down and into herself, anticipating the feel of its feet, their clutch, the tearing. Skin—it might want her skin too, to turn into a new surface, to lay as a damp cupping atop sticks and twigs.

She could feel now on the skin of her neck and cheek the crawling weight of what the birds might lay on it after they'd taken it from her, and the pacing of their taloned feet.

Now she heard the cries of the other birds and felt their stirrings around her in the air. Flying around her, in front of her, behind her, calling and calling to one another about their imminent theft of her eyes, skin, hair, clothing—all their plans to pick her bare. What they wanted to turn her into.

She whirled and ran to save every part of herself.

She ran only for a moment. As soon as she couldn't hear the cries anymore, as soon as she couldn't feel the air moving and all the places on her where she might lose something, her fear fell away.

She stopped, turned around, and looked back at the birds where they were gathered on the lawn still. They were pecking now and not watching her at all.

We are only birds. What else?

How fanciful, how absurd, to believe they'd been attacking her with some sort of purpose.

Thankfully no one had seen. Caroline spun in the cold quiet and all around her saw nothing but space, grass, trees. She'd revealed herself to be a fool only to herself—less righteous and rational than David or Hawkins or her father. But then none of them had been here. She had been. Who was to say the birds had not been trying to take out her eyes? And that her fingers did not hum and tingle? And that all decisions about the girls' illness were best made by others with more distanced understanding than the girls themselves?

These girls they were trying to teach to be as sure as anyone and to know when they had seen a thing.

Caroline turned to walk back to the house—she would walk and not run, she could do this, she had it in her. And there was Hawkins after all, standing just outside the front door, watching.

How long had he been watching?

"That was quite something, Caroline," he said.

She squared her shoulders. Until she came close to him, she did not allow herself to alter her pace. "They startled me, that's all."

"I could see that," Hawkins said. "Are you often startled in that way?"

"No, I find it takes something like birds flying at my head to do it," she said.

"Well, they're birds. They do fly. And you were walking toward them."

"It was only a reaction."

"Have you been feeling nervous lately?" Hawkins asked.

Hysterical?

"We've all been feeling nervous—how else should we feel?" Caroline said.

She walked past him, through the door.

Just inside stood Samuel. "I've just told David and Hawkins," he said. "We were coming out to meet you. I've had time to consider now. I think it's best we begin the treatment immediately."

"What? Papa, I've been thinking." Hawkins came in behind her. "I've been thinking, and I'm really not sure we can."

"Of course we can," Hawkins said.

"We'd be deciding for them, and we aren't their parents."

"Their parents have entrusted them to us," Samuel said loudly.

"But to take this sort of action? What if it harms them?"

"*Harms* them?" Hawkins said. "I understand this has been a . . . trying time, Caroline. But really, how could it harm them?"

Caroline looked only at Samuel. "You wanted to shape their souls," she said. "I thought that's what we were doing."

"Of course we are. But now their souls are ailing, in particular, specific ways that Hawkins has seen before and that have nothing to do with our project—other than that they must be addressed before the project can continue."

"*Addressed?*" she said.

Her father and Hawkins looked at her.

Are you being hysterical, Caroline?

But his fingers, she wanted to say. *But his hands. But those words in those books, so tight and small, no room there for an actual girl.*

She would have said it all, in a different room, in a different life. She knew she would have. In this one she did not trust her voice or the body it came from.

"We'll try it," Samuel said in his best reasonable tone. "We'll try it for one round of treatment, and we'll see how they do. Just one, Caroline."

One for Abigail, one for Tabitha, one for Livia, Meg, Julia, Eliza, Felicity, Rebecca. One, one, one. Animals inside animals inside animals, all of them made to lie down.

15.

TREATMENT

*"Sometimes so many presences afflict me I am sure I shall
come asunder," she cried.*

—MILES PEARSON, *THE DARKENING GLASS* (P. 360)

Hawkins said they should all attend the treatments. "At
times the change is almost instantaneous." He snapped
his fingers. "How often do you get to see instantaneous change?
Not like teaching."

Not like teaching, no.

"Oh, I—I don't think . . . ," Samuel stammered.

"Yes, surely not," said David.

Both of them cringing, slinking away from the idea.

"Please, gentlemen. This is nothing troops of medical school
students haven't seen," said Hawkins. "Far less, actually. Then
we'd even have the coverings off to show how it's done."

"They'll be covered?" David asked.

"Ah," said Samuel. "That seems—that seems more—yes." He
fiddled with the heavy round orb of clear glass that was always
on his desk to weigh down his papers, against the possibility perhaps of a great whirling wind inside his study.

Sophia was looking back and forth between the two of them,
David and Samuel, as if she'd never seen them before.

"With whom should we begin?" Samuel asked.

"Not Miss Bell, of course," Hawkins said.

"Why not?" Sophia said. "Why not, if she's sickest?" She sat quietly beside David on the sofa and yet somehow gave the impression that at any moment she might leap up screaming. *Screaming what?* Caroline wondered. If she knew, she might scream it herself.

Though when had Caroline ever stopped a thing in her life?

"In her case the ailment and the belief in the ailment are worn in so deep it will take some doing to dig them out," said Hawkins.

"I don't understand," Sophia said. "Is she sick or isn't she?"

"Of course she is," Hawkins said. "And we will treat her. But it's an unusual kind of illness. The patient's approach to treatment can make quite a difference in that treatment's effects. In the event she's resistant I would prefer to have already made some progress with the others."

"Abigail, perhaps?" Samuel ventured.

"Or Meg? Meg might be better," said David.

Which features were they evaluating? They seemed to be discussing the girls themselves, not their particular symptoms. Which attributes? Times when the girls had held their eyes? Dropped them? Spoken loudly, quietly, not at all?

Hawkins's face pursed as if he were considering a particular taste.

"Rebecca," he said.

*

Caroline wasn't sure who moved her body up the stairs behind her father and David and Sophia, Hawkins leading them at the front of the line. It did not seem to be her. She did not feel as if she were really present. The world tilted and straightened as the group progressed—they were like that troop of medical students after all—but whatever was moving her feet didn't mind. It didn't mind either about the faint sibilation of the soles of those feet as they all stepped toward the door of Abigail and Rebecca's room, as Hawkins knocked. As if the house were hissing but none of the others could tell, and even Caroline couldn't tell, only her feet could.

Abigail and Rebecca were lying on their beds. They propped themselves on their elbows. Rebecca's hair had tufted above her braid on one side where she must have been leaning against her pillow. Caroline looked at her face, trying to see it as Hawkins had in choosing her: for its softness, maybe, or the quietness in the set of the mouth.

"You'll be pleased to know, ladies, that I have diagnosed your ailment," Hawkins said.

"You have?" said Abigail.

"What is it? What's wrong?" Rebecca said.

"Just as I suspected—nothing more than a . . . call it a nervous tension."

Abigail's eyes darted to the arc of teachers in the space between the beds and back to Hawkins. "What do you mean—*hmm*—call it that?"

"Miss Smith, please," Samuel reprimanded, though he had been the one to teach her that the names for things mattered. Caroline wanted to say this to him, but she found she couldn't speak. Just like that night in the woods when she'd been unable to step out from her hiding place and say anything, when she'd been too afraid to act and Eliza had not.

But she wasn't hidden now—she was right here in front of them. Why was she only watching them with polite concern, like a person who didn't even know them? Why was that all she could do?

"I mean it *is* that," Hawkins said. "And nothing I haven't seen a hundred times before. You will be unaware, of course, of the many precedents for your symptoms."

"You've treated people who—*hmm*—make noises without meaning to?" Abigail said.

"And the tipping over, just falling? It happened again on my way up the stairs," said Rebecca. "Meg caught me or I'd have broken my neck."

"How can it all be—*hmm*—from feeling nervous? I don't feel nervous."

"The nervousness is in your body—you might not even be aware of it," Hawkins said. "I'm sure it all seems extraordinary to you, but not to a physician of my long experience. And the treatment is quite uncomplicated, quite effective."

"What treatment?" said Abigail.

"A simple pelvic manipulation, leading to hysterical paroxysm."

Abigail squinted at him. *"Hmm,"* she said, as if agreeing. Rebecca tilted her head.

"If you're waiting for him to be clearer, you have a long wait coming," Sophia told them.

"Really, there isn't any need to trouble yourselves, girls," Hawkins said. "It won't hurt."

Their eyes grew.

"Miss Smith, if you could please wait outside."

"Can't I stay?" Abigail asked.

Run, Caroline wanted to tell her; Abigail didn't know how close she'd come to being first.

"Yes, please, I want her to," Rebecca said quickly.

Both of you, run.

But the arc of the teachers would have arrested them. And here Caroline was, part of it. She could feel her polite expression still stuck in place.

"Miss Smith will have her own treatment shortly," Hawkins said. "There's no reason at all for concern."

Abigail reached out, took Rebecca's hand, and pressed it between both of hers, wincing with seriousness. Then she stood up to leave, her face reluctant but her legs young and healthy and adamant about carrying her from the room. Caroline and her father moved apart at the shoulders to let her through, then closed in again. Whatever was in charge of Caroline's body did this for her.

Hawkins unfolded the plain white sheet that had been draped over his arm. "All right, Miss Johns, you may lie back on the bed."

She did. He wafted the sheet down and over her, the material of it so horribly like skin, like bloodless, untethered skin—as if they were remaking her and this would be her new surface—and Caroline thought of the trilling hearts and the theft she had expected of them, and of her mother's skin over hers in the post office.

"Now," said Hawkins, "you'll need to remove your drawers and loosen your corset. It won't be necessary to remove your dress."

Rebecca flushed all the way up to her hairline. "What?"

Samuel flinched slightly. On her other side, David angled his attention away, toward the wall. Sophia caught Caroline's eyes with hers, and then they both looked back at the girl on the bed. Caroline imagined the visitors' couch lined up against one wall, Mr. Thoreson on it, watching.

Allow us to show you the current phase of our project.

"You can just shift the skirts up, that will be all right," Hawkins said.

Rebecca's lips trembled. "Can I talk to Eliza first?"

"Not just now, I'm afraid," Hawkins said. He turned to the teachers. "Quite common for there to be this resistance."

Though that was something the books hadn't mentioned, not the body books, not the mind books, and not Hawkins's notes. Had he needed to chase the fine society girl around his examination room, pin her to the table?

"Come now, do it yourself or we'll do it for you."

"I only just remembered something I need to ask her. Please," Rebecca said.

"It can wait," said Hawkins, moving in, but she shrank away to the wall. Again he turned to the teachers, expecting perhaps that one of them would make Rebecca lie still. When none moved, when Samuel and David wouldn't even look at him, Hawkins sat at the foot of Rebecca's bed.

"Miss Johns, you're making this much more difficult than necessary. You seem like a reasonable sort of young lady to me. I'm sure your father has always been proud of you for being so sensible and reasonable. Hasn't he? Did you know that I know your father, Miss Johns? He handles one of the accounts for my practice. Very decent man, Stephen Johns."

At the sound of her father's name, Rebecca's brow wrinkled.

"I can tell you're the sort of young lady who can understand the best thing to do. If you lie still as I ask, this will all be over very quickly. You'll be astonished how much better you'll feel."

"I don't want to," Rebecca said.

"I wouldn't want to have to write your father a letter and explain how you'd behaved."

She sat up straight. "Please, don't tell him."

"I wouldn't like to, of course."

"Please," Rebecca said, easing off the wall. She lay down on the bed and adjusted the sheet over herself. Beneath it she made some movements. Caroline heard Hawkins breathe in and settle, her father beside her breathe in and settle, David on the other side.

Hawkins stood up. "Good girl. There you go now," he said.

Rebecca was loosening her stays underneath herself and bunching her skirts up around her waist. She lifted her hips to slide down her drawers and the movement dislodged the sheet, showing her body, almost blue in its paleness, blue-purple veins running like strings over the jut of her hip bones, the small mound of her pubis with its dark, downy hairs. Caroline looked away while Hawkins pulled the sheet back down. When she glanced back Rebecca's eyes were closed, and Caroline hoped the girl hadn't noticed about the sheet and would never know.

"All right. Some pressure now," Hawkins said. He worked one

hand up under the covering. He adjusted the fabric with his other hand, then put it on Rebecca's lower belly and leaned down. The hand beneath the sheet was doing something. The elbow began to work.

For a few minutes, it seemed that nothing else was going to happen.

Then, slowly, Rebecca's face began to take on a distance. She opened her eyes and directed them at the ceiling, and her feet and legs began to shudder.

"A fit?" Samuel asked.

"Shh," Hawkins said.

The movements were smaller than a fit, though there was that violence to them, and that sense that they weren't of Rebecca's own doing, as if she were being puppeted on threads suspended from the ceiling.

Paroxysm.

Rebecca watched and watched the ceiling while her body moved like something separate from her.

Rebecca stopped twitching. Hawkins withdrew his hand and wiped it on his pocket handkerchief. "Very good, Miss Johns. You'll feel better soon," Hawkins said.

Rebecca made no move to rearrange herself beneath the sheet. "I saw things," she said. "A big light sky, and the way our garden looked as I went back and forth on my swing when I was small. I don't understand. What happened?"

Since that word *paroxysm* had gripped her, Caroline realized, she had been expecting to recognize this treatment from her own dreams. The movements themselves had looked familiar. But Rebecca's face, its lostness, did not—had nothing to do with the dreams' thrill through the core of her, that sense of taking into herself the whole world.

"You'll feel better soon," Hawkins repeated. "You may cover yourself now."

When she had, Hawkins took the sheet and folded it and asked her to please go and send Abigail in, and wait outside.

*

The sheet was folded and unfolded, wafted down on top of each girl. Abigail cried, before, during, and after. Livia jerked theatrically. Meg, before Hawkins could cover her, bared and poked at her rash, great red streaks now all down her legs, but during the treatment she lay as if enervated.

"How many will we treat today?" Caroline asked Hawkins. Her voice grated in her throat; she had up until now been so silent.

"We ought to get them all in," he said.

But they adjourned to eat something and allow food to be brought up to the girls. Hawkins ate his cut of pork, then pushed back from the table and went into the other room—to write up case notes, he said. Caroline suspected him of wanting to gather himself before approaching Eliza.

The four teachers looked at one another across the table, whose plane warped in Caroline's vision. She blinked, blinked.

Sophia pushed her plate away. "I thought I could eat, but I can't eat," she said.

"This isn't the time for theatrics," David said tiredly.

"No, we're much too busy, aren't we?"

"I must ask you, Sophia," said Samuel, "to either say clearly what you want to say or stop speaking."

"I will say it." Sophia's lips trembled but her voice was loud. "These treatments are wrong. They are—they are making these girls feel—feel *womanly* things. Things only for marriage."

"Sophia!" David said.

"That is quite absurd," Samuel said. "These girls are receiving a medical treatment. That is all. There is no penetrative instrument."

Caroline's father was wearing his best teaching face, the one that put even Eliza in her seat and that made him the equal of those busts on the shelves in the barn, as immovable and as certain.

"But—"

"I have to insist you stop now, Sophia," David said. "To suggest such a thing of a respected, established physician—"

Sophia whirled on Caroline. "*You* must see," she said.

Now Sophia's face too was full of lostness. Caroline planted her humming hands on the bending tabletop and thought, *If I say I don't, who will I be?*

"Yes. I question this treatment," she said. "I think it might be ... pulling something out of them." That was how it had looked to her, as if something were being yanked forth. "I think we need to pause and consider their age, consider our role."

"Their age is only some three years younger than your mother was when she married me," Samuel said.

"Hawkins isn't proposing to marry any of them, is he?"

Samuel rose. "Unless one of you has become a physician without my knowledge," he said, "I think we must bear in mind that Hawkins knows rather more than either of you."

Yes, from reading all those books, books, books, no girls anywhere in the words, no room for the meat of them.

"Papa—"

"No, please, excuse me. I find I am greatly upset, Caroline. I would not have expected this of you."

Caroline's face burned. *I wouldn't want to have to write your father a letter and explain how you'd behaved,* Hawkins had said to Rebecca.

"I will see you when it is time for us to resume," Samuel said.

The door closed behind him.

Sophia stood. "All right. I'm going home." Her lips trembled.

"What do you mean? What do you mean, Sophia? You *are* home," David told her. "You're with your husband."

"You know what's in my heart, but I can't stay here. I'm going back to Mama's. I can't watch this."

David's mouth, his chin, worked.

"Please don't start it all, not again," Sophia said, though Caroline didn't think David would have managed to say anything even if she hadn't stopped him. "I don't understand everything, I know that, but I understand enough."

This was true, Caroline realized. She looked to David, but his eyes were directed at the tabletop, so that it almost appeared they were closed.

Sophia moved toward Caroline now and took her hands. Caroline could only barely feel the touch of her fingers. "I don't think you should watch it either. I think you should go too."

"I have to stay. I can't leave the girls," Caroline said. This was also true.

And one last terrible truth: in all her life, Caroline had never left her father.

"I can't," she said, and Sophia nodded and dropped her hands.

*

"My wife isn't feeling well," David told Hawkins as they made their way back up the stairs.

"Not feeling hysterical, is she?" Hawkins said, chuckling.

"Oh no," David said quickly.

Caroline's father wouldn't look at her. He stood as far from her as possible.

Julia trembled before Hawkins ever touched her. Tabitha kept making sounds, and when the treatment was finished, she vomited on the floor.

"Not unusual," Hawkins said. "The inner rearranging this provokes can cause some passing nausea."

Mrs. Sanders was sent for and went in to clean up as they were all going out.

In the next room waited Eliza, sitting up in her bed, her hair gleaming down on her shoulders as if it were sucking the life out of her.

"Hello," she said. Her head bobbed to the side, righted itself.

Caroline sat down on Felicity's desk chair, unsure her legs would hold her, craving and dreading her father's eyes—had he ever withheld them before? It seemed spiteful in a way she wouldn't have believed of him. She wouldn't have believed so much of this.

"Ah, my old haunt," Hawkins said. "This was my room when we lived here, did you know?"

"I didn't," said Eliza.

"Well, Miss Bell." Hawkins seated himself on her bed. "In your particular case, before we begin the treatment itself, I've been thinking we might benefit from a bit of discussion."

"What would you like to talk about?"

"I suspect—we suspect—that some of the tension from which you in particular are suffering stems from your ideas about your time here. Yours and perhaps also your father's."

"What about my father?" Eliza said. Her voice was still cool but color began to stain her cheeks.

"You may be glorifying him in your mind, idolizing him. And in turn reading all kinds of significance into his book, with its very specific mood, in terms of your own experience at this school. In ways you yourself aren't fully conscious of, even." Hawkins was making himself comfortable, shifting, extending his knees. "All understandable, of course, but not, I suspect, very good for your own health. So I thought Mr. Hood and I could tell you a little about what your father was like."

"They claim not to remember much." Eliza nodded toward Caroline and her father as if they were one person.

"How mysterious."

Caroline thought of the last thing Hawkins had told her about

Miles Pearson. Beside her, she saw her father's face tighten too, and there it was, confirmation, had she needed it. How could she not have seen and known all along, from a hundred small moments like this?

How? By believing, always, her father above herself, even when this belief required averting her attention, suspending her judgment, putting out of her mind what she had seen, deciding she had not, after all, understood anything.

"Well, I do remember. Would you like to hear?" Hawkins said.

Would you like it if I gave you what you've most wanted your whole life, Miss Bell? What's eluded you even as you walked where it once was? Even as you've tried with everything you have to catch it and draw it close to you?

"Yes," Eliza said, the word cracking.

"Of course, when he was with us, Miles was very young. From across the room he was one thing: so tall, with all that dark hair, an intimidating sort of look. But up close he was different, especially once you began to talk to him. He had all these *ideas*. Sam, how would you describe Miles's ideas?"

As her father looked at Eliza, Caroline watched layers of feelings twist in his face. Here was a soul in pain, a fatherless girl, and he wanted still to help her, steer her, soothe her. But beneath that generosity was a desire too to punish. Because here she was, the poison seed.

"I would call them naive," Samuel said.

"That's generous," said Hawkins. "Your father, Miss Bell, had a blindness about the world."

"Blindness?" Eliza said. "He can't have been blind. He wrote a book so many people love—he saw plenty."

"The adoration of crowds is not perhaps the most useful proof of any kind of vision," said Samuel.

Eliza narrowed her eyes. "You're only jealous of him. That and you don't like what he wrote about you."

"Of course I don't," Samuel said. "It was hateful of him to imagine in such a direction. I'm sure anyone in my position would say the same. As for the other charge, I have been guilty of many sins in my life, but here I think I may safely exculpate myself. Never, not once, have I envied either your father's writing or his insights about the world."

"Please, Papa," Caroline said quietly. She was trying to remind him of how Eliza would be fastening every word he said to a wall in her mind from which none of it could ever be dislodged.

"What, Caroline?" Samuel said. "It's all true. Do you know, once I sat next to Miles at supper, and he spent the whole time telling me what the future of civilization would be like. He said in a few generations' time we would all be in communion with both the living and the dead. That, he thought, would become the measure of a *spiritual life*."

"We must have a very spiritual life, then—we're communing with the dead right now," Caroline said. She couldn't bear this.

"He mooned around this place like he'd never heard of working," Hawkins said.

"You're lying," Eliza whispered.

"We aren't," Samuel said. "He used to take morning swims in the stream, though it was so shallow he could barely get himself all the way in. He called them his 'ablutions.' He proposed we speak only in ancient languages to one another, in the interest of purity."

"Remember when a tree fell on the barn, and the roof needed fixing?" Hawkins said. "He disappeared for three days and walked back just as we were finishing."

"He'd come across some rune in his readings and he would sing it while he walked because he said—"

"Stop," Eliza said. "Oh, stop, please. I see what you want me to, about him. My father was a silly boy. That's what you mean to tell me."

"Miss Bell," said Samuel, "we have no desire whatever to be cruel. But since you came here you've seemed to be questing after some connection with your father, and it's clear the obsession has grown to unhealthy dimensions. Best for you to know the truth about him. Sometimes the ideas we have about the people in our lives aren't helpful to us."

Is that true of the people in your own life, sir? was what Caroline expected Eliza to say next.

Instead she said, "All right. I understand."

"You understand?" said Samuel.

"Miss Bell?" Caroline said.

Eliza looked at her then. Caroline wanted to tell her that she didn't need to understand this, that such an understanding was more than what she needed to ask of herself; or even lie and say that she could remember Miles after all and what they were saying wasn't true, he'd been nothing like they were telling her. But she was thinking of her mother, of all she'd never seen about Anna, and that stopped her for a moment, and in that moment Eliza looked away again. Something collapsed in her face. "I do. I do understand," she said. "Might I have my treatment now?"

Hawkins raised his eyebrows. "You're ready?"

"I'm ready," Eliza said. "If this treatment might make me better, I'm ready. I can't stand to feel like this anymore."

Like what? Caroline wanted to ask her. *Like yourself?*

Eliza lay back, and Hawkins wafted the sheet down over her, her body just like all the others' bodies, nothing so mysterious or powerful about her at all. She was only a girl.

"That's very good, Miss Bell. You will feel much better soon," Hawkins said.

16

PAROXYSM

❦

*"Only you can save me, though it costs
us both," she told him.*

—MILES PEARSON, *THE DARKENING GLASS* (P. 403)

Alone in her bedroom that evening, Caroline lay down and then realized she'd forgotten to put out the light. She rose again to do it, and the world swung away from her like a loose door pushed open.

She lost some time then—she wasn't sure how much. When she awoke she was lying with her cheek to the floorboard, goose bumps stippling her arms. Cold down there, on the floor. Had her body made a sound, falling? No one had come to check on the thump, if there had been a thump.

The lamp on her desk still gave off its domestic glow. She crawled across the floor to reach it—staying low enough that she couldn't fall again—and snuffed the flame, then crawled back and hoisted herself into bed.

By the time Caroline came downstairs in the morning, Sophia was already gone: Mr. Sanders had driven her into town before daybreak to hire a coach to Boston, where she would board her Ohio-bound train. The house without Sophia in it felt so much closer to dead. Caroline could not believe her own bereftness.

Samuel clasped David's shoulder at the bottom of the stairs, when he came down alone. "It will be all right in the end," he said.

"Will it?"

From the dining room, Caroline could see how hollowed out David's face looked.

"She will come to understand. Once we've properly gotten our feet under us, once this course has a chance to take effect. When you can write and tell her of recoveries, she'll be back, mark my words. Nothing like results to win them." There was a forced cheer in Samuel's voice, as if he were jesting about a customary lovers' spat, the middle act of some comic play in which the shrewish wife is at her temporary pinnacle of unreason.

The explanation David gave Hawkins, when he emerged from his room, was that Sophia's mother was ill and she'd been called home.

Over breakfast, Hawkins said, "We should try to get them all in again today."

"Again?" Caroline said. She couldn't catch her breath.

"It's important to provide the release several times in quick succession at first. In some cases a cumulative effect is beneficial."

Samuel had work to do in his study, David had writing to finish in his room, and so neither would attend. After all, no need to learn an identical lesson twice.

"And you, Caroline?" Hawkins said.

"I'll go with you." If no one were presiding, Hawkins might whittle the girls away like dry wood.

Those who had resisted yesterday were mostly calmer today. They understood what to do without being told, so almost nothing needed to be said, and that helped—some of the words involved were themselves so incensing. They lay back obediently. Hawkins set to work with only brief instructions to each, and no explanations.

Today tears gathered only in the corners of Abigail's eyes.

"Will we need to do this many more times?" she asked when Hawkins had finished.

"Not many, no—not if you continue to make progress as I expect," Hawkins told her.

He folded the sheet and handed it to Caroline as if she were his nurse. She took it and the world leaned again, and she tilted forward, fell—she kept her eyes open but could not stop herself from falling to her knees. She was scrambling up again when Hawkins turned to her.

"I stumbled," she said, clutching the bedpost for balance. Abigail was watching her absently, as if half asleep.

"Miss Hood, a word outside, please," Hawkins said.

Caroline went into the dim hall, heart pounding: *caught caught caught caught*. She faced him.

"Tell me, Caroline, how long has this been going on?" Hawkins said sternly.

"I don't know what you mean."

She made herself as tall as she could. This wasn't anyone else's but hers, to do with what she would, and she wouldn't be made to feel she'd failed to confess a sin. What could he do, if she insisted it was nothing? If she used her very best teacher-voice to say so?

"I assume you've been keeping this from Samuel. He would have mentioned if he considered his daughter to be among our patients." Hawkins shook his head. "You know I'll have to tell him."

Ah, there it was—there was what he could do.

"Dr. Hawkins, I would ask you, please, as a friend"—the word almost gagged her—"not to do that."

"I must. He's my friend too, Caroline—my old friend, one of my oldest. It wouldn't be right to keep such a thing from him. You know it wouldn't. And you can't go on like this."

"But you don't understand—I think it might kill him. Truly, having to worry about me in this way, he couldn't withstand it."

Her voice broke, but she would not, would not, cry in front of Hawkins.

Hawkins sighed.

She breathed, breathed, breathed while she waited.

"One thought," Hawkins said finally. "If we started you down the right path, and if I felt that you were improving, I might feel better about keeping the situation between us."

Caroline still had the clammy weight of the sheet draped over her arm. *The right path.* Between her and Hawkins she wanted nothing except space. She didn't want him anywhere near her. Hawkins was suggesting that he see now beneath her dress, as she'd always suspected him of wanting to do, and at the recognition of this she flinched, a full-body flinch, as if something had pricked her spine and the hurt traveled in every direction at once.

But her father's face, when Hawkins told him: the way it would crumple as all of his worst moments returned to him. As he remembered Anna falling, and kicking at the air, and losing herself, and failing to return, one day, from a walk he had let her take alone. The way Caroline would feel, watching his face, knowing she'd made it look that way.

Here again was the pattern Hawkins had used with Rebecca and with Eliza too: the father brought in at the critical moment to make the daughter tractable. Caroline could see well enough what he was doing, but seeing didn't help her.

And Hawkins had said that she couldn't go on like this, and she thought that might be true. Caroline of course wanted to be whole and well. The books, the doctors, made a long line in front of her and each of them said that yes, this was the way to wholeness and wellness. At the back, so far distant she could barely see, Hawkins and David and her father, just as sure as the rest and only part of this pack of sureness. Her father who—if all of this were the way they thought—would never have to carry the weight of what was wrong with her. All together they were loud. They all wanted her to listen to them, as they always had.

What did Caroline know?

Hawkins was watching her face.

"When?" she said.

*

Caroline waited in her bedroom. At least she knew what was coming and could loosen her corset and take off her drawers ahead of time, so she wouldn't need to fumble beneath her skirts with Hawkins in the room. She positioned herself on the bed, positioned the sheet over her. Soft and a little damp-feeling against her legs. She would lie like stone in the shape of a woman: like the statue on a sarcophagus. She would be in all respects stony. Not a word would she say to Hawkins, not the whole time. She would in fact pretend he was not Hawkins but only a physician, the anonymous physician all the books referred to. And she herself only the anonymous patient. *First the physician should instruct the patient to . . .*

There was her ceiling above, the same as ever. It seemed impossible that the familiar water stains and ripples would look down on something like this without intervening on her behalf.

But then what would this be, after all? Only a treatment for her body, which had been disobedient, which would now be taught to obey. Every one of their girls had survived this, and the fine society girl too, and so many others. Things had been happening to Caroline's body that she didn't understand—this would be one more thing. Maybe this thing would do what was promised and fix the others.

She pulled in air.

Hawkins knocked. He entered.

"All right, Caroline," he said.

She said nothing. She did not look at him. She looked at the ceiling.

He seemed then to understand her sarcophagus terms and came to the bed without speaking again. The sheet clung to her legs as he slid his arm beneath it.

And there were his hands. She'd been right about the place they touched and tried to move.

If she kept her eyes on the ceiling, she found, Hawkins was entirely out of her line of vision. She didn't have to see anything about him.

His hands' motions were causing a sort of jittering in her legs that seemed to have nothing to do with her. A mechanical effect from a mechanical cause. Caroline herself was nowhere in what was happening, and so this was nothing like her dreams, where her whole self swelled. She felt only an unpleasant friction, easy enough to hold at a distance. When she lay as still as she could, everything under the sheet seemed not to be hers. It all seemed to belong to the patient.

She glanced down once and found that Hawkins's eyes were on her face, where she'd caught them so often before. She looked back at the ceiling. She would not think of reciting Latin in a white dress with Hawkins watching from his chair. She would not think of him across the parlor watching her. Watching her flee from the birds. Those were thoughts of Hawkins, and this was not Hawkins but the physician, giving the patient a treatment, dealing in bodies.

With her eyes on the ceiling she waited through the movements of her legs—the patient's legs. They were moving beneath the sheet and Caroline could wait out the moving. Waiting she was good at.

"All right. All right. That will do for now," Hawkins said.

He wiped his hand as he had done after each of the others.

He left. Caroline lay quiet. She was still stony. She was afraid of what would happen in the first moment she moved again, of what she would feel.

At last she sat up. She whisked the sheet away, wanting to be free of it.

And there she was, uncovered, herself as always. Nothing he'd done had left a mark on her. She thought of all the unmarked girls around her, in their rooms.

The walls seemed to blur a little, her fingers seemed to tingle, but maybe that was only the last gasp of the blurring and tingling, the last breath of them on her before they left forever.

*

Next there were hours for Caroline to last through. She reminded herself that she was waiting now for a cure to take effect. Each feeling that visited her the rest of the day might be the start of becoming well, becoming a person clean and empty with newness.

The feelings themselves mattered almost not at all.

She walked into town so as not to be in the house. How did her legs feel on this walk? She could not have said with any certainty. She tried to breathe in the cold air deeply and feel only new.

At the post office she found a letter from Miss Sterne waiting for her.

Oh, I was so very sorry to read the news your last letter brought. Despite the challenges she posed, I quite liked Miss Bell; I felt for her. I do so wish there were some strategy I implemented that I could tell had an effect—I would gladly share it with you now—but no, our episode persisted and then passed for no discernible reason, something like the way weather does.

I will be thinking of all of you.

Unexpectedly Caroline's eyes welled at the thought of Miss Sterne sewing capably in a quiet room and thinking of her. It felt as if Miss Sterne had reached out and found her, the real her, and gripped her hand.

*

At supper Samuel passed Hawkins the plate of salted beef.

"How are the treatments progressing?" he asked.

"Quite well, I think," Hawkins said. "We're starting to make some real strides forward. Wouldn't you say, Caroline?"

She was not going to look at him, not ever again. She would remain stone where Hawkins was concerned. "I suppose so," she said.

"So you think they're beginning to recover?" Samuel said.

Hawkins sipped his wine. "I do. I think we're beginning to see real changes. I feel very pleased with how it's all going. We all should."

He raised his glass, and Samuel and David raised theirs in return. Caroline remembered herself and raised hers too.

17

BODIES

*His yearning for her was pure as the breath of the very
soul—pure and stainless as she herself.*

—MILES PEARSON, *THE DARKENING GLASS* (P. 407)

The third morning of treatments, Julia had a fit as Mrs. Sanders was distributing the breakfast trays. She fell off her desk chair and struck at the air with her hands and feet while the others, alerted by Tabitha's scream, flew to her—the girls from their rooms, the teachers and Hawkins from downstairs, everyone running. The girls encircled her where she lay on the floor. Samuel stood in the doorway, looking as if he wanted to close his eyes.

"Please stand back," Hawkins said. They made way for him, and he lowered himself beside Julia and plunged his hand into her flailings to find the pulse at her neck. He kept his fingers pressed there until she was still, then stood up again. "Let her lie there for a moment. Then someone can help her onto her bed."

"Why is this happening?" said Caroline. "Why is this still happening?"

She had allowed the treatment to happen. Here, in this room—and all the other rooms, her own too—she had allowed it.

"What has it all been *for?*" she shouted.

"Miss Hood, surely you weren't expecting instant results," Hawkins said.

"You yourself said the results would be instant."

"Ah, I said they *can* be. One possible course—a rare one, I ought to have explained. In most cases it's several cycles at least before we begin to see real change. We may find that it takes months."

"Months," said Eliza, from the floor near Julia's head, her hand woven into Julia's hair; Julia's eyes flicked to her. They looked like a classical portrait of dying sisters. Caroline had been a failure of a guard. She dug her nails into her palms.

David was watching them too, and his face looked grief-stricken.

"Why yes, Miss Bell. I'll be a part of your company for a while," said Hawkins.

As they were leaving, Caroline touched her father's elbow. "Papa."

"Caroline, I do not wish to hear it, not again," he said.

*

Caroline went to David's room, after. She knocked, then slipped inside and closed the door behind him, startling him as she had that day when Sophia's dress had sprawled across his chair.

No dress there now, no Sophia, only David in the chair, reading at the center of a bare room.

"I need you to help me talk to my father," she said. The room was dimmer than the hallway outside and some special light seemed to flicker in her peripheral vision as she looked at him.

He didn't rise. "You don't need any help speaking, Caroline."

So he assumed that when she was quiet it was because she wanted to be.

"I've tried. You've seen me trying," she said. "We need him to listen, and he isn't listening to me. To you, he might."

"Why would you think that?"

"He loves you. You love him. If we could have filled this school with you in replicate—eight versions of you in pretty skirts—all would have been well."

David leaned his face forward into his hands. He'd rolled up his sleeves, warm perhaps from the fire in this small, dark honeycomb chamber of a bedroom where they'd put him to live, across the hall from all the best light. Caroline watched the muscles of his forearms, veined like a map, tense under the weight of his head. "Please, Caroline. I'm too tired."

"It's a difficult time for you."

"How do you manage to do that, I wonder? Make such a sentence into an insult?"

"I'm very sorry, David, that your wife went home without you. But we are still here. We must, must do something."

"About a course of medical care?" David said, but she heard his doubt.

"You said you wanted the reasons and the methods to be the same. That's what you said when you told us why you'd come here. You wanted to be able to look at either of them. I watched you, during the treatments. You couldn't look at that."

"I—"

"And now—what was the purpose of it, even? It isn't even working."

"The purpose—"

"What are we thinking?"

"All right!" he said, standing. "All right." He met her eyes, sighed, set his shoulders. "Yes. We'll talk to him."

"Thank you," Caroline said. She found herself surprised—she hadn't really thought she'd be able to make him do anything. "Tonight?"

"Tonight."

She watched him across the room. He was as still as he had been that first day she'd found him on her doorstep, the world's false promise to her.

"You're merciless, Caroline," he said, and at last his face was full of all the longing she'd always wanted to see there.

Perhaps she might try that, being merciless. As merciless as others had been. Eliza, chasing always what she needed, what she thought she might need. Caroline's mother, taking what she pleased from everyone. Hawkins, and her father, requiring from Caroline everything, and Sophia, free to leave when she chose. Here Caroline was, still inside one of the chambers of her father's dreams, for which she had paid and paid, though they weren't hers.

Perhaps she might find out what this room could hold for her.

Close up, David would look only at the floor, but he did reach out and take her hand. She closed the space between them. She pressed her body hard to his, and he made a sound like lifting a heavy thing. For a moment, she watched the ceiling above his shoulder and pretended he was lifting it off her, to open a space through which she could reach the sky.

Then at last there was the sweet full offering of his mouth. His hands moved to her arms, clutched them. She put her palm to the ridge of his cheekbone and slid her fingertips into his hair.

She felt suddenly sure that in spite of everything hers was a strong body, that if she asked it to, it could take her great distances, relearn its shape as many times as necessary.

He opened his eyes—hers had already been open—and trailed his fingers softly down to her elbow, then back up. Then to her face. His soft fingers on her cheek, her forehead, her hair—too soft, not enough, not as much as she wanted. She closed her hand tight on his wrist, and he pushed her up against his desk. His hands were on her breasts now, and not so reverent. She felt herself straining up through her dress to meet his skin. It was the feeling of her whole fullest self rising up in her. Above the ceiling, she knew the sky unreeled.

A red wave began to build at her center. Pictures pushed bright through her, flooding her to her fingertips.

Running after William through the field, sun on her face. She should have caught him. She'd been able to run as fast as anyone.

David at the breakfast table, his hand just beyond the reach of hers.

David on her doorstep on the first morning. Red birds spinning through the space behind his head, even if she couldn't yet see them.

David on the day of the sheet sewing, the day of the walk, the day of the nest, the day she'd fainted, all the days she had not touched him, had thought she would never touch him, and she was touching him now.

His mouth was moving down her neck, harsh enough that she couldn't tell if his lips or his teeth were closing on her. She gasped at the need. Inside her the cresting built and built.

She fumbled at her skirts, lifting the endless cloth. He was lifting too, until his hands found her thighs.

He tried to move back then. Into the space he left between their bodies crept, for a terrible moment, Hawkins and his hands, and a brief panic flooded her. She took David's hand and pulled him nearer and the panic left.

"We can't," he said.

Caroline could.

She pulled harder until all the space between them was gone, and he closed his arms around her again. Then his fingers moved, filled. He pushed her hands out of the way and undid his belt himself.

Pushing, pushing.

Her head full of light.

The wave broke and its breaking was the moment of containing and releasing both, it was both, she could do both things at once, amazing animal that she was.

Another moment and he twitched, parted from her, and she knew he'd pulled back for the end. They were both breathing in quick, warm puffs in the chill, dark space of this room, which they had flooded.

He pulled out a handkerchief and turned away. She pulled her skirts back down.

*

In her room, Caroline surveyed herself. There was a rawness between her legs and an almost pleasing soreness in her arms from pulling and being pulled, but mostly she felt the same, except more solid. Here was her whole, real self—she was surer about that self than she'd ever been before. Its facts felt realer now that someone else knew them too, and now that she knew the facts of someone else.

Bodies, in the essays of Samuel Hood, were only incidental housing. In his life he never much discussed them. Though as a child Caroline felt warmly enveloped by his love, in actual practice he'd sometimes gone days without touching her.

"Papa," she'd asked one night when she was about ten, as they were reading by the fire, "what's so exciting about a wedding? Ginny was going on and on today about a wedding they went to, for somebody named Celeste Matthews. She kept talking about the dress. She said it was *exquisite*."

"You have some doubts about its exquisiteness?" her father asked, smiling.

"I don't understand why it's so interesting to Ginny, is all."

"The dress ought perhaps to be less interesting to her than it is. I'm sorry if that troubled you, but glad too that you were troubled."

Caroline was relieved to learn that he wasn't sending her to these girls only to turn her into them.

"I do think, though, that the fascination with these material things springs from a fascination with the larger ritual, and that is appropriate, if a little premature in this case. Marriage is the great ceremony of a woman's life."

The use of the article alarmed her—*what* woman?

"It joins all her gifts, passions, pursuits with another's. It is a great bestowing of herself on a man she feels will appreciate and make wise use of that gift."

Caroline imagined herself approaching a shadowy boy, putting a box into his hands.

"I am glad that you asked me about this," Samuel told her.

As she grew up, then grew older, Samuel had sometimes gazed at her with a misty preoccupation and asked if she was lonely. She knew what answer he expected and she delivered it promptly, but each time resented his asking, his making her inspect her life. If she had been meant to outgrow its fit, he should have said so. The question raised a faint dark suspicion that he'd been keeping some truth from her.

But now here it was, as she paced her bedroom for the feel of the tendons in her knees catching and letting go, for the smooth weight of her arms. Now she could see that truth whole, and it consisted only of these arms, these legs, this mouth. All the actions these could take. It didn't look to her like anything Samuel, or anyone else, could ever have known about before.

*

David was shaky and tight-faced when Caroline went to him that evening. He smiled as if sick but laughing a little at the sickness.

"It will be all right," she said soothingly. She had a good soothing-voice after all this time. She took his hand, kissed it, and he gave her another smile, more real this time.

When they knocked at the door of Samuel's study, she dropped David's hand, but still the moment felt very like the start of a scene in which a suitor announces himself and his intentions.

"Come in!" Samuel said.

He stood before his bookshelves. Caroline knew what he'd been doing a second before: surveying all those spines, searching for something, running his fingertips over them to help his search. She imagined instead the bare spines of the girls turned toward him. His outstretched fingers.

"What is it?" Samuel said quickly.

"Oh, nothing, no—nothing new," she said—the soothing-voice again, and she stopped, because that voice had no place here. "But we do need to talk to you."

"Oh?" Samuel said. His eyes darted between their faces.

There was no reason to think he could see what they'd done together. No reason to think that anyone could. This was one more secret Caroline's body would keep, like the secret of the tingling she could feel even now in her heels. She would have liked to tell David about the sureness of this inaccessibility, that he didn't need to worry.

"We've decided we can't let it go on," Caroline said.

"We've been through all this, Caroline. You're speaking about an accepted course of care for a documented condition—"

"Which their parents don't even know they have. For which none of them has given permission to have their daughters treated." It felt different to be speaking with David beside her— together they were more than Samuel was, and she felt the shift in weight, as if the room were a scale, moving. "And that isn't even it, really. It's what it's doing to them. You must see."

She knew Samuel had been trying not to look at the girls' faces, but it was written everywhere on them, even on their spines, the bump bump bump of where knobs of bone stretched skin.

Her father watched her quietly as she spoke. Then he gave that quiet face to David. "Now this is your opinion too?" he said.

Yes, David would say.

"I am concerned," David said.

Caroline had been so sure of his *yes* that she almost heard it. She turned, slowly, to look at him.

"Well, of course you are. It's concerning," Samuel said.

David looked imploringly at Samuel, which was the wrong expression to wear when they were the ones on the side with more weight, the side that was winning. "It does seem we have an obligation to make certain—I have feared that the effects on the girls are—"

"What, in your expert opinion, *should* the effects of this particular medical treatment be on patients?" Samuel said.

"I don't know, of course," David said. "You're right, I don't know."

"He's *right?*" Caroline said, but David was still looking at her father.

"I just fear it might be—I just fear we might be overstepping."

"We're not overstepping but *stepping*! Taking steps!" Samuel thundered. "We're taking care of the girls in our charge. We are doing what medical science says must be done for them, and we are guarding our vision, and we are doing all of that because it is the right thing. Because of the importance—the critical, the *essential*, importance—of what we are trying to provide."

Here David began to nod.

"A life that no one else could ever have shaped for these girls. You *know* all of this."

"I do."

"Qualms mean no more than the presence of complication."

"And certainly we have complication."

Caroline should have been expecting nothing else. This was David. David who, yes, had stood on the doorstep, had summoned a wave in her, but who had also shown again and again how easily he said fine things. Who had talked to her all the time he knew he was married and she did not, and taken joy in the talking. Who'd talked beautifully to Sophia earlier and after too. Who'd said his fine things even to their girls, who'd so loved their love of him.

And long before David had ever come to Trilling Heart, when he opened his mouth to speak the best of his words, it had been Samuel he'd been imagining every time as listener.

"You do see, then? We are in agreement?" Samuel said.

"I think so, yes," David said, still not looking at Caroline. He hadn't looked at her once since coming into the room.

Together the two men turned toward her. The cue for her own *yes*, the one she'd given them so many times. The scale was moving again as David climbed between its platforms. Caroline could not outweigh them both. She was expected to move now too; it was what she had always done, what she'd practiced.

But if she had practiced assent, long assent, and given each time every required thing, she had also practiced anger. Anger growing with each year.

She let the anger and not the assent move her. Without a word to either of them, Caroline turned and left the room. David and her father could stand there as long as they liked. Let them practice holding nothing.

18

NEST

❧

*"I cannot explain how I know," she said, her breath now
failing, "but oh! I do know."*

—MILES PEARSON, *THE DARKENING GLASS* (P. 420)

Caroline's body took her on a walk. She took her body on a walk. A weight was moved; she was moving it.

At the place where the birds had swarmed her, she stopped. There were no birds here now, only frozen earth and the skyward reach of the trees. She paused and watched the clouds of her breath dissipate. Look at her body, breathing so well. Able to do so many things, and what would she make it do now?

She made it walk into the woods, the way she'd tried before the birds had stopped her. Branches cracked under her shoes, making sharp, slight sounds in the cold air. The ground was uneven with frost heaves, catching her arches and heels awkwardly. She could see so far with no screening leaves—trunk after trunk before her. Above, branches and more branches, like blood vessels pulled out from skin and muscle and frozen high in the gray light, doing nothing to break up the weak sun.

Up ahead of her, though—were those leaves after all? A cluster of trees with lines blunted by brown clumps of something. Perhaps leaves that had somehow fallen and frozen there. She moved closer.

Not leaves. Nests.

Nests upon nests, mound upon mound upon mound of them, heaped and splayed like an enormous soft-angled body across the trees. Many nests—she could see all the dark circular dappling openings, too many to count—but also one, all joined into a single structure, a sort of roughly molded haystack, that spanned this stand of trees, hanging from the branches it had swallowed. The length of several Carolines, the height of several of her stood on end. The shape was irregular, unpredictably curving in and out, like the shape of that smaller nest she'd found before and pulled from the tree. As if that nest had doubled and redoubled itself here—the first chamber of a many-chambered thing.

It was loose and messy at its edges, riotous with hay, with twigs, so much she couldn't believe the birds had made it without plucking the hillsides bare. Tighter and more compact near the openings, all those openings. A beast with so many mouths.

Though a beast was not quite what it looked like: that curving, that swelling and receding, the narrowness of it in places and the thickness of it in others. Here was the shape that had evaded her when she'd seen only part of it, in the bits that had crashed through the ceiling and then in that smaller nest. It was rough, yes, loose, shrouded, but she recognized it. A joining together of girls, buried girls. One standing, two sitting, two lying down, none of them free to move because of the way they'd been covered over and woven together into this one large supine body. Hips, heads, waists, shoulders.

There were trilling hearts here, she saw: a few in the trees, a few perched on the body of the nest itself. They were quiet and mostly still, just a ruffle here, a shifting there. Then one flew toward the nest, slowing as it neared, flapping once and twice, choosing one of the small dark openings, winding its way inside.

From within, it could probably go anywhere. One chamber to another. The bird might weave its way along a path from the body of one girl to the next, from Abigail to Tabitha, Eliza to Livia, Meg to Julia, Rebecca to Felicity to Caroline herself. Caroline was so sure of this impossible thing. Of course she knew that the real girls were all outside the nest—some in their beds upstairs in the farmhouse, some circling the parlor, she herself standing in these woods—but somehow they were also here in the nest, because she was seeing them, mounded and joined and made to be still.

She had known the birds were taking little bits of things from all of them. Now she saw that had been only the visible tip of their ambitious thievery. What the birds wanted were the girls. The girls, whole. What other shape could an infinite hunger take? What shape other than their own?

That one red bird, Caroline seemed to feel it making its way toward her in the nest. She felt it navigating the net of their bodies and shaking that net with its weight, causing a tremor in one body that passed to every body, bound as they were. A percussion, a repercussion, from each thing that happened, from every traveling point of red.

Caroline closed in on the place where the bird had led her. The birds on the outside of the nest flapped and fluttered farther away and perched again on its surface to watch her. Up close the nest seemed so quiet, though inside she knew it must be boiling with birds.

She could reach the lowest opening by stretching. She prodded, releasing that smell again, even more potent—feathers and rich, varied rot—and from within the nest an unseen bird pecked at her skin, not hard, but still it startled her and she whipped her hand free, tearing the weave of the nest. A piece fell. She bent to lift it. Caught in it was a scrap of paper.

She pulled the scrap loose, yellowed and crisp.

told you in my last letter

Livia's large, looping hand.

From the next hole Caroline pulled a shred of fabric she recognized from the new gown, deep blue silk, that Rebecca had brought back with her from her time away at Christmas.

She moved to the other holes she could reach. She brought forth, from the next: half a ripped page of a book on the natural sciences. A pen nib pocked with marks of teeth. Felicity's missing earring—a suspended crystal dewdrop.

From the next, a little to the left: a tangle of light brown hair. A silver locket, tarnished, nothing at all left inside. A scrap of black lace from the hem of a shawl she'd seen on Eliza's shoulders. Three words in Julia's cramped hand: *greed cannot whose.* A scrap from her own day dress.

More pieces of fabric too: white, black, brown, burgundy, blue. Silk and linen, cotton and velvet. Meg's green paisley from Christmas. Some swatches coming apart between her fingers, some fresh.

As she collected—some of the bits requiring untangling, some only resting on the floors of their caves—the birds inside sometimes poked and picked at her hand, not gently but not painfully, broody as nesting hens.

Another new hole and a small ceramic dog the size of a fingertip she'd once seen on someone's desk—she could not now recall whose. A large piece of what seemed to be a fingernail, a thick dull-white parenthesis. A bit of rag soaked in what looked like brown-red blood.

When she reached into the next hole and brought out a tooth, brown encrusted at its base, she cried out, then dropped it as she'd dropped the rest.

The birds outside the nest, the ones she could see, rustled a little at the noise she made.

Who knew what else there was just beyond her reach—the whole structure studded with parts of them. Finding each object, she felt as if the girl inside the nest were pushing it out toward her. The way a person in a cell might push a message under the door.

Here I am. Here is proof that I am here.

The way Caroline herself might push one, might hope for someone to find it.

*

ON THE TRILLING HEART SCHOOL

by Caroline Hood

Lately my father, Samuel Hood, undertook—and I and others along with him—a grand educational experiment, the establishment of the Trilling Heart School for Girls. My purpose in writing this brief essay is to declare that experiment finished. I feel that only in so writing can I ensure its final conclusion.

My father sought to demonstrate with our school the truth and importance of certain principles. While I am certain of nothing, I believe our failure lies not in those principles themselves but in the discrepancy between them and the world in which we live. There and in a ruthlessness that awoke in those of us who had charge of the school, defending ourselves past the point of defense. My father set out to show that women have as great a capacity as men to learn anything that might be learned, and in this I feel he did prove himself correct. The girls of Trilling Heart, our girls, did all that boys might do.

Yet our girls were not boys. The world does not consider them boys, and in the end we could not either. We both knew and did not know who they were. Were we nobler than the rest of the world, which does not know them at all? I think, though I am no longer sure, that we were. But it did seem that in the divide between our knowing and our not knowing—between the girls' minds and their bodies; between the sense we tried to give them of their possibilities and the actual state of those possibilities—a strange suffering flourished. In our approach to this suffering, we were less interested in preventing further pain than in preventing the world's discovery of that pain.

For that offense, I am sorry. I find I cannot quite be sorry about the whole of Trilling Heart itself, though I know that it is right for the school now to close. We were, I think, making girls for a world that does not exist. That cost them.

I wonder still what we ought to have been doing instead. Perhaps the answer is just what we were doing, except that we should have made it clearer—to everyone—that the girls themselves mattered more to us than our or anyone's ideas about them.

To the families of our girls, I offer my deepest regret. To our girls themselves too.

And also, always, if they will accept it, my love.

*

Caroline sent Mr. Sanders into town to post the essay to the editor of *The Examiner,* a Mr. Nathaniel Lewis, enclosed and sealed inside a much briefer letter. *Word of the start of our school appeared in your pages. I thought it only fitting that word of our end appear there as well.*

Caroline watched Mr. Sanders walk away with it. Past the woods, which hid the nest, though she could see it clearly in her mind. She would until she died, she knew. She had written the essay because she needed to name its shape in some useful way.

Then she went to her father's study to tell him what she had done.

They sat there. The two Hoods, alone, as they had mostly been.

What did Caroline mean? Just what she had said.

"They won't publish it," Samuel told Caroline. His eyes were open so wide the gaze looked painful, turned on her, as if on too fierce a brightness. "Nathaniel wouldn't do that, something so damaging to me."

"I think he will. It's a story, isn't it?"

"A *story*. Is that what you saw yourself doing? Writing a story?"

"After living it."

"Explain yourself, please," he said. His willfully level voice made her so angry.

"That was always how we began, wasn't it, when I did something displeasing? But I'm grown now, Papa, and I've been explaining and explaining myself, and if you haven't heard me, that no longer seems to me to be my concern."

Samuel leaned back. "There was always," he said softly, "such a viciousness in you."

Caroline held her face still.

"I never knew where it came from."

"I never did either."

"Your mother would have been so—"

"Oh yes. My mother the angel. My mother the white light. Did you know Hawkins told me about her?"

She watched his face absorb this without changing. "What about her?" he said, as if there were nothing Caroline could say that could trouble him. For as well as she knew his voice, even she wouldn't have been able to hear the lie there this time.

"The truth of what happened between her and Miles Pearson."

"If he did, then he told you nothing more than what many people have always—"

"And he told me you knew."

"Knew?" Samuel said, just as carefully, but she could sense that care beginning to slip beyond him.

"Papa."

His expression changed, sagged toward grief. "You don't have any idea how unbearable this is, how impossible—there are things it would only hurt you to know."

Now was the dangerous moment, when he was only asking her to save them both by withdrawing her question, by not making him answer after all.

"Let them then," she said.

She could see, ever so briefly, her father's disbelief that she would do this to them. She allowed no mercy to cross her own face. *I am doing this, and you must also. I am demanding this of us.*

Samuel's mouth set and hardened. "I came upon the two of them once in the hayloft. Walking by in broad daylight, I heard . . . something. So I went in."

His vision would have adjusted slowly from the brightness outside. Pigeons cooing in the rafters. The smell of all that hay the Birch Hill men had gathered to try to feed their animals into health. And above, a tangle of dim, dusty shapes. She saw and heard and smelled all of it as if she had been there.

That was her real mother, up there in the hay. No wonder Caroline had never quite been able to get to her before now.

"They didn't hear me, and I left. I don't think Anna ever knew I knew. I never spoke of it to her."

"How could you stand it, not saying anything?" The restraint this would take—to carry on after, sitting down for tea, saying good morning, sharing a bed, kissing a cheek—seemed to her miraculous.

Samuel's voice shook. "She was so young. So beautiful. The great unexpected gift of my life. I put myself in mind of the vastness of human imperfection. I thought eventually her own conscience would come to show her the wrongness of what she'd done, and she would come to me herself and beg me to forgive her."

"Would you have?" Caroline asked.

"Of course."

He didn't know he was lying. Just as he didn't know that few men could have denied themselves the expression of such a rage.

"Later, after they'd all left—I almost managed to convince myself I'd dreamed it."

"Yes," said Caroline. She could understand that feeling.

"And then when I found her there—"

"What do you mean? When you found her where?"

He stopped. She watched him close his teeth on his lower lip.

New panic came over Caroline, the sense of drifting down and down in deep water. "You always said she died of a fit, out for a walk."

"She did. I just didn't tell you . . . the particulars. I couldn't. She said she was going walking. After, I went into the barn for something, and there she was, broken at my feet. She must have been up in the hayloft, and the fit took her at the top, and she stumbled off the edge."

Her father looked at Caroline austerely now.

"And I know how that sounds, Caroline. You may trust that I've considered it from every angle, as much as anyone could. I knew her, and I knew her mind. It was a fit."

You may trust.

Caroline peered at him, weighing. How deep did the lie go? If Anna hadn't been on a walk, if she'd been up in the hayloft, where had he been?

Samuel saw this question in her face, the way he'd always seen so much of what she wanted to hide from him, when he cared enough to look for it. "If you could actually wonder such a thing, I was with George Crammer, from *The Continental Review*, in my study that whole morning. George died five years ago, but he gave a statement at the time. The examiner was perfectly satisfied." He inhaled, fixed her with a bitter stare. "Of course, he was not a daughter."

"No," Caroline said. There was relief in learning she had to revise only so far.

Still, the revising dizzied her. Her mother might have made a choice not just to leave *wife* and *mother* behind but to leave her whole self. It had not been her body directly that killed her. Maybe her body's demands, but not her body.

"How, how could you not have told me, Papa?" Caroline said.

"Telling you would only have caused you pain."

"Pain? Don't you understand? The fit didn't kill her, then, if it even was a fit," Caroline said. She was choking.

"What does it matter? She's dead—what does it matter how?"

"What does it *matter*? Do you know I've lived my whole life fearing I'd get sick like her, and die of it?"

Samuel breathed in, deeply. He closed his eyes. "Well, who isn't afraid?" he said.

From within her body, with its head-swimming, its tingling, Caroline watched him—her body that, it turned out, had all along been as survivable as anyone else's. She need never have read particular meaning in its signs, even now need not assume they pointed anywhere. With a survivable body, a person could do anything she wanted.

Caroline raised her body out of the chair. She moved to her father's desk, she lifted the glass globe, she threw it through the window, so she would always know the sound of all that she could do.

19

PROVISIONING

❧

*Some part of him had always understood
that so must this season end.*

—MILES PEARSON, *THE DARKENING GLASS* (P. 431)

A carriage removed Hawkins to Boston. He would see more patients there soon; he would not concern himself much with those he'd seen here. If he spoke after of Trilling Heart, Caroline knew it would be for titillation. Caroline managed not to speak to him again before he left. It turned out this was simple. When he walked into a room, she walked out of it. He wasn't going to chase her.

She'd been wondering how much he knew about what he did to the girls and women he treated. Perhaps he'd worked not to know very much, like her father or David, like all the men who'd written all those medical books, who'd implemented this treatment of a territory from whose borders they averted their eyes. Though she would always suspect some animal part of Hawkins of understanding more, and relishing.

David and Caroline spent a week avoiding each other, a dance of abandoned spaces and broken glances. Then he took a train back to Ohio. The morning he left she looked at her face in the glass, still and solemn, and thought of the first morning David had come to live in the farmhouse, before the school had opened,

how his closeness had seemed a taunting, a yanking at her teth-
ers to a self that would always be the same and that would never
see the consummation of anything. The consummation, when it
came, had also made her feel tethered to herself. But to a self she
suddenly understood, suddenly trusted.

She was sure this must have been the pull for Anna too, toward
Miles. One's self could be felt most easily in its desires and in its
sufferings. Anna had been trying to choose.

But Miles must have disappointed Anna in the end—he had
left, after all—much as David had disappointed Caroline. David,
who had turned out to be so much less than she'd imagined. What
they'd done together had left a mark on him, a sort of wincing
in his back, and though she'd been trying not to look directly at
him in the days before he left, even in the periphery she noted the
new, tentative way he held his shoulders. Sophia would see it as
soon as he came off the train.

*

Caroline's essay had not appeared yet but would, Mr. Nathaniel
Lewis had written, in next month's *Examiner.* Caroline met her
father in hallways, pressed his hand, dropped it. Practiced drop-
ping it.

By the time the essay actually appeared, she knew, she would
be gone.

*

The girls' parents hurried to them and hurried them away as
they might have during a plague—they understood that this was
one, even if they didn't quite understand its nature. No one had
told the parents much. Samuel knew that the essay was coming
and that it would be better if the girls had left by the time it came,
and so he had written a brief letter stating that there would be a
recess of indeterminate length, outlining with as little sensation

as possible the nature of the girls' ailment and disclosing that a treatment had been started, but it had been decided the course would best be pursued by each family individually. Those were the phrases Samuel used, *had been started, had been decided.* There was authority in this anonymous starting, deciding force, and for now the parents seemed jumpy and daughter-consumed enough not to press beyond a few vague threats of future demands for answers. Later, after the essay, after the news spread, Caroline thought there would be letters, and perhaps lawyers, but now the parents only clutched at their girls and bundled them away.

Upon each daughter, Caroline wished she could bestow a different part of her father for the girl to take with her. This would be fitting: a last giving of gifts, of specialnesses, which despite everything she still knew that he had. The trouble perhaps was that he had too much of them.

She imagined Samuel diminishing behind his closed study door as she wished these parts off him.

Tabitha, she thought, Tabitha who could never think of anything to say, should take Samuel's voice. That sureness he'd used in lectures once, and then in teaching Caroline, and then the others. Through the glass of her parents' carriage Caroline saw Tabitha wave, her fingers scratching at the glass, and she thought, *Be sure. Think of things to say and say them.*

Rebecca could take Samuel's writing hand. Caroline watched Mr. Johns stare in confusion at his daughter, so whole seeming— he hadn't yet seen her dramatic slumping, and her rash was hiding under her sleeves. Perhaps he wouldn't ever see, if Rebecca could take the writing hand, which had always persevered and could give her relentlessness.

For Abigail: Samuel's imperturbability. The way no one but Caroline could spy when something had rattled him; the way his words and movements came at their own pace always, not the pace the rattlers would set. Soon, when Abigail's mother squeezed her shoulders and cried, Abigail would not flush so crimson. Whatever she felt, she would be able to decide what she wanted to show of it.

Meg could take Samuel's grace, the lightness of his step when his thinking was going so well he had to pace with it. The impassive like-faced parents who came to collect her would see her new way of walking and know that she had moved beyond them, the way people, most people, hope their children will.

Julia could have his laughter. That sense of the joy of living that so rarely deserted him. Julia's mother, all boniness and flaring nostrils, had scented and stomped out all threats but also all joy in Julia's life. Now Samuel could give her his.

Livia needed Samuel's kindness. Caroline wanted her up on a stage somewhere, her white-gold hair its own light, accusing them all—but she also wanted Livia to look on some deserving faces with the kind of love that had always come easily to Samuel.

For Felicity: the set and sureness of Samuel's shoulders, to bolster further that courage she'd always had. A spine that stayed straight, so that Felicity's smallness would hereafter be a screen behind which she could set all the terms.

That left only Eliza, and for Eliza Caroline had trouble thinking what would be enough.

Before Eliza left, Caroline went to see her in her bedroom. Everything she had brought with her had been packed back into her trunk. She sat on the mattress. Caroline sat too.

"I wanted to tell you that I'm sorry," Caroline said. "I'm so sorry that I didn't understand in time about him. You are . . . much too good for what happened to you." Her voice trembled a little. "But he's gone now, back to Boston. It's over."

Eliza looked at her curiously. "Hawkins, you mean?"

"Who else?"

"When you said *him* I thought at first you meant your father. And of course they aren't the same, are they?"

"No, of course," Caroline said, pleased that they could agree on at least this much.

"Your father's worse, I think," Eliza said.

Caroline stared at her. "Worse than *Hawkins*? How can you say that? You *don't* really believe what's in *The Darkening Glass*, do you?"

"Don't be absurd," Eliza said sharply. "I mean that after all of this, after everything, he still thinks he sees more than everyone else. He still believes, however it went wrong, it can't really have been his fault. He'll write about it. You'll see, he will."

Was this true? Caroline didn't know. It might be. It had been true of nearly everything else that had ever happened to her father.

"I came here wanting so much to find something I never had," Eliza said, her eyes welling. "I don't know what, but I've always missed it. Somehow I thought it might be here. And he *let* me believe that. He let all of us."

"If it matters," Caroline said, "I do think he believed it himself."

Eliza considered. "I suppose so."

In the end, as Eliza's stepfather carried her to the coach, since she still felt too weak to walk down the stairs, Caroline decided Eliza should have Samuel's anger. That rage he had treated as an unwanted, unnamed, unacknowledged child—at all those who'd wronged him and every current he'd fed that had somehow passed on without carrying him where he expected to go. Eliza had anger already, but Caroline looked at her quiet, pale face, before the closing of the carriage door hid it, and wished her more, a mountaintop of rage on which she could be distant and safe.

After they had all left, Caroline understood that perhaps these pieces she wanted to give the girls were pieces not just of Samuel but of herself too. That perhaps they belonged to her just as fully. She thought about which of them she would choose to take with her, into the life that would come next.

*

The next morning, Caroline would leave for Boston. Mr. Sanders would drive her.

In the middle of that last night she took her lantern and went again to the nest in the woods.

She'd decided that before she left she should set the massive nest shape on fire, so that she could turn it into a dream that had passed. This was something she could do with her brand-new strong body, which was not going to teeter into death at any moment and which was whole enough to carry and unleash a destructive force. The image of the nest would continue to haunt her, but after this it would be only an image, only a haunting. And only for her. She'd had no desire to tell anybody else about it—not David or Hawkins, before they left, and not her father. It didn't belong to them.

Not the girls either, because it did.

She walked in the lantern's circle of light through the dark and to the nest. Then she stood, looking.

How easily it would catch. Two more steps, the lifting of the lantern's glass case, the touching of the flame to the parts of the underside she could reach. The whole haystack of it would burn and, with it, all the stolen scraps she hadn't found. If there were birds in there, well, birds had wings.

This act was the same one she'd feared Eliza would take, that night in the woods with the stick and the fire, and there was no reason to assume the fire Caroline would set would stop with just the nest. It might devour that and then just keep devouring: tree after tree, until no trees stood. That wasn't what she wanted, but if it happened she was prepared to consider it necessary.

She imagined the slow lick of the fire's first contact, then the wild orange rush, trilling hearts flying straight upward from it like great sparks.

The undoing of the girl shapes.

Caroline ran her eyes now over the nest that linked those shapes, the path made solid that any tremor would take to register there, and there, and there. She stood for a last moment looking at this nest that was itself the shape of receiving all the signals of the world.

Birds again now. Several, then more, coming out of the nest, flying toward Caroline. The light, she understood—they were drawn to the lantern she held—but before she could put it down one had landed on her, on the soft inside bend of her elbow, as if on a branch. The clench of its feet through her sleeve was like strong, warm wire—but the bird's body was so light, impossibly light, her arm wasn't aware of holding any new weight at all. A second landed at her feet. Her skin shivered, her heart thrummed, but it didn't seem they were trying to take anything from her. Others landed near the one on the ground. All of them faced the lantern. They didn't seem very aware of Caroline herself. The one on her arm was straight from her dream of red sleeves except it moved, darting now in its reptilian way a little closer to the light, lifting now its wing. The birds on the ground shifted, hopped. Movements she couldn't have dreamed for them, designs she couldn't guess at—remote as the impulses that had built this nest, or as the ones that had produced, from Caroline's own unreachable heart, the trembling and numbness and fainting— all of theirs.

Animals within animals within animals within animals, stretching far too deep to see.

Best, maybe, not to burn down things that you couldn't see.

Because everyone, she decided, should be allowed that dark. She looked again to the nest. Everyone should keep the space of a haunting.

One day she might tell the girls about this nest after all. She imagined them returning here as women to find whatever remained: perhaps nothing, or perhaps a layer of debris just a little thicker than the layer of pine needles and leaves elsewhere, littered, on inspection, with their own artifacts. Or perhaps the nest would last whole somehow and they would stand here to look at it. Just here, where they could face the shapes they'd had as girls.

Caroline blew out the lantern and felt the small, small shift of the bird lifting off and leaving her.

*

In the morning, Caroline knocked at her father's study door a final time. "Come in," he said. When she did he was reading, or pretending to. Behind him a board still covered the space of the windowpane she'd shattered.

"Mr. Sanders is on his way now to drive me," she said.

"What are you going to do once you arrive?" He stood, her diminished father, and stepped toward her.

"I'll be all right," she said.

"Dearest, I still don't understand what you're doing, going there."

"I know," she said.

She moved in and put her arms around his neck. She breathed in the smell of her childhood, leather and paper; a childhood at last done no matter how she had loved it.

"I'll write once I'm settled," she told him.

Outside Mr. Sanders hefted her into the carriage and settled her case at the back. Not much in it. Most of what she had in her little room hadn't seemed like proper material for a new life. "All right, Miss Hood?" he said.

"Yes."

He closed the door and clambered up in front, and they began to move. Slowly, then faster. Caroline did not let herself look out the windows for last glimpses of the landmarks of her life. She kept expecting a sudden snap as some band reached its limit and returned her. Then she expected her father on horseback, galloping abreast, leaning toward the glass to say, *Back!* Leaving was not a thing that was, in her experience, allowed.

Yet she did seem to be doing it.

She hadn't been to Boston since she was fourteen, for the last of Samuel's lectures. In Boston, he had been young and famous and built intricate ideas like gold machines with many whirring parts, he and all his friends—most of them sent to Harvard by their fathers to become ministers, but becoming in the end something else in spite of those fathers. Caroline was in a fine tradition, going there in spite of her own. She wondered if she'd recognize the city when she saw it.

She closed her eyes, and eventually she slept. When she woke the hills were flatter, the trees shorter and scrubbier, the land being pulled tight like a stitch as they neared the sea. There were houses, and more houses. More, then more again. A steady hum began to build outside the carriage. Finally Caroline could see only slivers of sky between buildings, they stood so close together. Brick facades next to wood-painted, next to wood-painted, next to stone, every roof a slightly different height, reeling past the window, so she seemed to be watching the line of the horizon jump and then dip, jump and then dip again. People everywhere—in carriages, on the street, passing under awnings, standing in doorways, every one of them moving. Even the ones who were standing in place were moving, reaching into a pocket to check the time, swiveling a head, turning a face up into the snow that had started to fall. The breath and warmth of them and the steam of their horses and the smoke from their fires fogged the street. How was it possible there were so many people in the world?

Caroline's memories of those early lecture-trips here held the smells of the streets, ripe and sour, and stuffy rooms full of men and women in rows, and then the relief of coming home again to run across the grass and sprawl with books across her bed. To eat supper with her father and see him smile at her across the table. Home that quiet she'd craved until it had become all she had.

The hum Caroline was hearing now was the sound of all these people's moving bodies. They ferried all their terrors and joys like incidental luggage along with them, not hidden, not really, but not much looked at, since all the others were occupied in carrying their own. They were lovely and scurrying as ants. *How beautiful,* she thought, *to be so busy going somewhere.*

20.

CLASSROOM

Her sweet face would always be so luminous in
his memory he could not believe he would
never see it again in life.

—MILES PEARSON, *THE DARKENING GLASS* (P. 442)

M iss Gloria Sterne was not as Caroline had imagined her. Instead of pincushion-stout, she was broad and tall, and younger than expected. Daunting, a gray iron ship of a woman.

"I must say, I was surprised to receive your inquiry," Miss Sterne said.

"Oh?" said Caroline, taking her seat. The room swam for a moment. She closed her eyes forcefully. These feelings still came to her, not often, not rarely, but she'd stopped fearing they made up a narrative. Now she considered them telegrams from some sender who had ceased to exist.

"Yes. I appreciated our correspondence, of course—but I read about Trilling Heart, back before it opened. In your father's essay in *The Examiner*. Forgive me, but I'd imagined you might consider yourself above our sort of school?"

Miss Sterne read widely then, for a sewing instructor—though why should a sewing instructor not? "I didn't write that essay," Caroline said.

The one she had written had also appeared, as promised, in *The*

Examiner, two weeks after she'd arrived in Boston. It had made people talk about Samuel—subsequent essays had appeared, in *The Examiner* and elsewhere—but Caroline's name hadn't even been on it. "By the daughter of Samuel Hood," the author line had read. Seeing those words, she'd felt as if she'd stood up in a crowd of people, knees shaking, blood pounding, to scream with anger, and discovered as the scream left her mouth that she was separated from all of them by a veil, and that they could hear her, yes, but they still couldn't see her.

One of the essays that had followed her own was by Thoreson. "A Strange Final Chapter." Its tone had been gently, condescendingly bemused; its stance had been that Samuel and his every idea were relics; and its final paragraph announced the founding of Thoreson's next school. That school, she'd heard, had filled almost instantly.

Samuel had written Caroline a letter that arrived two days after her essay appeared. *I forgive you, dearest*, it read, though she hadn't asked for forgiveness.

If Miss Sterne had read Caroline's essay, she wasn't saying. "That isn't an answer," she said, smiling.

"I imagine I did see things that way once."

"And now?" Miss Sterne asked.

Caroline took in a breath, let it out in the close, hot air of Miss Sterne's sitting room. In Boston in the summer, everywhere was hot, and the buildings seemed on the verge of melting, the roads of sliding down the hills like sweat. Something in Caroline also sliding, too massive to stay fixed. Her mind had been too full of her need to get away for her to make specific plans before arriving. For months now she'd been paying her room and board out of her earnings from tutoring the ten-year-old daughter of a solicitor, and the girl was cheerful about working her simple sums and reading aloud, but their sessions left an unused vastness within Caroline. She needed to find somewhere to put it.

She had remembered how Miss Sterne's note of sympathy had touched her like the touch of a hand and wondered if this might be a place.

"Now," Caroline said, "I think we must find productive ways of living in the world as it is. Living in it and meanwhile changing it in the ways that are available to us, small ways at first, that might if we're fortunate add up to something larger. I'd like to help my students to find those ways."

She had been hoping for months that the girls of Trilling Heart were finding ways of their own, teaching themselves to carve out and modify as needed the spaces the world presented to them. She thought on the whole they probably were. For most of them, the months of Trilling Heart, the faintings and the red rashes that had crept across their bodies, were probably like the strangeness of a dream in the moments just after waking, when there was a choice: clutch closer, look, wonder, or open the fingers.

Every night before she slept, Caroline pictured each face. *Open, open*, she told them.

Skin healed. Fainters awoke again.

"Do you know," Miss Sterne said, leaning back in her chair, "my father idolized yours. He knew him only on paper, of course—he was a shopkeeper, didn't move in the same circles, but still your father made quite an impression. *If everyone could listen to this man,* my father used to tell me, *the world would have no problems at all.*"

"I spent my life listening to my father. That has not been my experience," Caroline said.

Miss Sterne stared at her. Then she let out a creaky startling laugh. "Well," she said, "Sarah Truman is always complaining that she has too much work to do. She might not mind giving up the literature sections, if you'd like to teach them. I'll have to talk to Miss Marsh, of course, but—you'll excuse my saying so—it's likely she'll listen to me. The pay won't be much, I'm afraid."

"I don't need much," Caroline said. In this context it was true.

*

On the Tuesday after her appointment with Miss Sterne, Caroline thought she saw Sophia at the post office, where she'd come to mail a letter to her father. Impossible, of course. She'd had these sightings often since coming to Boston—she would think she saw Livia or Tabitha or Rebecca. Samuel in a corner-of-the-eye glimpse of someone's gray beard, and she'd feel sure he'd come to spy on her and gather ammunition for the writing of some letter so powerful it could make her come home once and for all. Or David, in the set of a stranger's shoulders or chin, and a heat would rise in her, still. Though she knew so well now the word that named him best: *coward.* She thought if she did see him again she might even say it.

Or Hawkins. Caroline avoided the streets surrounding his practice, but still she'd seen a man's familiar broad back once and had to hurry two blocks to shake off the fear, even after the man had turned his head and proved not to be Hawkins after all. She had names for him too—*usurper, trespasser, wolf, thief, thief.* She was disappointed in herself after, for having run like that instead of turning to call Hawkins, had he turned out in fact to be Hawkins, by his rightful names. She had thought she'd become surer of her own voice.

Today, spying this woman's yellow hair from a distance made Caroline's breath come fast at the prospect of all she might tell her. The imposter's gold braids were coiled in a knot, and her shoulders rounded like Sophia's.

Then the imposter turned. Somehow she was not an imposter, but the woman herself.

"Sophia!" Caroline cried, without thinking.

"Oh!" Sophia said. She moved toward Caroline. She clasped her hands as if they'd been dear to each other.

"What are you doing here?" Caroline asked her.

"We came to get an endorsement," Sophia said. "From a judge here, quite a public figure, if you'll excuse my saying it. He and David have been writing back and forth. David would have been happy to see you, I'm sure, but he's already gone on without me, for a meeting with some potential donors in Hartford. I'm taking the train later today to meet him."

"Endorsement?" Caroline said.

"Oh, I'm sorry—I thought you'd have heard. David's running for the Ohio legislature," Sophia said proudly. "As a first step into public life. It was my idea. It's going well. It never does to count on these things ahead of time, but"—she waved a hand—"through God's grace. We're very thankful to Him, both of us. David's been coming to church with me again, you know. I can't tell you how happy it makes me."

All the imposter Sophias had filled Caroline with imagined confessions, apologies, many genuine wishes of happiness. *I have harmed you in these ways, and I am sorry.* But in those scenarios David had been languishing in a dark Ohio bedroom, and Sophia had been out of her mind with worry and frustration that nobody could tell what was wrong with him, and they could not forgive each other.

Sophia in the flesh did not look worried. "How are you?" Sophia said. She looked at Caroline with new attention.

Some reckoning it seemed had happened all on its own, without Caroline. David had come home and told Sophia some things and not, Caroline was sure, others, but the mess of him had communicated enough to Sophia for her to understand, and out of that mess Sophia had managed to build a new life for the two of them. Sophia didn't need to hear most of the things Caroline had been planning to tell her. Caroline would be saying them only for herself.

Open the fingers, Caroline told herself, *open them.*

"I'm quite well," Caroline said.

Sophia glanced down at the letter in her hand. "For your father?"

"Yes."

"I hope he's well too," Sophia said savagely.

"Well enough. Does he know about David's run?"

"David wrote to him about it, I think."

"Ah. He didn't mention."

"Well," Sophia told her, "I was going to say we'd be grateful for his support, but I don't think we would, not really."

"No." Caroline smiled.

"I'm glad it's done. For all of us, you too," Sophia said. "I'm glad you're here and not there anymore."

"So am I," Caroline said. She caught Sophia's hand. "I told myself that if I ever saw you again I'd tell you how I admire you, for seeing it all first."

"Oh, admire," Sophia said, and wrinkled her nose. "You did see it too."

"But you acted. You were braver and better. I am sorry I was not." She looked into Sophia's eyes. This part she could say after all. "I am so very sorry."

Sophia pressed her hands. "Thank you," she said.

"Please tell David I was happy to hear the news."

"Take care." Sophia surprised Caroline by embracing her. "Find the best way of taking care," she said, and then she pulled away and walked out the door.

David before a crowd, behind a lectern, speaking. He did speak well, of course. Caroline wondered whether he was standing straighter these days, whether Sophia had noticed his hollowed-out sagging and prodded at his back until he looked more like himself again.

Caroline put her letter in the mail. It was like all the letters she sent to her father: she wrote perhaps three for every one she actually sent. In deciding which to post she judged them by the quantity of their revelation of her real self: true things but not the truest. She was willing to show her father her hands, her arms, the back of her head, but never her face. *I miss you,* and *Remember that afternoon when we reenacted the picnic scene from* Pickwick*? and Please remind Mrs. S you aren't to have too much salt.* She didn't send the letters that said that she loved him but thought she might never forgive him; that she still felt the weight of all he had ruined; that despite a newness here that made her giddy, she still seemed to be pulling that weight forward with her through her new life.

He always wrote her back. She tried not to imagine the airless, silent hours from which he sent these letters. *Mrs. S seems to have taken your injunctions to heart; I find there is no taste I can recall to reassure myself that I have, in fact, already had dinner. When, my dearest, are you coming home?*

She was not.

*

Caroline wondered if all the Trilling Heart girls were finding that, like her, they were mostly all right when not in rooms alone. Rooms without other people in them sometimes seemed to Caroline to hold too many thoughts of Hawkins and his hands. Though *thoughts* was the wrong word, really: too many *relivings* of him, of those hands, and then the stoniness would creep over her again in a way that felt like dying.

When this feeling came, she tried instead to remember the afternoon with David, the way she had taken then what she wanted. Except in reliving it she changed him into the person she'd thought he had been.

She wondered how the girls were managing, so much younger than she was, with so much less to steady them. She wondered and worried about the dreams they were having, while sleeping and while awake, and what their feelings about these dreams were, whom they blamed. She wondered what it would be like for them when they married and another man touched the places Hawkins had touched. He had shown them all something they would always know now about the violability of their own boundaries.

Caroline worried most of all for Eliza, who had been so eager to exceed the boundaries of herself even before she came to Trilling Heart.

So it was to Eliza that Caroline wrote, just one letter, the week before the term would begin at Miss Marsh's. She wanted to write much more than she did. She wanted to say that she hoped Eliza was finding ways to get out of her house sometimes, and that she had a good lamp beside her bed, and that she still had her father's painting to look at. That Caroline had come to believe some mysteries were beyond solving but a person could still live with them, around them, inside them. She wanted to tell Eliza that she'd be teaching at her old school—imagining a correspondence in which Eliza would write her back with her opinions of the teachers, and Caroline would reply with her own, and eventually they would come to really know each other, and this might make some difference.

In the end, all Caroline actually wrote was that she thought of Eliza often and wondered how her health was. How was she spending her time?

Astoundingly, a letter came back. *I was pleased to hear from you,* Eliza wrote. *I find I am reading and sleeping a great deal. My fond regards.*

Caroline made herself keep this letter, this call from a ship sinking far off in the distance. She put it in her desk drawer, atop her plain paper, where she would see it, not daily, but often, lest she ever begin to forget about costs.

*

There were trilling hearts even in Boston by summer's end. Instead of leaving they seemed to be expanding their territory.

The first time Caroline saw one stalking the roofline of a building on a busy street, she stopped, and the man two paces back bumped into her. The bird didn't look in her direction, and why should it? The meaning between them ran only in one direction. Caroline was doing her best to live in other directions herself.

The *Boston Daily Advertiser* ran a story on them, several pages in. "Scientists Investigate Bird Species' New Range." The words of the article held no indication of awe. The birds had done something new for reasons that existed somewhere and wouldn't stay unknown indefinitely.

She imagined what the scientists would think if the birds began their exaggerated nest building here. Great, wild, sculptural, ensnaring thickets in the crow's nests of the great ships in the harbor, on the broad and somehow horselike back of Faneuil Hall, on Harvard Green, in the doorway of the statehouse, so that the men trying to come and go would find their way blocked. Everywhere this great city of men made to bear the shapes of girls and women.

Here we are. Look. Look.

When Caroline first saw the newspaper headline, her breath stopped, because she misread *range* as *rage*.

*

Early September, a sweltering second-floor classroom in Miss Marsh's school. Caroline perched against the edge of the blackboard and waited to meet her students.

She had dressed herself with care that morning, lining up the shoulder seams of her good dress exactly with the tendons of her neck. Smoothing her hair, patting her cheeks, she'd been pleased with her eyes' steadiness in the glass. She looked like a person who belonged to herself.

She'd felt like such a person since the first time she'd bled, after David. A red streak, a question answered: her body was only hers.

Inside her body in this classroom now, though, there was fear with Caroline, fear inside her nose and mouth and chest. She kept clearing her throat to try to dislodge it. She would be all right once the girls were there in front of her and she could see that none of them had Livia's face, or Rebecca's, or Abigail's. Not one of them Eliza's, or Caroline's own.

The door creaked open. A girl came into the room and sat down. Caroline registered her brown hair, her blue dress, and her serious face, without meeting her gaze.

Two girls came, then, and a group of three. Another girl, and another. Caroline knew there would be nineteen in total, but she had the feeling that perhaps they would just keep coming forever until they stuffed the room.

Almost exactly two months later the Great Boston Fire would begin, one evening after the students and teachers had all retired to their rooms for the night. For a few minutes it would seem as if Miss Marsh's would be in its path and would be impossible to save. As it would turn out, the wind would shift, and the fire brigade would arrive, and their hoses would work well enough to stop the flames from quite reaching their door. But in that brief, tense, infinite time, Caroline would flee from room to room, rounding up the girls, coughing on smoke and panic, sending them all out to stand with Miss Sterne in the street. An orange glow would fall through the windows, bathing floors and walls and faces like a sunrise, and she would think of the nest she hadn't burned. She would feel so afraid of somehow missing a girl. One of them might be in an unexpected room where she'd fallen asleep, and no one would notice her absence until too late. Caroline would remember then this first morning she met them, when they seemed a crowd to her, with many interchangeable faces. She would feel like she was remembering a different person's life.

Now Caroline turned her desk chair toward the blackboard,

sat, and flipped through the pages of her lesson plan, so that she might look busy to the girls. She'd be teaching the plan on Shakespeare's sonnets from her first lesson at Trilling Heart. In bringing it into this room she saw she'd tried to smuggle in an artifact from another time.

The clock on the wall said she should begin. She turned to face them.

In rows—no circle here—they watched her. In this quiet room.

The hayloft where Caroline's mother had sat on the last day of her life would have been quiet too, and sunny, sweet smelling. The most peaceful place on earth. Sitting in the hay, her mother had been safe, but her body was made of text. Her substance was only all the words that men had written and said about her. Motionless, she was linear, slight, transparent as a series of sentences.

Only when Anna stood and moved did she take on flesh.

Caroline rose behind her desk, pushing her chair out so it scraped across the floor, and the girls shifted forward in their seats.

Her mother had neared the hayloft's edge, next. Each step made her more real and more solid. Her skin was ordinary skin. Her cheeks were ordinary cheeks. She curved and wept in all the ordinary ways.

Caroline stepped out from behind the desk and moved forward, to the edge that divided the space that was hers from the space that was the students'. The lip of the hayloft must also have seemed a meeting point of spaces. The hayloft was Miles's, and the floorless space in front of Anna belonged to Samuel. Or the other way around. Or maybe the space behind her—that solid floor and pillowing hay—belonged to Miles and Samuel both, and the floorlessness in front of her, that was hers.

It might be she took no step, no conscious step; that she'd meant only to walk to that line and show herself what the choices were, and there—something unexpected and toppling. A fit, just as Samuel had always said. Except Caroline was almost sure not, seeing now her mother's flesh and the way it knew from years of practice which way to fall. If something beyond her own choosing had happened to her, it must have been something less expected. On the line between the floor and nothing, thinking of Miles's hands, his lips, the feel of his face in her palms, she could have heard the squawk of a bird, Samuel calling for her, Caroline's own child-voice, crying out from deep in dreams. Anna opened her mouth to call something back and the weight of whatever she was about to say had changed her balance there on the edge of the world.

Caroline took another step forward, over the line. Her mouth filled with red feathers. Through them, she found she could still speak.

ACKNOWLEDGMENTS

This novel's events and world are invented but do have real-life debts. Some books that were especially helpful in anchoring and directing my imaginings: *Record of a School*, by Elizabeth Palmer Peabody; *Republic of Words: The Atlantic Monthly and Its Writers, 1857–1925*, by Susan Goodman; *Eden's Outcasts: The Story of Louisa May Alcott and Her Father*, by John Matteson; *The Peabody Sisters: Three Women Who Ignited American Romanticism*, by Megan Marshall; *The Technology of Orgasm: "Hysteria," the Vibrator, and Women's Sexual Satisfaction*, by Rachel P. Maines; *Mass Hysteria in Schools: A Worldwide History Since 1566*, by Robert E. Bartholomew and Bob Rickard. Caroline's teaching of Shakespeare is informed by Helen Vendler's analysis in *The Art of Shakespeare's Sonnets*, because my own understanding is informed by that analysis in ways I can't escape. Louisa May Alcott's *Transcendental Wild Oats* sowed some of the seeds of Birch Hill, and had I not read her *Little Women* countless times in childhood, I'm quite sure this novel wouldn't exist at all.

Working with the team that has brought *The Illness Lesson* into the world has been a gift beyond my wildest dreams. Lee Boudreaux saw this novel for its real self so clearly from the very first—the kind of seeing that is a rare, rare gift—and made it immeasurably better, and I am so very grateful, for this brilliance and for her passionate devotion to her books. She is extraordinary, and being edited by her has felt like a fairy tale. My bottomless thanks also to everyone at Doubleday, especially Cara Reilly, Michael Goldsmith, and Emily Mahon, who made me the most beautiful jacket I've ever seen; and in the UK, to the wonderful Harriet Moore, and to Lizzy Goudsmit and the whole amazing Transworld team. Thank you also to Michelle Kingdom, for the use of her glorious embroidery art on the jacket.

My faith that my agent, Michelle Brower, is the very best there is, in every way, just grows and grows. I am the luckiest.

Writing any book is a long road, but this one felt especially long—maybe in part because I had two babies along the way—and communities of all kinds sustained it, and me, through the years. In two life-changing strokes of luck, the National Endowment for the Arts and the Sustainable Arts Foundation funded stretches of writing time. The feedback I received on portions of the book at the Sewanee and Bread Loaf Writers' Conferences was invaluable, and the chance to be part of those communities even more so. I am so grateful to all of these organizations, and to Lookout Books, especially Emily Smith and Beth Staples, who published my first book, the story collection *We Show What We Have Learned*, moved mountains for it and for me, and will always be part of my literary family. Many thanks also to the Pittsburgh Writers' Collective, where I did much of the work of revising *The Illness Lesson*, and to its members—Jonathan Auxier, Mary Auxier, Katie Booth, Danielle Chiotti, Becky Cole, John Fried, Maggie Jones, Geeta Kothari, Irina Reyn—whose wisdom and generous advice have meant a great deal to me. My life is so much better since we all banded together to make ourselves a creative home.

Then there are the brilliant writer-women without whose guidance on early drafts this book and I would have been lost. Michelle Adelman jumped in and read the whole thing at a crucial juncture and helped me steer it right. Keri Bertino, among her many talents, has such an innate sense of the heart of a story, and she helped me to understand where I was and wasn't being true enough to this one. Ruth Galm, I really don't know how you do it, but you always know where the magic is, often before I do. I will never be able to thank any of you enough—for the particular help you've given me with this particular book and for your fellowship as writers and mothers in this world.

Friends old and new, thank you for your support and listening and encouragement. Our Boston crew, I continue to miss you desperately. And I feel so lucky to have found a group of friends in Pittsburgh that has helped me weather this writing-books-while-parenting-small-children season: Elizabeth and Rob Felter, Michelle Gil-Montero and Roman Antopolsky, Meg Goehrig and Bryan Brown, Sara and Dan Lindey, Megan and Alex Poplawsky, Lauren Shapiro and Kevin González, Anjali Sachdeva, Becky Tuch, I am grateful for all of you. Then the far-flung but dear: Lydia Nycz, Amy Wu Silverman, Anna Mirabile, and Kate Schlesinger, what a joy to watch you shape your lives, and how lucky I feel to have you in my corner as I shape mine.

I have wanted to be a writer almost as long as I can remember, and my family has helped me in uncountable ways with the pursuit of this particular dream (and, really, all dreams). Thank you a million times over to my mom and dad, Ann and Mark Beams, for their endless belief and their endless love—and to my mom for being, always, my first reader. My thanks and love to my brother, Owen Beams; my sister-in-law, Eden Beams; and my nieces, the wonderful Madelyn and Cadence. And thank you to my incredible in-laws, who have often stepped in to help make things work on the home front.

Thank you to my husband, Finnegan Calabro, for building with me this life, for living it with me, for filling it with more joy and love than I think I would have believed possible.

And to my miraculous daughters, Tess and Joanna. This book is for you, because you have changed everything.

ABOUT THE AUTHOR

Clare Beams' short-story collection, *We Show What We Have Learned*, was published in October 2016. It won the Kirkus Best Debut and was a finalist for the PEN/Robert W. Bingham Prize. Clare lives in Pittsburgh, where she teaches creative writing, most recently at Carnegie Mellon University and Pittsburgh Centre for the Arts. This is her first novel.